INTERNATIONAL ACCLAIM FOR VINCENT McCONNOR'S FIRST NOVEL, *THE FRENCH DOLL*

"A crackling good suspense novel."

—*Los Angeles Times*

"Ceaselessly suspenseful action and a loving picture of Paris . . . make it highly readable."

—*The New York Times Book Review*

"There are several lively thrillers this spring. Among the most beguiling . . . *The French Doll* by Vincent McConnor."

—*Time*

"Deliciously fast and exciting."

—*The Observer*, London

"*The French Doll* is a doll of a thriller. It is among the very best we have read. . . ."

—*MD Magazine*

Bantam Books by Vincent McConnor

THE PROVENCE PUZZLE
THE RIVIERA PUZZLE

THE PROVENCE PUZZLE

VINCENT McCONNOR

An Inspector Damiot Mystery

BANTAM BOOKS
TORONTO • NEW YORK • LONDON • SYDNEY

*This low-priced Bantam Book
has been completely reset in a type face
designed for easy reading, and was printed
from new plates. It contains the complete
text of the original hard-cover edition.*
NOT ONE WORD HAS BEEN OMITTED.

THE PROVENCE PUZZLE

*A Bantam Book / published by arrangement with
Macmillan Publishing Co., Inc.*

PRINTING HISTORY

Macmillan edition published April 1980

Bantam edition / September 1981

*All rights reserved.
Copyright © 1980 by Vincent McConnor.
Cover art copyright © 1981 by Bantam Books, Inc.
This book may not be reproduced in whole or in part, by
mimeograph or any other means, without permission.
For information address: Macmillan Publishing Co., Inc.
866 Third Avenue, New York, N.Y. 10022.*

ISBN 0-553-14596-7

Published simultaneously in the United States and Canada

Bantam Books are published by Bantam Books, Inc. Its trademark, consisting of the words "Bantam Books" and the portrayal of a bantam, is Registered in U.S. Patent and Trademark Office and in other countries. Marca Registrada. Bantam Books, Inc., 666 Fifth Avenue, New York, New York 10103.

PRINTED IN THE UNITED STATES OF AMERICA

0 9 8 7 6 5 4 3 2 1

For Raymond Thomas Baker

There have been several short stories printed about Chief Inspector Damiot of the Quai des Orfèvres since his debut, some years ago, in a story called "Soufflé Surprise."

Herewith his first appearance in a novel, but Damiot is in his native Provence instead of in Paris.

The village of Courville may not be found on modern maps of France, but you will discover it driving south from Arles, between the town of Figment and the village of Rêve . . .

1

The unmarked black police car moved straight as a bullet up the dark and deserted street.

Chief Inspector Damiot remained silent, seated beside Borell—his leather-jacketed chauffeur—feeling unnaturally calm, as usual, when entering enemy territory.

Nobody knew how many *agents de police* the Valzo gang had killed. Tonight he must find some clue—anything—that would connect Valzo to the murder of that Laurent woman. . . .

He didn't usually get involved with types like Valzo, but the death of Nicole Laurent had raised an outcry from the Paris press. Another Valzo murder, one headline had called it, demanding immediate action from the Quai des Orfèvres.

There had been a conference this morning that ended with the Director-General ordering Damiot removed from all other investigations and assigned exclusively to the Laurent murder.

Nicole Laurent had been Valzo's latest mistress until he handed her over to one of his lieutenants, who in turn had discarded her to a minor member of their gang. Her bullet-pocked body had been found in an alley last week.

Conveniently, Valzo had been in London on business when the Laurent woman was eliminated by one of his faceless killers.

Today a police informer had reported that Valzo was in Marseille. The gang was known to be involved in the kidnapping of some Arab oil potentate from a private jet in Algeria. Valzo, behind the scenes, would supervise the ransom deal. He never permitted his lieutenants to handle anything that important.

The Préfecture wasn't interested in the kidnapping. For the moment, that was beyond their jurisdiction. They wanted Valzo for murder. Any one of a dozen suspected but unproven murders. Nicole Laurent was the latest . . .

Damiot had a hunch that he was getting close to the truth. That pimp, Chulot, picked up last week, was about ready to talk. Another day without drugs and he should spill everything. Chulot was known to have bought heroin from the Laurent woman a few hours before her body was found.

"What's in this warehouse, M'sieur Inspecteur?" Borell asked casually. "Where I'm taking you . . ."

"That's what I'm hoping to find out, mon ami. We only know it's a cover for the Valzo crowd."

"Valzo?"

He heard the note of fear in Borell's voice. "Valzo's in Marseille with most of his gang. Gives me an opportunity to take a look inside the warehouse. I had Graudin watch the place this afternoon, but there was no activity of any sort. It's used to store motorcycles for a chain of outlets Valzo controls around Paris. I suspect this may be where he keeps a supply of drugs and sends off deliveries with the motorcycles. There's only one night watchman, an old man who sleeps on the job, and no armed guards. That's to make us think the setup's legitimate. We've raided it several times, but found nothing. I suspect the narcotics are stored in underground vaults with access from other streets."

"Am I coming in with you?"

"No. I'll have a quick look at the place. Nothing more."

"Yes, M'sieur Inspecteur!" Borell sounded relieved.

"Park here. I'll walk the rest of the way."

"Yes, M'sieur Inspecteur." Borell slowed the police car to a stop, as though for protection, behind a battered truck that looked abandoned.

"And keep alert! This won't take more than half an hour." He started up the narrow street, passing a row of shops metal-shuttered for the night.

As he walked, not hurrying, he wondered whether Sophie would be asleep or reading one of her romantic novels.

God only knew where Olympe would be at this moment. His mistress always had friends to see. Singers and musicians. They sat in some favorite café near the Comique, drinking and gossiping . . .

Reaching the cross street and staying close to the high wall, he turned toward the warehouse entrance at the middle of the block.

The double wooden doors were locked, but a small metal door to one side swung in at his touch. No need to use the special device he carried on his key ring.

He went inside, closing the door silently, and waited until his eyes adjusted to the darkness. That watchman must have slipped out for a beer at some nearby bar and left the entrance door unlocked. Reaching an inner door, Damiot was surprised to find that it too was unlocked. With the boss in Marseille, somebody had been careless.

He pushed the door open and slipped inside into complete darkness, closing the door behind him before pulling a hand torch from his overcoat pocket. Its beam revealed a large storage room containing rows of shiny new motorcycles. They seemed to form one monstrous machine with hundreds of wheels.

There was a whisper of movement at the far end of the room.

Damiot snapped off his torch.

He didn't move, barely breathing, listening . . . Was someone there? Waiting for him in the darkness . . . Had he walked into a trap?

Perhaps he only imagined that something had moved. The place would be infested with rats.

He stepped forward in the dark, and struck one of the motorcycles with the toe of his shoe. The unexpected clatter echoed like the crash of a metal gong.

A machine gun blasted and its spitting fire revealed a man's face. Bullets smacked into metal and plaster, motorcycles clanged and crashed. Something hot burrowed into his left hip.

The impact knocked him back. Into a bottomless void . . .

2

The black Peugeot nosed off Route Nationale 7 through heavy rain, onto a secondary road that twisted higher and higher into the hills.

Damiot, at the wheel, glimpsed a village far below, at the bottom of a deep valley.

Provence! Empire du Soleil, they called it, but there was no sun this morning.

His doctor had agreed that his hip should heal more quickly under the hot Provençal sun. He would learn to walk again without a limp.

And he should be able to make decisions here. Plans for the future, about Sophie and their marriage. About Olympe . . .

Once again, Sophie had left him. Would he be able to persuade her once more to come back? That required a drive down to Cannes, and long arguments while her mother listened to every word.

His hip was hurting much worse now. Waves of pain. Probably caused by climbing those steps to the plane, then sitting in a cramped position on the flight from Paris to Nice.

The doctor had warned him that he must avoid strenuous exercise. A little walking—half an hour, twice a day. He had already done much more than that today.

Eleven years since he had been back to Courville! That last summer before he met Sophie . . .

He looked forward to seeing his birthplace again, the old stone building his parents had owned at the northern edge of the main village street. Only half a dozen blocks in length, but they called it Avenue de la République!

Chez Damiot. Restaurant and kitchen on the ground floor and three small bedrooms upstairs. His room had been the smallest.

He'd grown up there. Always underfoot. His father wearing a chef's hat and white apron, busy in the kitchen, while his mother ran the dining room with a series of youths from the village working as waiters. He was thirteen when he got a black suit with his first long trousers and took his place helping in the restaurant.

That's where he had learned about people. Observed their stupidities and peculiarities. How they ordered dinner, the way they ate, and the ways they complained. What they said when they thought he wasn't listening.

He slowed to peer at the sign beside the road, smiling as he read the name aloud. "Courville!"

The road at once became the Avenue de la République. Such a pretentious name for the narrow street lined with plane trees, running south to north from one end of the village to the other.

He slowed again to inspect a row of small shops on his right.

First the florist. It had always been here, as you entered the village. There was a new name above the entrance—Sibilat Fleurs—so old Lorois must have died and somebody had bought his business.

He realized, as he went on, that the avenue had been widened and that the sidewalk edging the churchyard wall on the other side had been eliminated.

At least the ivy-covered stone wall hiding the cemetery behind Saint-Sauveur—the only church in Courville—hadn't been touched.

His parents were buried in there . . .

As the avenue curved toward the heart of the village, he saw unfamiliar names above several other shops, their interiors so dim that he was unable to glimpse anyone inside.

Everything looked so shabby! Like some grubby foreign village he'd never seen before.

He discovered to his surprise that he was hungry. Been hours since breakfast and he had eaten nothing on the flight from Paris.

Slowing for a new traffic light at the corner of rue Provence, facing the Place de la République, he saw the ancient pissoir on the far side of the square, faded posters peeling from its stone sides. Beyond the pissoir, behind a row of umbrella pines, was the small railroad station where no train had stopped since before the war.

He drove on when the light changed, staring at everything. Straight ahead were the town hall and the Hôtel Courville, across the square.

The stone fountain in the center wasn't spouting any water in this rain. Only a few cars were parked around its marble basin, but on Saturdays, when an open market was held here, farmers came from the surrounding countryside and filled the square.

The Hôtel Courville looked seedy and dilapidated. It was the only hotel in the village, but he didn't care to stay there.

As he approached the town hall, he saw that it needed a coat of paint. The clock in the small tower had stopped with both hands straight up. Noon or midnight? Its chimes would no longer sound the hours.

Another new traffic light, corner of rue Voltaire, turned green, and he continued up Avenue de la République.

Madame Mussot's pâtisserie on the far corner, where he used to buy apricot tarts, seemed unchanged.

Eleven years ago he had stayed at a new motel on rue Voltaire, behind the town hall. It had been comfortable but served no meals. Should he stay there again? With his injured hip, he would miss having breakfast in bed.

Easing the Peugeot over the railroad tracks, he slowed past the final row of shops and the filling station that had been built after the war. Today, in the rain, it seemed old and dirty. A mechanic working on a truck in the cramped garage watched him as he drove past.

He wondered if that girl still lived in the village. The one he had met the summer before he married Sophie. What was her name? Blanche? Blanche Carmet!

Must find out what had happened to Blanche. A pleasant girl with brown hair and blue eyes. Solidly fleshed body . . .

That had been his last holiday as a bachelor. In the spring he had written Blanche and told her he was going to be married. She had never answered . . .

He drove past some handsome seventeenth-century houses with carved doors and graceful balconies. A child's swing, hanging from a tree in a deserted garden, was swaying almost imperceptibly in the rain.

Next a row of crumbling stucco houses, dingy and narrow. Beyond these, at the end of the avenue, was his old home . . .

He would have a quick look at it before he found somewhere to stay.

The whitewashed stone building in its small garden. He had planted flowers in front, vegetables along both sides and in the rear. Every morning he had cut fresh flowers for his mother to arrange on the restaurant tables and had picked vegetables for the kitchen.

Rain was flooding his windshield, in spite of the hissing wipers.

"Empire of the Sun?" he murmured. "Not today!"

Pray God the weather would clear. He needed sunshine for his hip. The pain was almost constant. A steady monotonous throbbing . . .

He could see the roof now, beyond the last of the plane trees. "Mon Dieu!" Someone had painted the old house yellow.

A wooden sign hanging from a metal arm extended from a vine-covered post. Two words, neatly lettered.

Auberge Courville

Damiot slowed the car and turned off the avenue into an unfamiliar cobbled courtyard. The Peugeot came to a stop at the place where he had planted his flower garden.

He sat there, both hands clutching the steering wheel, staring.

The old building had been enlarged and painted a soft yellow with white trim and shutters, walls barely visible under a thick cover of young ivy leaves. Big new windows in the dining area, plants in white window boxes, and dark yellow awnings.

Perhaps he would be able to find a room here. Actually stay in his old home!

Eleven years ago the building had been in complete disrepair. He was told then that it had been vacant for several years.

Maybe the place was closed. March was off-season in Provence. He picked up his hat from the seat and clamped it onto his head. Opening the door, he pushed himself out, favoring his injured hip. The stab of pain was immediate, and continued as he limped across the wet cobbles.

The old entrance had been replaced. Instead of a wooden door there was a clear pane of thick glass. Stepping inside he realized that the former narrow hall had been expanded into a shallow entry leading to a small circular lobby. A faint glow of warm light came from a shaded lamp above a tiny reception desk in an alcove that had never been there in the past. Pale gray daylight filtered out of the dining room. This restaurant was much larger than the old one. At least fifteen tables!

Limping past the reception desk, he saw that the old staircase was still there, curving up into the shadows. Stairs to climb if they gave him a room.

He reached out to grasp the wood handrail. Smooth to his touch. How many mornings had his mother polished that! And how many times had he slid down it when nobody was around to see.

Beyond the staircase a new wing had been added. He looked into a lounge with comfortable sofas, several fauteuils, and a television set resting on an antique chest. Green plants in large earthenware pots. An old-fashioned hooded fireplace. Framed paintings on the walls. Impossible to see, in this light, what they were. A row of tall double windows faced a small terrace with a flower garden beyond, barely visible through the rain, where part of his vegetable garden had been . . .

"M'sieur?"

Damiot turned to face a skinny red-haired boy coming from the dining room, wearing a striped apron over his denim work clothes. "I was beginning to think you must be closed."

"We open at seven. Never for lunch."

"I was hoping to find a room . . ."

"La patronne has gone into the village." He edged behind the desk. "But I could give you a room. How long does M'sieur plan to stay?"

"I'm not certain. Perhaps a week. I would prefer something quiet."

"If you'll sign our guest book . . ."

Damiot wrote his name on the empty page, adding only Paris, without giving his home address. "I'll bring my luggage from the car."

"Leave your key in the ignition and I'll park it for you."

"Won't be necessary. I'm going out for some lunch and I'll drive around to the back when I return. May have a nap before dinner. How's the food here? You have a chef?"

"The best in Courville! M'sieur Michel's from Marseille. He worked in a famous restaurant there and before that in Toulon and Cannes."

"Then I'll certainly dine here tonight."

"I will ask la patronne to reserve a table." He bowed and hurried ahead to open the glass entrance door.

Damiot brought his suitcases from the Peugeot and awkwardly carried them inside to where the garçon waited, key in hand.

"My name's Claude, M'sieur. Let me take those."

"Merci, Claude." He set his luggage down. "I'll have to go up these steps slowly. I was in an—an accident recently."

"I noticed M'sieur was limping. So I've given you a room on the ground floor." He handed the key to Damiot and picked up his bags.

"That was very considerate." He followed, pain spreading through his hip again, down a tiled corridor leading to the rear of the new wing. A single window at the far end was opaque with rain, but soft light came from behind handsome sprays of copper leaves on the orange-brown walls. The garçon led him to the second door and swung it open, snapped a light switch, and stood aside for Damiot to enter.

He went through the door unprepared for what was probably the most comfortable room he had ever seen. A large bed with simply carved headboard, an armoire, a comfortable bergère near a small fireplace. All the colors were muted: browns, yellows, and deep greens. Several handsome lamps and interesting paintings. Two pairs of French windows with long curtains that matched the flowered bedcover. The entire room had a curious feeling of security and peace.

"This will be satisfactory, M'sieur?"

"More than satisfactory. I may stay longer than a week." He continued to inspect the room as the youth set one bag on a bench at the foot of the bed, then brought a collapsible luggage rack from a cupboard and set it up for the other suitcase. Watched as he turned on lights in a bath, tiled in green and white, with a large tub—he was delighted to see—as well as a modern shower. He dropped a generous tip into the youth's hand.

"Plaisir, M'sieur Damiot."

"You know my name?"

"Saw it when you signed the guest book. I can read upside down." He grinned. "You are in Courville to look at property, perhaps? For the new hotel?"

"I'm here for a vacation."

"La patronne, Madame Bouchard, will see you at dinner." He started toward the door. "Madame will wish to welcome you."

"She is the owner?"

The garçon turned at the door. "Madame and her husband

opened the Auberge four years ago. Unfortunately, M'sieur Julien died in a skiing accident. He and Madame had gone to Mégève for their winter holiday. Service, M'sieur . . ." He departed, closing the door.

Damiot limped across to the bed and pressed his hand on it, testing the mattress. Firm but not too hard, unlike that pallet of rocks at the hospital that they had assured him was good for his spine.

Walking to the windows, he looked down into a garden flooded with rain. Gravel paths ran between neat flower beds. Nothing in bloom, but everything was green. In the old days this too had been part of his vegetable garden . . .

Madame Bouchard and her husband had created an attractive place here. Pity the husband had died. Madame would be running everything. Middle-aged, plump, and wearing black . . .

At the café on the southwest corner of rue Woodrow Wilson, facing the square, he had a steaming bowl of *petite marmite du pêcheur* and then, still hungry, ordered a ham sandwich with a glass of beer.

This was the oldest of Courville's two cafés, but he didn't recognize any of the men drinking pastis and playing billiards. He was aware, as he ate, that they were watching him, although they were careful not to stare directly at his table. All of them wore faded work clothes and bérets, old and soft, flat as crêpes on their heads.

His sandwich was excellent, fresh bread with a decent slice of pink ham, the beer exactly as he liked it, not too cold. In Paris these days, beer was served so cold it had no taste. That was how the American tourists wanted it. And the ham in most Parisian cafés was sliced too thin, with absolutely no flavor.

It was good to get away from Paris. He would be able to put all problems, professional and personal, out of his mind. Sophie and Olympe! And those two cases he had been working on before he went into the hospital. Let his assistant, Graudin, lose sleep over them . . .

He wondered whether Olympe had reached her destination. She hadn't mentioned, when she surprised him with a phone call at the hospital, whether she was going to Mexico by ship or plane, and he had asked no questions. Delicious Olympe! Her golden beauty should be a tremendous success in Mexico City . . .

Then, two days later, Sophie had sat on that white plastic chair like a stranger, telling him that their marriage was finished and she was leaving for Cannes to stay with her mother. He had asked her to wait, at least until he was out of the hospital, but she had whispered her accusations, eyes on the corridor door. "You think more of your murderers than you do of me!" Then she had started to sob, quietly, as she accused him of having a mistress. Thank God she didn't know that for a fact!

He had lost his temper and shouted at her until she hurried out of the room. Should have sent one of the nurses running after her but he didn't, convinced that her threat to leave would be forgotten. When he phoned the apartment next morning, there had been no answer.

His wife and his mistress! Both gone . . .

Olympe had informed him on the phone that she had fallen in love. His name was Bruno and she was going to Mexico City with him. They must have met before he went into that damn hospital . . .

A battered gray Citroën, its left rear fender crumpled and rusty, was parking near the fountain.

The rain wasn't so heavy now, but what he could see of the square through the drizzle was depressing. The terra-cotta tiles on the roofs of the low buildings were rose-colored in this dull light.

A young man got out of the Citroën, wearing an old waterproof over dungarees and opening a green silk umbrella. It was a girl! Once the umbrella was raised, she pulled off the cap covering her hair and shook it free—straight blonde hair that fell below her shoulders. An attractive face that somehow didn't look French. Probably American . . .

His hip continued to pain. Eventually, he had been told, it would give him no trouble—except in damp weather . . .

His doctor had been delighted at the idea of his coming to Provence but had warned him not to climb hills or attempt anything that might result in a fall. Better to stay on level ground when he did any walking. Get plenty of rest at night and take a nap every afternoon. Above all, he must keep his hip warm at all times. Soak in hot tubs . . .

He eased the hip, changing his position on the hard café chair, and felt an instant wave of fresh pain.

"Another beer, M'sieur?"

Damiot looked up to face the beefy, thick-necked *type* from behind the *zinc*. "Yes, I will." As the man returned to the bar, Damiot saw that the others were still watching him. The locals were always curious about strangers. He wondered if his father had known these three. Probably not. They looked much younger than his father. In their fifties . . .

His father would be eighty-four if he were alive!

Must remember to send the address of the Auberge Courville to his office at the Sûreté. That's if he decided to remain longer than a week . . .

He had phoned yesterday afternoon and told the Chief he was coming to Provence for a few weeks. The old man had urged him to take as long as he needed. Two months, if necessary.

Nobody in Paris knew where he was at the moment, and that's how he would keep it for now. Maybe phone Graudin on Sunday . . .

Damiot looked up as his beer was set on the table.

"M'sieur is a stranger in Courville?"

"I'm staying at the Auberge for a few days."

"They say the food's first-rate there."

"Nothing wrong with this ham of yours."

"My wife buys hams from a local farmer. Cooks them herself. Better than you get from Mauron, down the street."

"Mauron?"

"Hercule Mauron. Owns the charcuterie . . ."

"Hercule Mauron!"

"The only charcuterie in Courville. He's also the mayor."

"Was his father a butcher?"

"That's the one! The old man's been dead for years." He leaned closer. "M'sieur has come to Courville about the hotel?"

"What hotel?"

"The one they're supposed to build next year. Some say in the hills but others think it will be here in the village."

"I'm in Provence for a vacation, not business. Who's building this new hotel?"

"Some rich men from Paris. They've looked at many properties. Their hotel will be twenty stories high! With a big swimming pool and fancy restaurant."

"You want such a hotel here?"

He shrugged. "It would be good for business. Give jobs to our young people, keep them from running off to the cities.

There are many, of course, who are opposed to the idea. Mostly the old ones. They say it will bring too many outsiders and ruin the village."

"I agree. People don't come to Provence to stay in fancy hotels. Enough of those in Cannes or Nice." He looked up at the man's flushed face and realized the *type* was much younger than he had thought. Shrewd eyes and a hard mouth. "Have yourself a drink and put it on my bill."

"Merci, M'sieur." He headed back to the *zinc*.

So Hercule Mauron was mayor now!

He remembered him from school, a pig-faced fat boy whose father was the village butcher. Hercule had bullied all the smaller boys. Until one day Damiot had tricked Hercule into chasing him into the pissoir.

Damiot smiled, staring through the rain at the ancient pissoir, as he recalled that sunny morning . . .

He had run inside and around the edge, close to the walls, where the stone floor was always dry. Hercule had slipped in the slime and fallen on his face. When he came outside, a stinking mess, the other boys had laughed at him, and Hercule never bullied anyone after that.

Hercule Mauron! Mayor of Courville! *Incroyable* . . .

The mayor's office would be in the town hall across the square, a dark gray blur behind shifting veils of rain.

He had never been inside the old building. As a kid he had always avoided the police. When he left Courville to seek his fortune in Paris, he had no idea that one day he might become a detective.

Damiot paused just past the white-columned entrance, inspecting the restaurant. Only half a dozen tables were occupied.

The slim wooden columns, a pair on either side, were new.

"Monsieur Damiot?"

He turned to face a woman who had risen from a cashier's desk beyond the left pair of columns.

"I am Madame Bouchard. Unfortunately, Monsieur, I was out doing errands when you arrived. Your room, I trust, is satisfactory?"

"Most satisfactory."

"Claude tells me you wish to have quiet, and that is our most secluded room. I've reserved a table for you."

"Merci, Madame." She was neither middle-aged nor plump and she wasn't wearing black. As he followed her graceful figure through the dining room, he was aware of fresh flowers and lighted candles on each table. Two waiters moving among the tables, and one darting garçon. For a moment he didn't recognize Claude, in a black suit, long white apron tied around his waist. Then the youth saw him and grinned.

"You will also have complete privacy here." Madame Bouchard indicated a table set for one, partially hidden behind a low partition topped with green plants in white pots.

"Excellent, Madame." He eased his hip down onto a comfortable armchair with a petit point seat, his back to the wall.

"The chef assures me that the woodcock is unusually good tonight. Bon appétit, Monsieur."

He watched as she went back toward her desk, pausing at several tables en route. From a distance he could get a better impression.

An attractive woman. Wearing a smart gown she had surely bought in Paris. Made of some soft, dark green material that clung to her body as she walked. Copper-colored hair, brushed away from her face and arranged in a heavy knot at the back.

Damiot looked up to find a young waiter at his side.

"I am Jean-Paul. Would you care for an apéritif, M'sieur?"

"A dry vermouth."

The waiter bowed and hurried away.

There was a diffused glow of light from the candles on the tables and the candelabra on the walls. The effect was handsome against the wallpaper, which was a rich mustard color with cream stripes. More green plants in white pots, hanging from the ceiling and set on low pedestals. Curtains at the windows, patterned with white flowers against a yellow background. And all the chairs had petit point seats . . .

Two people were seated at another table shielded by potted plants, across the room. It was the blonde girl he had noticed earlier in the square, dressed attractively, her hair neatly arranged now, dining with an older man. Her companion had a thick crest of silver hair and a striking face, deeply tanned, with prominent jaw, twisted nose, and shrewd eyes. Was he the girl's father or her lover? Could be either, from the possessive way he looked at her as they ate their dinner.

The waiter served his vermouth with an order of *tapenade* and placed a menu within easy reach. "I can recommend the woodcock, M'sieur."

"Merci, Jean-Paul." He picked up his apéritif, realizing that he hadn't felt so relaxed in months.

When he had returned to the Auberge after lunch, he'd left his car in the parking lot and had sensed someone observing him from the kitchen windows as he limped through the rain around to the front. The lobby had been silent, the registration desk unattended.

His room was warm and inviting, lamps lighted, bed turned down. Somebody had closed all the curtains and started a fragrant fire of olive logs in the fireplace.

He had soaked himself in a hot tub until the pain in his hip subsided to a bearable ache. Put on fresh pajamas and eased into bed.

Oblivion came quickly. No dreams about Valzo or his gang! Nothing to make him twist in bed and start his hip throbbing . . .

"M'sieur has decided?" The waiter hovered beside him.

Damiot glanced at the list of hors d'oeuvres again. "I think, to start, the thrush pâté. No soup. Then, perhaps, the grilled lamb . . ."

Dinner was a miracle of many perfections.

As he ate, he studied his fellow diners, mostly married couples, some with teenage children. The men appeared to be businessmen; their wives were expensively dressed. All of them seemed to know Madame Bouchard who, from time to time, made a discreet inspection tour of all the tables. He was the only person dining alone.

After his lamb was served, he saw the chef come through the swinging doors from the kitchen in white-aproned uniform, starched *toque blanche* perched on his curly black hair, visiting each table, bowing to the men and kissing the ladies' hands. Young, and surprisingly, for a chef de cuisine, not an ounce overweight.

"How is the lamb?"

He looked up to face Madame Bouchard again. "Excellent! You have a first-class chef."

"I'm delighted that you think so. Pardon, Monsieur . . ." She moved on toward a table where a family of four was studying the elaborate display of pastries their waiter was offering from a chromium cart.

Damiot remembered his mother, an apron over her plain cotton dress, taking orders and moving among the tables. Arguing with some of the diners, most of them old friends, but always smiling . . .

The chef bowed on his way back to the kitchen, and Damiot nodded.

As he ate, his thoughts returned to his last dinner with Olympe. More than four weeks ago! The night before he was shot, they had gone to Drouant for supper. As usual, she had been full of plans. Someone wanted her to join a new opera company for a tour of the provinces. That must have fallen through—like so many of her other projects—or she wouldn't have gone off to Mexico. He had been more disturbed by her sudden departure than about his wife going to Cannes . . .

Sophie would come back. All he had to do was phone her in Cannes and apologize.

Not this time!

Yet he loved Sophie in a way he had never loved any other woman. In fact, he hadn't looked at another woman seriously, after his marriage. Not until Olympe . . .

Damiot finished the last of his wine with one of the small *Banons,* a local goat cheese wrapped in chestnut leaves, which he could seldom find in Paris.

"Coffee, M'sieur?" the waiter asked.

"Black, please."

"Since M'sieur is a guest, he might prefer to have his coffee served in the lounge."

"That sounds fine."

He sank into a comfortable fauteuil upholstered in deep yellow, near the blazing fireplace in the lounge, aware that his hip had barely twinged in the last hour. That Châteauneuf-du-Pape he had enjoyed with dinner was better than any medicine.

"Your coffee, M'sieur . . ."

"Ah, Claude!" He watched the garçon set a coffee tray on a low table. "Was it you lighted a fire in my room?"

"Thought it would be warmer for M'sieur when he returned from the village." Pouring the steaming coffee as he talked. "Service, M'sieur." He bowed and scurried away.

Sipping the scalding coffee, Damiot observed the last of the diners crossing the foyer toward the entrance.

He was aware that Madame Bouchard had left the dining room and, after pausing at the registration desk, was coming into the lounge.

"Would you like me to switch on the television, Monsieur?"

"I rarely watch television."

"Nor I. But it is here for our guests. More coffee?"

"Thank you, no. I wonder . . . Could I have a Calvados?"

"Certainly."

"Would you join me?"

"That's very kind, but I must complete my duties for the night." She smiled and turned back toward the restaurant.

Damiot finished his coffee before Claude returned, almost running.

"Your Calvados, M'sieur." He set the glass of brandy down. "Will there be anything more?"

"Not until morning. Is it possible for me to have breakfast in my room? I intend to sleep late. Perhaps nine o'clock?"

"Of course, M'sieur. Nine o'clock. Sleep well, M'sieur."

"Good night, Claude." He watched the skinny boy hurry toward the dining room with the tray. When he was that age, he too had always hurried.

Damiot cradled his glass in both hands, warming the apple brandy. Sleep until nine? Why not! He had nothing planned for tomorrow or, for that matter, all of next week. Certainly he would stay here at least that long. His room was comfortable and dinner had been better than any meal he had eaten in Paris for months . . .

Tomorrow he would drive through the countryside and up into the foothills. Explore some of the places he had known as a boy . . . He relaxed, staring at the flaming logs, feeling their warmth on his face as the Calvados warmed his body. No pain in his hip tonight!

It had been wise to leave Paris. Get away from his problems . . .

Sophie had her mother, and Olympe should have no problems in Mexico. Not with her Bruno in attendance. Another month, of course, and she would start worrying about her career. That's when the accusations and recriminations would start.

Chère Olympe! Give her six months, at most, and she would come flying back. Full of new plans . . .

What was he going to do about Sophie? Drive down to Cannes next week? Try and persuade her to return to Paris with him? Sit in that spotless white salon and argue while her mother scowled and sighed. Did he want to repeat that ridiculous scene?

Lucky he and Sophie had never produced any children. "Your murderers are your children!" She had told him during one of their arguments. "You never wanted any others!"

Maybe she was right . . .

"Monsieur Damiot?"

He looked up to see Madame Bouchard again. "Madame?"

"I did not intend to be rude, a moment ago . . ."

"Not at all!" He set his nearly empty glass on the table and pushed himself to his feet.

"Do not disturb yourself. I have finished my chores for the night and can now accept your invitation." She sank into another fauteuil, facing him. "Jean-Paul will bring more Calvados."

"Splendid!" Damiot lowered himself carefully onto his armchair. He was aware of her perfume, subtle and delicate.

"I understand that Monsieur is recovering from an accident."

"Yes." Better not say that he had been shot, or an explanation would be expected. "It was necessary to have surgery on my hip. My doctor advised me to rest, and I've come to Provence hoping to find the sun."

"There was much rain this winter, but soon now it will be spring and we'll have plenty of sun." She looked around as the waiter appeared with a bottle of Calvados and two glasses on a tray. "Merci, Jean-Paul."

Damiot tossed off what remained of his first drink as Madame filled the fresh glasses. "A vôtre santé, Madame."

"To your complete recovery from that accident."

"Merci!" He watched her sip the brandy. A serenely beautiful face, but her brown eyes seemed suffused with melancholy. Probably not yet recovered from the death of her husband. "I've not tasted Calvados like this in years!"

"My husband found this one. It was his favorite."

"I must compliment you, Madame. The changes you've made here."

"Changes?" She looked at him more closely, her interest aroused. "Then you've been in Courville before?"

"Some years ago. The restaurant was much smaller then and this lounge didn't exist."

"Julien and I added an entire wing. When we discovered this property it had been empty for many years, but we were told that at one time there had been a small restaurant here."

"Only half a dozen tables. And one guest room upstairs . . ."

There was a sudden explosion of barking as a small black dog raced across the foyer and into the lounge. Jumped into Madame Bouchard's lap, licked her hand, then faced the stranger and growled.

"Non, Fric-Frac! C'est méchant!" Madame laughed. "She protects me from all strangers. Never bites anyone—at least not yet—but her growl is ferocious."

"Fric-Frac? In the argot of Pigalle that means a caper—a bank robbery or some other planned criminal act."

"My husband named her. He had heard the word in a gangster film. She was Julien's dog . . ." Her fingers stroked the curly head. "He said the name suited her because she always capers when she's happy. Which is most of the time! He also called her Madame la Duchesse."

"Madame la Duchesse?" He smiled at the growling dog. She was completely black, except for a moustache streaked with gold.

"Julien found her one morning, sleeping in our garden. She had crawled there from the road, half-starved and filthy. He carried her into the kitchen and cooked breakfast for her. After she ate he stooped to pet her and she kissed his hand with the tip of her tongue. Thanking him. And Julien announced that she would remain as a permanent guest."

"What breed is she?"

"The vétérinaire in Arles suspects she must be part poodle and part Scottie. Probably about five years old now. He thought some tourists had lost her or thrown her out from their car."

"How could anyone do that to a dog?"

"People are cruel, Monsieur." She scratched the dog's head as she talked. "Fric-Frac's an affectionate little thing. She adored my husband and grieved for him when he died. It was more than a year before she gave any affection to me."

"Your husband died recently?"

"Almost two years ago . . . Please! Help yourself to more Calvados."

The dog sniffed at the rim of her glass.

"Non, chérie! You do not like Calvados. She adores white wine if you give her a few drops from your fingers."

"You and your husband created a fine restaurant here."

"Everything's exactly as Julien planned." She set the dog on the floor. "I was ready to give up after his death, until I found our present chef."

"Your chef is excellent."

"I am so fortunate! Michel was working at a restaurant in Marseille—not too happily—and driving through Provence on vacation. By some miracle he stopped here for dinner and, quite properly, complained about our food. I explained that I had recently fired my chef and was doing the cooking myself. Michel never returned to Marseille." She set her glass on the table and raised both hands in a gesture of surprise. "Monsieur! Observe what Fric-Frac is doing. I'm afraid she wants to be picked up."

He looked down and saw the dog seated at his feet, her paws stroking the air. Damiot put his glass down and the dog jumped into his arms. Wiggling and squealing her pleasure.

"You have been accepted, Monsieur. She has not done this with anyone. Not since my husband . . ." Her voice trailed away.

"I am honored." He settled the dog on his lap.

"I must say good night, Monsieur." She got to her feet. "We have a busy day tomorrow. Friday starts our weekend . . ."

He set the dog on the floor and stood up, grimacing as his hip protested.

"Your hip is bothering you?"

"It is nothing."

"Come, Fric-Frac!" She led the dog toward the foyer. "Time for bed."

Damiot followed, conscious of his limp.

"Let me know if there's anything you require for your comfort. I hope this weather clears and you get your sunshine."

"I trust so, Madame. Bonsoir."

"Bonsoir. Claude will bring your breakfast at nine."

"Bonsoir, Fric-Frac!" He turned down the corridor toward his room as Madame went behind the reception desk, followed by the dog.

An extremely beautiful woman! Probably in her early thirties.

"Here you are!" It was a man's voice.

Damiot slowed his steps from long habit, head slightly turned, listening.

"Thought you'd gone up to bed, chérie." The man's voice again.

"Soon as I get the cash-box . . ." Madame Bouchard's voice.

She must be talking to the chef. He calls her chérie?

"You think something will happen tonight?" she asked.

"There'll be no murder in this weather." He laughed. "The monster doesn't care to get his feet wet."

"Such nonsense!"

Damiot was scowling as he continued down the corridor.

No murder tonight?

He wanted no part of any murders. Or monsters . . .

4

Damiot opened his eyes reluctantly, reacting to a red glow that had seeped through his eyelids and wakened him.

Unfamiliar room? Brilliant diagonal bar of light . . .

Had he left a lamp turned on?

"Mon Dieu! It's the sun."

He pushed himself to a sitting position, in spite of a twinge of pain through his hip, and saw that the bar of light was an opening between two window curtains. When he had pulled them across the windows last night, they hadn't closed.

There was a thin strip of blue sky and, lower down, something green that seemed to be alive and quivering.

Slipping cautiously out of bed to favor his hip, he limped across the cold floor to the windows. Grasped the curtains with both hands and flung them apart.

The sudden glare of sunlight made him blink. Then he saw that the sky was indeed a brilliant blue. Not a cloud! And the quivering green was a tree branch covered with young leaves.

He padded back to the bedside table and snatched up his wristwatch. Not yet seven? Eh bien! Run a hot tub and relax in that for half an hour. Then back to bed and wait for breakfast.

He hadn't slept so well in months! Must have been that second Calvados with Madame Bouchard . . .

Damiot slowed the Peugeot to a crawl as he recognized a section of road he had walked hundreds of times in the past. Farther on there would be an old stone bridge across a small river where he used to fish.

He glanced at the dog beside him, seated on her haunches, muzzle thrust out through the open window. She had scampered into his room as Claude entered, and jumped onto the bed. Damiot had fed her bits of orange-flavored bread spread with lavender honey as he enjoyed his breakfast.

She had remained on the bed, watching him while he shaved and dressed, and followed him to the foyer, where he found Madame Bouchard.

"Bonjour, Monsieur! Did you sleep?"

"Without a dream. I feel completely rested this morning."

"I'm so glad." She glanced down at the dog. "Fric-Frac isn't being a nuisance?"

"Certainly not. In fact, I was wondering if I might take her with me this morning for a drive in the foothills?"

"You'll be doing my staff a favor. She gets underfoot when they're busy in the kitchen. And she adores riding in a car." Smiling as she ripped the page from her pad. "Will you return in time for dinner?"

"Long before that, I should think."

"Then I'll reserve your same table."

He saw that she was wearing a pullover sweater the color of spring violets, well-fitting gray slacks, and elegant black boots.

"Friday mornings I take the station wagon and drive from farm to farm picking up fresh meat and vegetables. Enjoy the sun, Monsieur . . ."

And he was enjoying the sun. First sun he had seen in weeks! It was spreading a golden haze across the orchards that provided the apples for Calvados, extending beyond the low stone walls lining the highway.

The farmhouses were old but appeared to be in good condition. Provençal farmers always kept everything in working order.

Fields and vineyards teemed with activity. Women in straw hats working among the grapevines. Smoke rising from bonfires of twisted roots. Farmhands in one recently tilled field, planting seeds. He could smell the rich earth, damp from the rains.

Groves of silver-gray olive trees trimmed on top, not as in some other provinces. Villages perched like toy houses on distant hills, their stone walls pink in the hot sunshine. Almond trees on the higher slopes and a row of dark cypresses like sentries, black against the intense blue sky.

A flock of ravens, disturbed by his car, shot up from a field with a clatter of sound, cawing and flapping their purple-black wings.

Passing a hedge of hawthorn, he was startled when a small boy straightened to stare at him. Probably crouched there searching among the roots for snails. He had done that many times, along this same road.

When Damiot reached the old stone bridge, he stopped the Peugeot and got out. The dog ran down to the edge of the bank and dipped her muzzle into the water.

He had fished here many times, another small dog beside him, although he didn't recall ever catching any fish. Had sat on this same bank for hours, dreaming in the summer sun . . .

What did he dream about in those days? He had no idea.

As he continued along the curved road, higher and higher, he realized that he was approaching the Château de Mohrt. For centuries the ancient castle had belonged to the de Mohrt family, but he and his young friends always called it Château Mort. Castle Death!

That was what the villagers, long ago, had named the place. Which gave the great estate a special fascination . . .

He and his pals climbed over the high wrought-iron fence to steal berries every spring and walnuts in the winter. There were plenty of both closer to the village, but they were supposed to taste better if they came from the dark forest surrounding the castle. Sweeter berries and larger walnuts! Many times when they got inside the grounds they had been chased away by a gamekeeper with a pack of fierce dogs. Huge gray beasts that came crashing and snarling through the underbrush . . .

Damiot realized that he was passing a high stone wall he had never seen before. They had replaced the old wrought-iron fence with a wall!

In the past you could see the front of the castle from here, beyond a sloping green lawn where sheep grazed. He had driven by several times with Blanche Carmet, and always slowed his car to stare through the trees at the distant château.

It was rumored that the de Mohrt family had died out or, if any members survived, that they were living elsewhere. The only tenant was said to be a caretaker. Some of the locals claimed that the castle was haunted. Lights had been glimpsed late at night through windows in the upper floors . . .

He slowed the Peugeot as he approached the entrance and saw the same tall wrought-iron gates that had always been there. Although not as high as he had thought when he was a boy. How the size of things diminished as you grew older.

The gates were closed, padlocked on the inside.

Damiot stopped his car and leaned across the open window, pressing against the dog, to look between the elaborate grilles.

A broad drive lined with poplars led up to the lower edge of an open courtyard from which, in a glare of sunlight, rose the impressive stone bulk of the Château de Mohrt.

It was this cobbled courtyard that had given the name of Courville to the village. The first houses, and an inn, were built centuries ago, at the place where two highways crossed. People were said to have traveled great distances to attend the famous trials held in the courtyard of the castle.

He stroked the dog's head, feeling the delicate bones of her skull, as he studied the distant château through the locked gates.

The enormous mansion appeared to be unchanged. But from here he could only see the western wing and a corner of the central part of the castle. Through the open space in between he glimpsed far-off hills at the rear. Ivy climbed the stone walls like rising smoke, winding around the balustraded upper terrace and spreading upward around the small tourelles to one of the massive high towers with its slits of windows. The other towers and the main entrance, under its pillared arch in the center, were no longer visible because of that new wall.

Suddenly the sound of pounding hoofs made him turn and peer

through the windshield. He saw a small figure on a black horse, racing toward him. Probably some farm boy. The rider would notice him sitting here and think he was a tourist, gawking at the famous château.

The dog began to growl.

"No, Fric-Frac." He reached out and patted her. "It's all right."

As the horse thudded closer, he realized that the rider was a girl. Long blonde hair flying. Wearing a man's sport shirt, riding breeches, and boots. Sitting the horse like a professional.

It was that girl he had seen yesterday in the village. She glanced at him as the horse galloped past, their eyes meeting briefly. The dog barked and tried to scramble across his knees.

"Stay where you are." He lifted her back to the window, where she settled down after one final growl.

The great château seemed to float in a haze of sunlight above the open courtyard. Perhaps, while he was here, he could do some research on the castle's history. There must be documents at the town hall. That would give him something to do for a few hours . . .

He saw that the grass edging the entrance drive had not been trimmed in a long time. Heavy coils of ivy hid the stone columns on either side of the gates. Barely possible to make out the carved gargoyle heads that glared down from the top of each gatepost. They were supposed to be the faces of de Mohrt ancestors . . .

Fric-Frac sat up again, her head thrust out through the open window, and began to growl.

A sharp crack of sound came from beyond the wall. A branch snapping under the weight of an animal? Wild boar or deer . . .

He had a momentary feeling that he was being watched.

Damiot drove on, following the high wall to the west boundary of the estate, then passed through a wooded area where ancient oak trees joined their branches in an overhead arch. No other cars in sight and the only sounds were muted bird voices from the forest.

This country air was giving him an appetite. In Paris he seldom had more than a sandwich with a glass of wine, but today he would treat himself to a real lunch.

He wondered where that blonde girl could have been going on

her black horse? Either in a hurry to get somewhere or anxious to escape from something. Or someone . . .

He drove past more vineyards and farms.

Heads turned, eyes following his car, but no arm was raised in greeting. These country people were never friendly with strangers.

He slowed down as he approached another farm. The old stone house, to his surprise, had recently been roofed and painted. A flower garden extended around both sides to vegetable gardens at the rear, with stables beyond. There was a long lane, lined with beech trees, where one car was parked. It was the gray Citroën that blonde girl had driven yesterday. So this was where she lived!

Damiot drove on into the foothills, through rocky canyons that led up to shallow plateaus. Olive trees clung to the steep hillsides with desperate roots.

After driving for another hour, he checked a map and took a different route back toward Courville. The road descended gradually, and he glimpsed deep gorges and rock-tossed streams. One brief view of a river, probably the Rhône, snaking through a city that he didn't recognize from this distance. Could it be Arles?

Several kilometers farther on, he passed a pleasant country inn with a small dining terrace at the side. Swerving off the road, he turned and came back. Slowed as he read a sign—La Terrasse—before he drove into the empty parking lot. Careful to leave his car under a tree, windows open, so that Fric-Frac would get air.

He followed a path to the dining area. All the tables, under yellow parasols, were empty, but a fat pigeon in a patch of sunlight was searching for crumbs on the stone terrace.

"M'sieur?"

Damiot turned as a swarthy waiter in shirtsleeves came from inside. "Are you serving lunch?"

"But certainly!" He led the way between the tables as he talked. "Yesterday, in the rain, there was nobody, but with this sunshine we should get several people today."

Damiot eased into a chair that the waiter pulled out and flicked with a napkin. "I drove past, but your terrace looked so inviting I came back. Such peace and quiet can't be found in Paris restaurants."

"At the moment we have too much quiet. Another month and

we'll get a flood of tourists. The quiet will depart, of course, but business will improve. An apéritif, M'sieur?"

"A vin blanc cassis. What do you suggest for lunch?"

"The chef has prepared wild quail today. With a special stuffing."

"I'll have that."

The waiter bowed and went inside.

Damiot realized that he was smiling in anticipation. He hadn't tasted wild quail in years.

His table was near a low brick wall enclosing a flower garden whose rosebushes were a solid mass of green leaves. Another month and they should be covered with buds.

And, faintly, he heard the true sound of Provence. Les cigales! There seemed to be only a few of them, close at hand, probably hatched by the morning sun.

A shy-eyed garçon spread a checked cloth over the table and then, swift as a magician, produced napkin and silver.

"M'sieur . . ." The waiter set his apéritif in front of him.

"Merci. And what do you suggest for a start?"

"Perhaps the snail fritters . . ."

"Bien! With half a carafe of Tavel?"

"Certainly . . . M'sieur is in Provence on business?"

"I'm here for a holiday. Staying at the Auberge Courville."

"Courville! Have they caught that monster yet?"

"Monster?"

"It was in one of the local papers. Another Courville murder! A young girl, like the first . . ."

"Why do you call the murderer a monster?"

"That's what the newspaper called him. The Courville Monster!" He shrugged. "All murders are brutal, but this man's a real beast. Pardon, M'sieur." He bowed and disappeared inside again.

Another young girl murdered? And they were calling the killer "the Courville monster" . . .

Certainly all murderers were not monsters. Some of the most interesting people he had known were murderers. Fascinating people! Gentle and pathetic people . . .

A monster loose in Courville? Mustn't think about that . . .

"M'sieur?" The waiter again. "Is this your dog?"

Damiot looked down to see Fric-Frac dancing on her hind legs, tail wagging frantically. "I left her in the car but the windows were open. Would it be all right if she sits here beside me?"

"Of course, M'sieur. Le patron has two dogs of his own."

Damiot stroked the small black head and watched Fric-Frac settle down beneath his chair, revolving several times as though she were making a nest.

The fritters were excellent, rolled around succulent snails.

The garçon removed his empty plate, and the waiter brought a steaming casserole containing two plump quail in a dark sauce, with baby carrots and small white onions.

Damiot sniffed the appetizing aroma rising from the stuffing. He detected herbs, tomatoes, mushrooms and sweet peppers, and a trace of Calvados.

As Damiot ate, he slipped bits of quail to the dog.

His hip was paining again, even while he sat absolutely still. The metal pin they had inserted must be adjusting to his first real exercise. All that therapy at the hospital had been easy—walking on moving belts, clutching handrails, and arriving nowhere—compared to his activity yesterday and today.

That night in Montmartre, he had been foolish to go into Valzo's warehouse alone. Once again he had taken an unnecessary risk. He should have waited until others arrived to back him up. But that had never been his way . . .

Valzo was dead, killed when he crashed his motorcycle escaping from the warehouse. Borell had heard the shots and was waiting in the police car when Valzo came out.

The informer who tricked Damiot into searching that warehouse had been arrested, and the pimp, Chulot, had spilled everything about the murder of the Laurent woman.

"How's the quail, M'sieur?"

Damiot looked up to see the waiter again. "Just as I remembered! I've come home."

"M'sieur is from Provence?"

"I was born in Courville."

"Welcome home, M'sieur!"

5

Damiot relaxed in the empty lounge, near the fireplace, drinking a second cup of black coffee as he watched the last of the evening's dinner guests departing through the foyer.

Fewer people tonight, because of the rain that had begun late in the afternoon.

"We are closing early."

"Madame Bouchard!" He pushed himself to his feet as she came toward him, carrying a tapestry workbag in one hand. "Won't you have a drink with me?"

"I've told Jean-Paul to bring the Calvados." She smiled as she sank into another armchair, resting her workbag on the tiled floor.

Damiot resumed his seat, facing her. Noticing the reflection of the fire on her copper hair, and the beige gown he had admired earlier in the restaurant. A single strand of pearls around her throat. "Dinner was excellent again. Especially the saddle of hare!"

"I will tell Michel. He thrives on compliments, like every chef, and he heard none tonight because he didn't leave his kitchen." She reached down to lift some needlework from the tapestry bag. "Usually, when it rains, we have at least a dozen for dinner. Tonight there were only seven."

"But of course you make up for this in the summer months."

"We turn people away every night. Actually, I don't mind this off season. No tourists arriving in a rush, wanting to be fed in a hurry! Only our regulars and an occasional stray."

"Like me?"

"Like you, Monsieur . . ." She smiled as she rested the needlework on her lap. "You won't mind my working as we talk?"

"Certainly not."

"It relaxes me at the end of the day. During these slow

months I'm always making more seat covers for our dining-room chairs. I can't do that in the summer."

He saw that she was stitching needlepoint on an oval frame. "Very handsome!"

"I do think they give the restaurant more character. We planned them, Julien and I, from the start. We wanted everything to be simple but quite individual." She looked up as Jean-Paul brought a tray with a bottle of Calvados and glasses. "Put that near Monsieur Damiot so he can refill his glass without inconveniencing himself. And you can pour us both a drink."

"Plaisir, Madame." Jean-Paul rested his tray on the coffee table, within reach of Damiot.

Fric-Frac, bounding with excitement, ran toward Madame Bouchard, yelping with pleasure as she pawed at her owner's skirt. Then she came straight to Damiot and jumped into his lap.

"Non, Fric-Frac!" Madame protested. "Naughty girl!"

"That's all right." Damiot stroked the curly black head. "She's welcome to stay."

The dog gave his hand a rapid lick with her pink tongue.

"Did she behave today while you were out?"

"She was a little lady."

"Sometimes she can be a large nuisance." Setting her needlepoint aside and accepting a glass of Calvados from the waiter. "Merci, Jean-Paul."

"Service, Madame."

Damiot raised his glass as the waiter departed. "A vôtre santé, Madame!"

"Vôtre santé . . ." She made a small gesture with her glass before sipping the brandy.

"Someone lighted a fire in my room this afternoon while I was out. Left a bowl of lilac . . ."

"Claude made the fire and I brought fresh flowers back when I returned from shopping. The first lilacs are so beautiful! I get all my flowers from Sibilat Fleurs in the village. Marc Sibilat is the best florist this side of Nice." Her needle flashed in and out as she talked. "Marc bought the shop two years ago, when the former owner retired."

Damiot made a mental note to visit Sibilat Fleurs tomorrow and buy some flowers for his parents' graves.

He watched her needle, with its thread of golden brown,

moving back and forth. She was apparently a woman who was comfortable with silence. "Madame Bouchard . . . What can you tell me about the Château de Mohrt?"

She looked up. "The château?"

"When I drove past there this morning, I noticed that the entrance gates were padlocked."

"They're always locked. No one is permitted to enter the grounds."

"Does anyone live there? In the castle . . ."

"I believe there's a caretaker on the premises." She dropped her eyes to the needlework again. "I've never been inside. Except for poachers, I don't think anyone goes there."

Damiot saw that the dog, curled in his lap, was asleep. There were other questions he wished to ask. "I noticed a girl in the village yesterday and again last night, dining here with an older man. Blonde girl?"

"That's Jenny Tendrell. The man's her father, Allan Tendrell. He's an artist—British—and, I believe, rather famous."

"Attractive girl . . ."

"They have a farm in the hills. Allan bought it, some years ago, and spent a fortune making the place comfortable. The night we opened this restaurant, they were our first customers. When Julien was alive we often dined chez Tendrell on the nights we were closed. They have an excellent cook."

"Then they live here all year?"

"Oh, yes! They're permanent residents. Although I fear the villagers have never really accepted Allan. They resent the fact that he brought his staff with him from Burgundy and hired none of the locals. Which, however, he had every right to do! They, including the cook, had worked on his farm for years. Allan moved south for the warmer weather. He suffers from arthritis."

"Is there a Madame Tendrell?"

"Not at the moment. Allan was divorced, years ago, and given custody of his daughter. I don't know the circumstances involved . . . Today Jenny's old enough to do as she pleases— which she most certainly does—but she continues to live with her father. They dine here at least once a week. Allan enjoys good food. Jenny, however, doesn't care what she eats!"

"You say Tendrell is an artist?"

"His paintings are in many museums, but I'm afraid they don't really appeal to me. I find most of them rather—unpleasant."

She hesitated, her eyes on the petit point. "I've been wondering, Monsieur, have you come here like the others—there've been several visitors recently—to look at property for the new hotel?"

"Certainly not! Matter of fact, I don't approve of these modern hotels springing up all over France." He darted his next question at her. "Tell me, Madame, what is the Courville monster?"

She faced him again. "How did you hear about that?"

"A talkative waiter where I had lunch today."

"Most waiters talk too much! I thought you had come to Courville about the new hotel."

He sighed. "I am with the Police Judiciaire in Paris. Chief Inspector Damiot."

"So! You were sent to find the killer?"

"I never heard of the Courville monster until today. I've come here to rest. As I told you, I'm recovering from surgery. When the hospital released me, my doctor suggested I get away from Paris and recuperate somewhere in the sun. That's why I came to Provence. But tell me, why is he called the Courville monster?"

"Because two people—two young women—have been brutally murdered. One girl from the village and another, a stranger, who has never been identified."

"How exactly did they die?"

"Their throats were cut . . ."

"And the murder weapons? Were they found?"

"I believe not."

"Where were these young women killed?"

"The first—the one who remains unknown—was found in a field surrounded by forest, across from the Château de Mohrt."

"I know that field."

"The second body, a local girl, was discovered in an alley directly behind the town hall. This, of course, has caused the villagers to make jokes about our local gendarmes."

"Naturally! Did you know this local girl?"

"Not really." She hesitated. "We would speak when we passed on the street or happened to meet in some shop. She was a femme de chambre at the Hôtel Courville. Everybody knew her." Her needle continued darting. "These murders have caused a mood of fear and suspicion to infect the entire village. No young girl will venture out after dark. Many accuse our gendarmes of incompetence!"

"That frequently happens. Even in Paris! I suppose both these young women were attractive?"

"The local girl was extremely pretty. The other one I never saw."

"How old were they?"

"Nineteen and twenty, according to the newspapers. The local girl was supposed to be nineteen, although I had thought she was somewhat older . . ."

"Is there much talk about the identity of the murderer?"

"Oh, yes! I see people, when I'm shopping, standing in groups. Men huddled together in the cafés, women gossiping on the streets. They usually stop talking when they notice me. I'm not really on speaking terms with many of the villagers. I'm still an intruder here and, I suppose, will remain one for many years. I do hear fresh rumors, every morning, from my staff. The waiters and kitchen help all come from the village or nearby farms. And, of course, many of the diners who drive here from a distance question me about the 'Courville monster.' I try not to discuss the murders but it is unavoidable . . ."

"What do the villagers say about this killer in their midst? Who do they think it is? People usually have their own theories, and even though they may be wrong, there can be a core of truth in what they think."

"They are confused . . ." She glanced at him, frowning, then lowered her eyes to the needlepoint again. "In the beginning, they said the murderer was someone from outside. That was after the first victim was found. It was thought she had been killed by a transient—we get many of those through here—but the discovery of a second body changed that way of thinking. For a time, many of the villagers believed it must be a madman who had escaped from some nearby clinic. That theory had to be abandoned when no such person was reported missing."

"And this is all the villagers are saying?"

"Not quite . . ." She hesitated again, needle moving in and out. "Some are saying that there is, vraiment, a monster. They say he prowls the countryside at night. Curiously, he doesn't seem to seek a victim in bad weather. Each of the nights when he killed, the weather was fine."

"Was there a moon?"

"I asked that myself. There was no moon, either time. Always a clear sky with stars."

"And what do the local gendarmes say?"

"I've no idea. They've brought an investigator here from Arles, but the villagers treat him as another intruder. Avoid his questions and make jokes about his intelligence behind his back."

"When was the last murder?"

"Three weeks ago."

"And now everyone's waiting for the next?"

"I'm afraid so. Yes . . . Some of the villagers seem close to panic."

Her hair, in the firelight, was like a bronze helmet. A genuinely handsome woman. Healthy looking. His eyes lingered on the firm weight of her breasts under the soft material of the dress. Strong, capable-looking hands. A simple gold wedding band . . .

"What is your own theory, Madame?"

"My theory?" She didn't look up from her needlework.

"About this 'Courville monster' . . ."

"I have no theory, Monsieur. None at all!"

He saw that she had turned slightly, toward the windows, as though listening to some sound from outside.

Fric-Frac growled softly.

Damiot stroked the dog's head. "Fric-Frac hears something."

"My kitchen staff may be leaving. Or the villagers could be passing on the road. They go up to the château when the weather is clear."

"But it's raining tonight!"

"Not at the moment. I glanced outside, as I showed our last guests to the door, and the stars were shining." She shrugged. "Everyone is nervous as a result of these murders. The slightest sound in the night, I am out of bed and at my windows. Fortunately, Michel, my chef, remains here at night. He has an apartment over the garage. The other staff members go home, so it is a great comfort to have Michel on the premises."

"You say the—monster only kills when there is good weather."

"So I'm told."

"Then he may be prowling tonight!"

"That's why the villagers go up to the château. Hoping to see him again."

"Again?"

"They've seen him several times. Or so they claim . . ."

"And what are the local police doing?"

"I assume they're waiting for something to develop. They

most certainly don't venture out at night, in their one ancient car, looking for problems. Unless they're summoned! They've warned the villagers they could get into trouble trespassing at the château."

"People can't be allowed to take the law into their own hands."

"Some of the villagers think the monster comes from the castle. Claude told me last week that they think he hides during the day in the cellars and comes out at night."

"Every old castle should have a monster." Damiot chuckled. "And a beautiful princess. They seldom do, these days . . ."

"Monsieur is laughing at me."

"Not at all." He finished his Calvados and set the glass down.

"The villagers watch the château from the road, but some have climbed over the gates to get inside the grounds."

"What happened?"

"One young man saw something moving through the trees."

Damiot remembered the sound he had heard this morning, behind those locked gates. "He probably glimpsed some animal . . ."

"I gather he didn't linger to find out. More recently, several of the villagers claim they actually saw the monster standing in a patch of moonlight. They say it was taller than any man! One moment the monster was there, in the courtyard of the château, and the next it had vanished. As though it had sunk through the cobblestones. One other thing! Before the monster appears they say a great bell tolls . . ."

"I wonder, Madame, would anyone have copies of the newspapers reporting those two murders?"

"We have no local papers, unfortunately, but there are weeklies, published in nearby towns, that some of the staff bring when they come to work. I will ask if there are any old copies. Claude is our squirrel! He saves everything. And he's fascinated by the idea of a monster . . ."

"Talking about that monster again, chérie?"

Damiot looked around to see the chef, still in his white uniform, entering the lounge.

"There must be one, Monsieur, because some of the villagers swear they've seen him!" The chef laughed, white teeth flashing, his brown eyes dancing with amusement.

"Ah, Michel!" Madame Bouchard motioned for him to join

35

them. "This is our chef de cuisine, Michel Giroud. Monsieur Damiot . . ."

Damiot put the dog down and got to his feet, extending his hand as the white-aproned chef came toward him. "You're a first-class chef!"

"Merci, Monsieur." He shook Damiot's hand. "It is a pleasure to cook for a man who appreciates food."

"Your saddle of hare tonight! Never tasted better in Paris . . ."

"Plaisir, Monsieur." He turned to Madame Bouchard. "Have you been spreading fresh rumors about the monster?"

"Certainly not! It's all nonsense."

Damiot realized, as Giroud talked, that Madame Bouchard's eyes glowed with affection for the young chef. He had left his *toque blanche* in the kitchen and his black hair was thick and curly. A real charmer! With his gypsy look and culinary talent he should go far . . .

". . . thought, perhaps," Giroud was saying, "I would take a drive, now that the rain has stopped. Clear my head of that kitchen."

"And I'm going to bed." She looked toward Damiot. "When we close this early I try to get an extra hour of sleep."

Giroud turned to Damiot again. "I hope you will have a pleasant stay in Courville, Monsieur."

"Merci."

"Will you be late, Michel?" Madame asked, eyes following him toward the foyer, as she returned the needlepoint to her workbag.

"You know I've no sense of time, chérie! Bonsoir, Monsieur!"

"Bonsoir . . ." Damiot remained standing as Giroud went through the dining room. "I think that I too may take a short drive."

"Yes, Monsieur?" Madame rose, closing the workbag.

"You have made me curious. I'd like another look at that château."

She walked beside him toward the foyer, the dog dancing ahead.

Damiot hesitated as they reached the corridor. "I would prefer, Madame, that you are the only one, at least for the moment, to know I am with the Police Judiciaire in Paris."

"I understand, Monsieur. A demain!"

"A demain . . ." As Damiot went toward his room to get his hat and waterproof, he realized that Madame Bouchard had been smiling.

A smile of amusement? Or complicity?

Damiot drove into the hills, through drifting eddies of white mist, passing several villagers carrying lighted lanterns.

They were walking close together in small groups, and when they heard his motor behind them they moved off the road and stood frozen, like wary animals. Only their heads turned, eyes following his car.

After he passed they would discuss his identity. If there were any among them who had seen him on his trips into the village, they would tell the others. Someone would certainly know he was staying at the Auberge.

Most of them wore cloth caps or berets. Old clothes and heavy work shoes. Muscular types, in their thirties and early forties, with a few teenage youths.

He caught up with a two-wheeled cart, drawn by a farm horse. Three old men were huddled on straw in the back, their ancient faces like Daumier caricatures in the wavering light of a lantern.

Last of all he passed a pickup truck carrying a group of younger men. The driver appeared to be in his thirties, with sandy hair and round face.

Damiot increased speed up the hill and around a curve in the road. His headlights soon revealed the high wall surrounding the château.

He slowed to a stop at the entrance. Got out and walked toward the closed gates.

The mist was much heavier here. Impossible to make out anything through the grille, except a ghostly section of drive revealed by his headlights. The distant château was invisible.

Damiot turned back to his car, hip throbbing and warning of pain to come. Hesitating, his hand on the door handle, he looked down the long road. As yet, no one in sight coming from the village.

He lowered himself into the Peugeot, careful not to strike his hip, and switched off the headlights. The night immediately became impenetrable—a solid black wall pressing against his car.

Damiot closed the window at his side. As though that could shut out whatever evil might be crouched behind those locked gates . . .

Better get out of here before the first of the villagers arrived. He turned on his headlights and drove slowly past the gates.

He recalled that there had been a rear entrance to the estate when he was a boy. He had forgotten about the entrance. He had forgotten how he had watched from high on a hill, stretched out on his stomach, as trucks and carts creaked through the open gates bringing freshly caught fish that dripped water along the side lane, or carcasses of beef and lamb piled under bloody tarpaulins. Some of the de Mohrt family still lived here in those days. The old lady—Madame la Comtesse . . .

Opening both windows, he backed the car until he came to a space where there were no tree trunks or underbrush. Only darkness . . .

Damiot eased the Peugeot off the road and immediately felt his tires sink into soft earth. The winter rains must have soaked this ground for months.

Branches slashed through the open windows, sending dried leaves and broken twigs flying across his face. The car filled with a rich scent of damp earth and moss. Rotting wood and decaying leaves.

The deep ruts in the lane were impossible to avoid. When he struck one, the car gave such a lurch that he bounced up and down. His hip protested each time, with instant stabs of pain. If he got a flat tire or the next rut damaged his axle, he would be in real trouble.

Finally, he saw where the wall came to an end at the rear of the estate. Slowing the Peugeot to a stop near the rear entrance, he left the headlights on and got out.

Damiot peered between the vertical bars of the padlocked gate and glimpsed more heavy undergrowth and trees. In the past, from this vantage point, he had been able to see the kitchen area of the château.

No point in staying here!

As he turned to leave he recalled that there had been another lane, directly opposite this rear entrance, leading to higher ground where you could look down into the kitchen courtyard. That was where he had stretched out for hours, watching the servants at their work.

He saw that the lane was still there.

Eh bien! After coming this far he would go all the way. He lowered himself into the Peugeot again and, backing a few feet, turned into the other lane. Felt the car lift at once as it followed the twisting curves.

He had neglected to close the windows, and the night air became colder as he drove up the hill.

To his surprise, he saw tire marks that looked fairly recent. The local teenagers must still drive up here with their girls.

The Peugeot rounded a final curve and came out into an open area where its headlights revealed a grassy ledge facing empty black space.

This was the spot he had remembered.

He eased off the lane and stopped the car parallel to the ledge. Switched off his headlights and was swallowed up by the night.

Leaving the door open, he got out and hesitated, unwilling to move closer to the rim. One stumble could pitch him over the edge.

Lights danced in the distance. Lanterns? Those villagers must have reached the front gates.

The silence was broken by the faint tolling of a bell.

A dog howled, somewhere below. Damiot shivered. Madame Bouchard had said that the villagers heard a bell tolling before the monster appeared.

The sound seemed to come from high in one of the château towers. A single repeated stroke, at regular intervals, deep and resonant.

That dog again. Barking now, but the sound seemed to be more distant. Was it one dog or several? Inside the château or running loose in the grounds?

The bell continued to toll.

His eyes must be adjusting, because the darkness seemed less opaque. He closed them, squeezing both lids together. When he opened them after a few seconds, he saw the dark bulk of the Château de Mohrt. Still, it was impossible to make out any details except for the massive stone walls and towers against the night sky.

From here he was looking between two wings of the mansion across the west terrace, just as he had done when he was a kid, over the open courtyard toward the entrance drive.

Squinting toward the distant gates, he could make out their wrought-iron grilles against a glow of lanterns. There seemed to be two lanterns inside the grounds, moving up the drive toward the château. Some of the younger villagers must have climbed over that wall.

Whisper of sound in the darkness, near at hand to his left. Probably some night creature prowling for food.

He glimpsed a faint blur of light in one of the castle windows, as though someone had passed inside with a candle or lantern.

Faint echo of voices from far below. As though the villagers were shouting from outside the gates.

Another glow of light from the château. This time it appeared to be on the terrace that surrounded three sides of the mansion. Could be someone walking there with a lantern, although this light didn't seem to be in motion. One of the villagers could have climbed up there and set his lantern down while he searched for an unlocked window.

Voices again. The villagers, beyond the gates, must be calling to their friends on the terrace, directing them or giving them encouragement.

Something moved into view on the terrace. Not much more than a dark shape in the dim light. A shadow cast by something not yet in sight . . .

The voices of the villagers were silenced. Damiot saw that the lanterns beyond the gates were motionless. The others, inside the grounds, had disappeared.

He tried to make out what was moving on the terrace . . .

Something seemed to be crawling along the base of the balustrade.

Suddenly, as he watched, a huge figure rose from the terrace.

The voices of the villagers sounded like a great wave rolling in toward a beach.

The monstrous figure stood without moving, looking down at the villagers outside the gates. Watching them. Damiot could see their lanterns, clustered together now, beyond the wrought-iron grille.

The giant form began to move toward the front of the terrace. Slowly and clumsily. Swaying slightly. Like some ancient figure in a long cloak that hung in heavy folds. It seemed to have a tremendous head with black hair falling to broad shoulders.

The bell was silent now.

Then, as suddenly as it had appeared, the monster disappeared and the light was gone.

It was as though the figure had vanished through the terrace floor. Just as Madame Bouchard had said! Only that floor must be solid marble.

Turning to look down toward the far gates, he realized that the lanterns were no longer there. The villagers must have fled.

He was alone. High on this dark hill, at the edge of a sheer drop that could kill anyone who stumbled over the rim.

And somewhere in that château there was a monster! Taller than any human being he had ever seen.

Damiot turned and started back toward the car. Stepping cautiously to avoid any loose stones.

He stopped and peered around, trying to make out some shape—tree or shrub—in the darkness.

Then, to his right, he saw a low dark bulk . . . The Peugeot! He stumbled toward it, eager to leave, grasping the door handle. Clutched the cold metal as though he had found a friend. Stood there, breathing heavily, his heart pounding . . .

This was ridiculous! He had never acted like this, in all his years at the Préfecture . . .

Of course this was the first time he had found himself alone, with an injured hip, on a dark hill above a castle containing a monster!

He looked around, still clutching the door handle, as he heard something moving stealthily through the underbrush. The sound came from in front of his car and it was getting closer.

Damiot released the door handle and, moving with caution, reached through the open window to fumble at the dashboard.

There used to be wild boars in these hills that would attack a man if they were aroused. His headlights should startle whatever this was. Man or . . .

He switched them on and the glare of light revealed a man.

It was the Englishman—Tendrell—holding both hands up to shield his eyes from the dazzling headlights.

Damiot faced him. Tendrell was shorter than he had appeared last night at the Auberge. Wearing an old leather jacket and dirty slacks. "What are you doing here, Monsieur?"

The question seemed to release the Englishman. He turned and plunged, arms flailing, away from the light.

Damiot followed, limping now, his shadow looming ahead of him like another monster, as he lurched in front of his own headlights.

Hip throbbing. Waves of pain shooting through his thigh.

The Englishman had vanished.

Eh bien! No point in continuing after him. Much too dangerous.

Starting back toward his car, he saw its headlights through a tangle of maquis.

Then he heard another car behind him, coming fast.

Glancing back, he saw the headlights rushing toward him.

Damiot moved aside, out of the way, as the gray Citroën sped past, but he glimpsed the Englishman at the wheel before the car disappeared around a curve.

7

Slowing the Peugeot, Damiot squinted at the stone farmhouse. Smoke was rising from a chimney, and two windows facing the road revealed a dimly lighted interior. He would have a talk with this Englishman.

He swerved into the lane, between long rows of beech trees, and parked behind the gray Citroën.

His hip throbbed sharply as he twisted his body out of the car and limped toward the house, eyes adjusting to the darkness, following a path between flower beds.

The stone farmhouse was built low to the earth, with shuttered windows on either side of a heavy wooden door. The lighted windows he had glimpsed from the road were not visible here.

As he raised his hand to knock, uncertain what he would say, the door swung open.

"Why the devil did you follow me? Who are you?"

Damiot noticed that Tendrell had removed his leather jacket and was wearing a heavy sweater. "Chief Inspector Damiot, Police Judiciaire." He brought out his flat leather case and flipped it open.

Tendrell stared at the badge. "Local police?"

"No, Monsieur Tendrell. Quai des Orfèvres."

"The big guns moving in, are they?"

"I am in Courville on vacation."

"In that case, come in! And welcome . . ."

"Thank you, Monsieur."

"I was having a drink. Bloody cold, up on that hill tonight."

"It was, indeed." He closed the door and, removing his hat, followed the Englishman through a dim passage. "Why did you run off when I spoke to you?"

"I had no idea who you were. Flashing those headlights in my eyes. I couldn't see your face. I heard a car arrive on the hill and wanted to find out who else was there. When I realized it was a stranger I took off." As they entered a shadowy sitting room, he peered at Damiot more closely. "Didn't I see you last night, dining at the Auberge?"

"I'm staying there for a few days."

"You're the chap! Aurore mentioned you to my daughter."

"Aurore?"

"Madame Bouchard. You're her only guest at the moment."

"Her name is Aurore?"

"Delightful, don't you agree? She didn't mention that you're from the Quai des Orfèvres."

"I hadn't told her."

"Do make yourself comfortable. May I fix you a drink? Whisky? Cognac?"

"Whisky would be fine."

Damiot glanced around the comfortable room as Tendrell talked. Low-ceilinged, with smoke-blackened wooden beams. Fine old furniture—French and English—and walls crowded with framed paintings and overflowing bookshelves. Logs blazing in a stone fireplace. He looked at the Englishman. "What were you doing up there, Monsieur? On that hill . . ."

"There were rumors that the monster might make an appearance on the first night of good weather."

Damiot sat on the sofa, resting his hat beside him. "You saw the monster?"

"No. Some of the villagers claim to have seen some sort of enormous figure, in the past, that was at least twelve feet tall. I saw nothing."

"They exaggerate. Slightly . . ."

"In what way?"

"I would guess their monster might be nine of your English feet in height. No more than that."

Tendrell came toward him, a glass of whisky in each hand. "Then you saw the monster tonight?"

"Yes, I did." Damiot took his drink from the artist's hand.

"You actually had the good fortune to see our Courville monster? And I didn't!"

"I saw it briefly." He took a large swallow of whisky. "It stood on the terrace looking down at the villagers, and then it was gone."

"I'll be damned!" Tendrell sank into a brown leather chair, facing his visitor, glass in hand.

"Before the monster appeared there was the sound of a bell tolling. Surely, Monsieur, you must have heard that?"

"I heard nothing."

"You couldn't have been too far from where I was standing . . ."

"From my vantage point, looking between the main section of the château and the west wing, it wasn't possible to see that upper terrace. Only the entrance drive." Tendrell tossed off half of his drink in one gulp. "I had thought the monster was supposed to appear in the courtyard where he's visible from the front gates. That's where those blasted villagers claim they saw him in the past. Actually, I went there tonight to observe the locals at their drunken revels."

"How often has the monster been seen?"

"Since that first girl's body was found, he's rumored to have been glimpsed several times, and at least three more after the second girl was killed."

"You don't believe in monsters, Monsieur?"

"Ah, but I do! I've known many genuine monsters, in my time. Including my former wife."

"What about this monster tonight?"

"I've already told you. I didn't see him."

"I mean—what do you think it is? Perhaps some kind of trick?"

"Might be one of the locals, having a bit of fun and games with his neighbors. There are those who say it's the ghost of some fellow who was hanged, centuries ago, in that meadow across from the château."

"It could be the murderer, of course! Whoever killed those two young women may be trying to frighten people away."

"He would be taking rather a chance, don't you think? Risking capture. Shouldn't you slip out of that damp coat for a bit?"

"Perhaps for a moment." Damiot set his glass on a table and rose from the sofa. Grimacing as fresh pain lanced through his flesh.

"Something wrong, Monsieur? Are you hurt?"

"Hurting, but not hurt. I came to Provence to recover from recent surgery on my hip." He slipped out of the waterproof. "Hoping to relax in the sunshine."

"We've had bloody little sun lately."

Damiot draped his waterproof over the back of a chair and resumed his place on the sofa.

"So you're stopping at the Auberge? Marvelous food! Though not up to what they served when Julien Bouchard was in charge of the kitchen. This new chef can't touch him, although he's jolly good. Aurore's in love with him. You must have noticed."

"No. I hadn't." The idea was somehow distasteful.

"She denies it, of course. Aurore's such an innocent! Except about running her restaurant. She's quite extraordinarily capable at that. Can I freshen your whisky?"

"Merci, no. Tell me, Monsieur, what do you know about these local murders?"

"Only hearsay, I fear. Mostly from my daughter who picks up all the local gossip. The villagers accept her, but they barely speak to me."

"Who was the most recent girl to die?"

"Lisette Jarlaud." Sipping his whisky, more slowly now. "Something of a beauty! Blonde and plump. Rubens would have enjoyed painting her. She was found three weeks ago in an alley behind the Courville town hall, where the gendarmerie is housed.

Which is, of course, a bit of a black mark for the local police lads."

"How could the monster get down there from the château?"

"And what makes you think the killer came from the château?"

"Isn't that what the villagers are saying?"

"Well, yes . . . Actually, that alley leads toward open country. Anybody could walk from the château across those fields and down to the edge of the village without being noticed. Or, for that matter, from a dozen farms in the area. Including this one!"

"Did the police find prints near the girl's body? Footprints?"

"I'm told there were several, but before anything could be done to preserve them, the rain washed everything away. The Jarlaud girl's clothing had been torn from her body and she had been raped."

"What was she like?"

"Familiar, shall we say, to one and all!" Tendrell moved around the room as he talked. "First time I noticed her, shortly after my arrival in Courville, I was having a whisky in one of the cafés. A young man, drinking with some chums, called out to her as she walked past on the sidewalk. From the nasty way they laughed, I gathered that all of them had known the girl. I learned later that she was a femme de chambre at the Hôtel Courville and rather a favorite with salesmen who book there overnight."

"You say she was raped. But that was not the cause of death?"

"Her throat was cut. Quite permanently."

"Did she have any family?"

"Lisette lived with her parents and two small children. It is rumored that the children belonged to her."

"Who were her friends?"

"I don't believe she had any real friends! Of either sex. Lisette was the sort of girl everyone knew. Yet, curiously, nobody knew her."

"What about the first victim?"

"She has not yet been identified."

"When was she killed? In relation to the second . . ."

"Two months ago. I believe it was mid-January when a farmhand stumbled over her body. She too had been raped. Her throat slashed."

"Footprints?"

"I'm told that dozens of people tramped there before the police arrived. When the body was taken down to the morgue, everyone in the village was asked to identify her, but no one recognized the unfortunate creature. I didn't want my daughter to participate, although I did go and have a look for myself."

"Had you seen her before?"

"Never. The police think she must have been a transient. Perhaps one of those hitchhikers one sees on the roads, more frequently during the summer."

"Is there a bus through here?"

"Not on this road."

"The Jarlaud girl . . . Did she limit her favors to overnight visitors at the hotel?"

"Not at all! Lisette apparently had many admirers in the village. Several shopkeepers have been questioned, discreetly, so that their wives would not find out. There are rumors she even had an occasional rendezvous with one of the local gendarmes!"

"Policemen too are human."

"You're quite certain, Inspector, that you weren't sent to solve these murders?"

"Paris doesn't get involved with unsolved murders in the provinces. Tell me, Monsieur. Was the first girl blonde, like the second?"

"She had red hair, but as a painter I can assure you the color came from the chemist."

"What a disgusting thing to say about that poor girl . . ."

Both men turned, startled, to see a slim figure in a yellow silk robe just inside the open doorway.

"What the devil are you doing up?" Tendrell exclaimed.

"Your voices wakened me."

Tendrell turned to the detective. "This is my daughter, Jenny. My sole offspring!" He set his glass down. "Come in, luv. Meet Chief Inspector Damiot from Paris."

Damiot got to his feet. "Mademoiselle . . ."

"So you're a flic!" She came forward, into the light. "I've seen you twice, Monsieur. First in the Auberge last night, at dinner, and this morning in a car parked outside the château." She curled herself in a corner of the other sofa, tucking both feet under her robe.

Damiot sat down again, facing her. She had a lovely face, pert nose, intelligent eyes.

"Aurore Bouchard told us about you, during dinner. A guest from Paris!" Jenny shook her long blonde hair away from her face. "But she neglected to say that you're a flic."

"Madame didn't know." He glanced at Tendrell. "And I beg you, Monsieur, not to tell anyone. I've no desire to have my holiday ruined by the local police trying to involve me with their unsolved murders."

Tendrell nodded, sinking into a leather chair. "I quite understand."

"Then you're truly not here to solve them?" Jenny asked.

"Certainly not!"

"Pity . . . It's been three weeks since Lisette died, and the gendarmes have no idea who killed her. Or, for that matter, the other girl."

"Do you, Mademoiselle?"

"Do I what?" She pretended not to understand.

"Know the identity of the killer?"

"I haven't the foggiest notion!"

"No suspicion?"

"Why are you asking questions, if you're not working on the case? And why have you been quizzing Allan! He never knows what's going on in the village or, for that matter, under his nose. Unless, of course, I tell him."

"Which you always do!" Tendrell turned to Damiot. "Each evening I'm given a report on everything that's happened during the day. From the running of our farm—which Jenny does, incredibly well—to the latest chitchat from the village. I get a full account at dinner."

"That's not true!" Jenny protested. "There are many things I don't feel are suitable for your innocent ears." She frowned as she looked at Damiot again. "You don't suspect Allan of these murders, do you?"

"Jenny!" Tendrell exclaimed. "What a thing to ask."

Damiot laughed. "I don't suspect anyone. I'm asking questions out of curiosity. Until yesterday I had never heard of these Courville murders. Then, tonight, I encountered your father on the hill above the château, and followed him home."

Jenny looked at her father. "Did you . . ." She stopped abruptly, as though uncertain how to continue.

"See the monster? No, my dear. I did not. But it seems that Inspector Damiot did."

She faced the detective. "What did it look like?"

"I saw a dark figure from a distance. It appeared for a moment on a terrace of the château."

"Was he quite huge?"

"Very tall."

"Could you see his face?"

"Only the back of the head and that not too clearly. One moment he was there and the next he had vanished."

"So the monster really does exist!" she exclaimed. "We've never been absolutely certain. You're the first outsider to see him. Until now only the villagers managed to catch a glimpse of the thing, and I, for one, never believed any of them. Allan has watched the château, most clear nights, but he's never seen anything."

Tendrell nodded. "We were beginning to wonder if the villagers weren't imagining their monster."

"Are you going to tell the police, Monsieur Damiot?" Jenny asked. "That you saw this—this creature?"

"Certainly not! They must have seen—whatever it is."

"No! They haven't. They've brought in a detective from Arles to handle the case. And he's completely stupid! Perhaps I shouldn't say that, but . . ."

"I'm sure they're doing their best!" Trendrell interrupted.

"This is their investigation, not mine." As Damiot's eyes moved away from Jenny's face, he noticed the framed paintings on the wall behind her head. One was a portrait. The head appeared to float in a mist, but the face was oddly familiar. Something about the eyes?

"Changed your mind, Monsieur Inspecteur?" Tendrell rose from his chair. "Another whisky . . ."

"I think not. Merci."

"Something for you, Jenny?"

"At this hour! Certainly not."

"I'll just have another quick one." He returned to the sideboard and busied himself with a bottle.

Damiot looked from father to daughter. "And what do you think, Mademoiselle, about this monster? Is it real?"

She shrugged. "You saw him, Monsieur. Not I."

"Which proves nothing. The whole thing may have been some sort of optical illusion caused by a reflection from one of the château windows. I glimpsed a moving light inside. By the way, does anyone live there?"

"A caretaker, I believe. I've never actually seen him but I know he's there because I have heard him, mornings, when I'm exercising the mare and ride past the gates. I suspect he's one of those strange old men who like to spy on young girls!"

Damiot saw that Tendrell's glass was half empty again. "Tell me, Monsieur, aren't you worried about the safety of your daughter?"

The Englishman looked startled. "What do you mean, sir?"

"My safety!" Jenny pushed her hair aside, away from her face.

"If there is, vraiment, some kind of monster hidden in the Château de Mohrt," Damiot continued, "you could be in danger. If the monster walked through those fields down to the village, he could certainly find his way here."

"So he could . . . Never thought of that!" Tendrell tossed off the remainder of his drink.

"But I should love to see the monster!" Jenny pretended to shiver.

"Why do you think the—monster—slashes his victims' throats with such violence?" Tendrell asked abruptly.

Damiot frowned. "Only the killer himself can answer that."

"The way he slashed both those girls, from what I've heard—and from seeing the first victim in the morgue—was quite expert. His skill with a knife would indicate some knowledge of anatomy."

"Indeed?"

"He might, of course, be a doctor. Possibly from some nearby city, since there is no resident physician in Courville."

"Or an artist . . ."

"Artist? Oh, yes! We all study anatomy."

"Even a farmer knows anatomy!" Jenny exclaimed. "Most of our neighbors do their own butchering. They're terribly expert at it."

Damiot saw the face in the portrait hanging behind her more clearly now. A young man's face with a prominent nose and petulant, sardonic mouth . . .

"What is it, Monsieur?" Tendrell asked.

He realized that the artist had been observing him. "I was intrigued by that painting on the wall."

"Oh?" He glanced at the canvas. "If you're interested, I would be happy to show you some more recent canvases."

"Another evening, perhaps?" He got to his feet. "I've intruded much too long."

"Not at all!" Tendrell rose, placing his empty glass on a table. "Always delighted to meet someone from the outside world."

"I think your monster is one of the villagers!" Jenny announced, following them out of the room. "Hoping to attract tourists to Courville this summer. All their little shops depend upon income from the people who stop off for a few hours, on their way to more important places. The season starts in another few weeks. I think the whole thing's a hoax to get publicity. And the local flics are in on it."

Damiot smiled. "But if that were true, who murdered those two girls?"

"I also have a rather large suspicion about the murderer!"

"Do you, Mademoiselle?" They had reached the entrance passage. "And what might that be?"

"I think he's a salesman who drives through Courville every few months."

"Why do you say that?" Damiot asked, shrugging into his waterproof.

"Because I've seen him. Twice! At least I've seen his car. A black Ferrari."

"What nonsense!" Tendrell exclaimed. "You've never told me this."

"You saw the man's face?" Damiot asked.

"Too dark, both times . . . And I'm much too sleepy, at the moment, to think clearly. Bonsoir, Monsieur Inspecteur . . ."

"Bonsoir, Mademoiselle." He watched her yellow robe disappear through the passage, into the dark depths of the farmhouse.

Tendrell moved ahead toward the entrance and opened the door.

"Thank you for the whisky. And for the information you've given me."

"Nothing but gossip, I fear. Drop by again, Inspector! And have yourself a pleasant vacation."

"A bientôt, Monsieur." He put his hat on and went down the path through a steady downpour. The Peugeot was streaming with water, so the rain must have been falling for several minutes.

The road was empty in both directions as he turned left toward the village.

This had been a curious evening. First that incredible figure on the château terrace! The villagers had certainly seen it from where they stood at the gates. And in spite of Tendrell's denial, he was certain that the Englishman must have glimpsed the monster.

Nobody lived in the château any more. Only a caretaker. Was he the one who wanted the villagers to think there was a monster on the premises? The fact that it only appeared on clear nights meant that someone wanted the monster to be seen...

He had liked the artist and his daughter. The Tendrells had talked like equals, not parent and child years apart.

Damiot turned off the avenue and slowed around to the rear of the Auberge. Through the restaurant windows he glimpsed a faint glow of light inside. Probably left burning for the night in the foyer.

As he eased the Peugeot to a stop in the empty parking lot, he saw that the garage doors were open, for the first time. Three cars were parked inside, with no room for another.

He got out and ducked into the dry garage, before plunging through the rain to look for the flowerpot where Madame had said he would find a key to the front door.

As he stood there, out of the rain, he noticed a shadow moving in a lighted room above the kitchen. Madame Bouchard's suite? He hoped that he hadn't wakened her...

Damiot glanced at the three cars. An old station wagon, a black Renault, and a dark green Jaguar.

A sound caught his attention, and he turned to see that the kitchen door had been opened and a figure was silhouetted against the light.

"Monsieur Damiot?"

"Yes, Madame!"

Damiot limped across the puddled parking area, his hip throbbing again.

"I heard your car and came down to open the door."

"That was very kind, Madame." He saw that her copper hair hung in twin braids and that she was wearing a dark brown robe of quilted satin. Her face, without makeup, was even more beautiful. "You shouldn't have waited up for me."

"Couldn't sleep. I was reading."

As he shook the drops of rain from his hat, he realized to his surprise that she had been concerned for his safety.

"I regret that on a night like this you can't park in the garage. Unfortunately there's only room for three cars." She closed the door behind him. "Michel and I always park there. He drives the green Jaguar."

"Tell me, Madame. Do you know anyone in the neighborhood who owns a black Ferrari?"

"Nobody in Courville could afford a Ferrari! Some of the tourists in the summer have expensive cars, of course . . . What happened tonight, Monsieur? You were going up to the château. Did you see anything?"

"I saw the monster."

"You saw . . ."

"And so did the villagers who were there."

"Then it's not their imagination!"

"No, Madame."

Fric-Frac arrived with breakfast, barking and dancing across the room, leaping onto his bed.

The garçon laughed. "Bonjour, M'sieur!"

"Bonjour, Claude." Pushing himself up to a sitting position, he saw a newspaper folded on the breakfast tray. "You've brought a paper?"

"La patronne said you wanted to read about the murders. This was the only paper I had saved."

Damiot read the brief story as he ate breakfast.

He learned very little. Two murders had taken place, and "these unfortunate young women would appear to have been killed by the same person." At no point was there any mention of the monster. Although the story did say that the first victim had been found in a field "adjacent to the famous Château de Mohrt, which for centuries has belonged to the illustrious de

Mohrt family." The last surviving member of that family, the Comtesse de Mohrt, had died several years ago in a Swiss sanatorium.

Like much reporting in provincial newspapers, the story was carelessly written and lacking in details.

Breakfast finished, Damiot shaved, showered, and dressed, with Fric-Frac waiting and observing from the bed.

She darted ahead of him, down the corridor and through the silent lobby, to the front entrance.

The sun was bright when he stepped outside. Swallows wheeled against a blue sky as he circled the Auberge to the parking lot, avoiding the puddles left from last night.

Fric-Frac splashed through each puddle, ran straight to the door of the car, and stood on her hind legs, pawing to get in. When he opened the door she jumped up and sat on the front seat, her tail thumping.

Traffic was heavy on the Avenue de la République as he turned left into the village. Big trucks heading down to Route Nationale 7. His first stop this morning would be that florist shop.

There was some activity in the village. Women going in and out of shops, wearing light coats over faded housedresses, scarves tied around their heads. Carrying string shopping bags or small baskets.

Of course! This was Saturday. Market day . . . He noticed a sign above a shop across the square, next to the corner bakery.

Charcuterie
Hercule Mauron

Hercule the pork butcher! Damiot smiled.

He parked across from the florist shop, glancing down at Fric-Frac as he swung the door open. "You wait here, Madame. I won't be long."

Crossing to the sidewalk, he saw the sign again—Sibilat Fleurs—above the entrance. This was the only shop in the village that had been painted recently, a soft gray with cream-colored trim. Today there was a bouquet of yellow roses in the display window.

A bell tinkled as he pushed the door open and went inside.

The interior was completely new. A refrigerated display case holding fresh flowers extended across the wall behind a long counter, which faced the entrance. A single shaded ceiling light was almost invisible among a jungle of hanging plants.

As Damiot approached the counter, he heard a woman's voice complaining to someone behind a curtained door. The curtain was pushed aside and a man appeared, in shirt sleeves, wiping his hands on a water-spattered apron.

Damiot realized that it was the young man who had driven the pickup truck he had passed last night on his way to the château. Same round face and sandy hair. Muscular but slightly overweight.

He reacted with obvious recognition when he saw Damiot. "Yes, Monsieur?"

"I would like two small bouquets of roses. Like those in your window."

"Certainly." He slid back a section of glass in the display case, lifted out a metal tub filled with yellow roses, and placed it on the counter. Moving expertly, he produced two sheets of green waxed paper, spread them flat on the counter, and carefully placed the roses, one by one, on the first square of paper.

"Monsieur is a stranger in Courville?"

"A visitor."

"But Monsieur has friends here!" He laughed, self-consciously, nodding toward the roses he was arranging. "Two friends?"

"Across the street. In the cemetery."

His face became solemn. "Forgive me, Monsieur. I am Marc Sibilat. The owner."

Damiot was aware of the curtain in the doorway moving slightly. The woman must be watching them. "I saw you last night, Monsieur Sibilat, when I was driving in the hills. You were at the wheel of a truck carrying several villagers."

"My friends and I were on our way to the château, hoping the monster would show up again. It only appears if the weather's clear, and last night was the first night this week without rain." He worked deftly as he talked, arranging a second bouquet. "I looked for you when we arrived at the gates."

"There was nothing to see. So I drove on."

"But you should have waited, Monsieur!"

"You saw the monster?"

"Oh, yes! He appeared on the terrace for a moment and stood there watching us."

"Cowards!" The woman's voice again.

Damiot looked toward the curtained door as a plump figure in black burst into the shop. Hawk-faced, with inquisitive jet eyes. White hair.

"My own son! Like all the others. Cowards . . ."

"Madame?"

"Grown men!" she exclaimed as she reached the counter. "They see the monster again but do nothing about it!"

Damiot turned to Sibilat. "You've seen this monster before?"

"Twice. In the past it has appeared in the courtyard, but last night it showed itself on a terrace."

"And the idiots did nothing!" Madame Sibilat's eyes blazed. "They should have caught the thing, whatever it is, and destroyed it!"

"I only hope that news about the monster will be good for business." Sibilat twisted plastic tape around the stems of each bouquet. "Most of the shopkeepers think the publicity will convince those people from Paris that our village would be a good location for their new hotel."

"New hotel?" Damiot frowned, reminded of what he had already heard.

"Some businessmen are considering building a modern hotel in this area. They've been looking at possible locations. Such a hotel would naturally mean more business for the whole village . . ."

"Then catch the monster!" Madame Sibilat exclaimed. "That would get you some real publicity!"

Damiot pulled a hundred-franc note from his wallet as the florist folded the waxed paper around the roses, and dropped it on the counter.

"At first, when the villagers said they had seen a monster, I didn't believe them," Madame continued, as she took the money and unlocked the cash drawer, "but then my own son saw the thing! So I knew it was true." She locked the cash drawer again and handed Damiot his change. "Merci, Monsieur . . ."

"Madame . . ." He took the bouquets from Sibilat. "You have an attractive shop here."

"We think so!" Madame answered. "My son studied to be a doctor—a surgeon!" she announced proudly. "His father was a well-known medical man in Toulon for many years. He had hoped that our son would take over his practice."

Sibilat shrugged. "I always preferred to work with plants and flowers. Living things! Not sick people . . ."

"Unfortunately," Madame interrupted, "my dear husband died. But he left enough money so that Marc could do as he pleased."

"I found this shop through an advertisement and, once my mother consented to live in Courville, I arranged to buy the property."

"Monsieur is visiting relatives in the village?" Madame's eyes sharpened with curiosity.

"I'm here on vacation. Staying at the Auberge."

"Our dear friend, Madame Bouchard! You'll be very comfortable there. My son and I dine at the Auberge at least once a month. We sell them all their plants and flowers."

"So I've been told." He bowed. "Bonjour, Madame."

"Monsieur . . ."

As Damiot went toward the door he was aware of their eyes following him. The mother's, black and penetrating, the son's, curiously dull.

Returning to his car, he swerved the Peugeot around and drove up the avenue. He turned left at the corner and parked along the edge of the square, across from Saint-Sauveur. "You'll have to stay here. Dogs aren't allowed in cemeteries."

As he approached the church he saw that the stone walls were badly cracked. The tiers of carved figures above the portal had always looked as though they were crumbling. They were supposed to be sixteenth-century, and Saint-Sauveur itself was said to have been built on the site of an ancient temple and to have Roman paving blocks embedded in its walls. The bell tower, which looked too small, had been added much later.

His mother had come here every Sunday to early Mass; his father preferred to sleep late Sunday mornings and then cook breakfast for the family after Mass . . .

Requiem masses had been sung here for both his parents. Those were the last times he had been inside Saint-Sauveur. Eleven years ago . . .

He tried the door but, as he anticipated, it was locked. Following the path around the corner, he entered the cemetery through a wooden gate. The graves he sought were toward the far end.

Ahead of him, to one side, was a brilliant spot of red. Someone had left fresh flowers on a grave. He saw that it was a bouquet of red carnations, placed in front of a simple marble headstone.

JULIEN BOUCHARD
1934–1976

Her husband! Madame Bouchard must have bought the carnations from Sibilat Fleurs earlier this morning.

Walking on, he continued to think about Aurore Bouchard, leaving fresh flowers on her husband's grave after two years. They must have been devoted to each other . . .

If he had died in Montmartre from one of the bullets fired by that gangster, Valzo, would Sophie still be placing flowers on his grave? Even one month later? Not likely . . .

He had reached a more familiar section of the cemetery. The two graves were side by side.

CLÉMENCE DAMIOT   PIERRE DAMIOT
1898–1961   1894–1961

His father had died first, after a siege of pneumonia that had weakened his heart. His mother, three weeks later, in her sleep. The doctor told him, when he flew down from Paris, that there had been nothing wrong with her. It was only grief . . .

He unwrapped the first bouquet and rested it on his mother's grave. The other on his father's. The yellow roses made twin pools of sunshine on the grass.

"Pardon, M'sieur . . ."

Damiot turned to face a tall man in a gray suit. Shabby gray overcoat, gray hat. He knew at once that this was a policeman.

"Jules Bardou, Sûreté Nationale . . ." A thin hand produced a leather case and opened it to show a badge. "You are a visitor in Courville?"

"That's right."

"One of the villagers saw you park your car and phoned the gendarmerie. I was asked to find out who you are, M'sieur. Your purpose here . . ."

Damiot reluctantly brought out his own worn leather case and flipped it open. "Police Judiciaire, Paris. Chief Inspector Damiot."

The bony jaw dropped, revealing tobacco-stained teeth.

"Who called you?" Damiot asked.

"Some man. Didn't give his name."

"One of those!"

"Has Paris sent you to help with this murder business?"

"I'm in Courville for a vacation. And I've come here because my parents . . ." He motioned toward the graves. "I was born in this village."

"Pardon, M'sieur Inspecteur. I would never have bothered you . . ."

"No harm done." He saw Bardou glance down to check the names on the headstones as he pulled a package of Gauloises from a pocket.

"M'sieur Inspecteur?" Holding out the cigarettes.

"I don't smoke any more."

"Some of the villagers saw you driving last night in the hills near the château." Lighting a cigarette. "You were a stranger, so they thought you might have some connection with the murders. Or with the monster . . ."

"You believe in this monster, do you?"

"I never believe in anything I haven't seen with my own eyes, M'sieur. But some of the villagers claim they saw him last night."

"What, precisely?"

"A tall figure. Very tall . . ."

"How many people saw it?"

"A dozen or more."

"A dozen people should be listened to—if they all saw the same thing. Do their descriptions of the monster agree?"

"I've questioned three of them this morning, but they change their descriptions, even as they talk. The monster had black hair and it had reddish brown hair. It was tall but they can't agree how tall . . . They were drunk, M'sieur! Believe me! They saw no monster. Last night or any other night. I've been through the château with the caretaker, and there was no trace of any monster."

Should he acknowledge that he had seen the figure on the terrace? Better not! "When I drove past those gates last night, the château was dark. I'm told nobody lives there."

"Only Pouchet, the caretaker. He's been there for years. More like a gamekeeper. He keeps people out and protects the animals in the forest. Some people think the place is haunted. The villagers claim they heard a bell tolling again last night, before the monster scared them away, but I've checked each of those towers and there's no bell in any of them!"

"Perhaps this is some trick of the caretaker's."

"Old Pouchet's not the type for that sort of thing."

"The villagers know he's there?"

"Oh, yes! They also know that he has a gun and, if necessary, will use it. Pouchet comes down to the village every two weeks for supplies, but he's not a friendly sort."

"Is it possible to get inside the grounds? Have a look around?"

"I'm on my way up there now, to ask Pouchet about what happened last night. If M'sieur cares to come along . . ."

"I would indeed!"

"My car's parked across the square, in front of the town hall."

"Perhaps I'd better take mine. Then you won't have to drive me back. I remember the château as it was years ago, when the de Mohrt family still lived there."

"I know very little about the place. My home's in Arles and I'll be returning there, once this business is finished."

"What about those girls who were murdered? Are they buried here?"

"One of them—the first—has never been identified. She's on ice, at the morgue, but the other one's over there. I'll show you."

Damiot followed. His hip was stiff but not paining too much. He came to a stop beside Bardou, facing a recent grave.

"Lisette Jarlaud. She was the second. Her family can't afford a headstone, but somebody's left flowers . . ."

From the soggy brown petals, Damiot saw that they had been roses. The rains had beaten them into the earth, but the small bouquet still had a twist of green waxed paper around its stems.

"She was only nineteen. Too young to die—even for her sort—but then, I suppose, any age is too young for the way these girls died."

"Who do you suspect killed them?"

"There hasn't been a clue. Except it must have been the same man. The method was identical with both."

"How do you know it was a man?"

"The autopsy reports show that both girls had had sex before they died."

"Must've been cold, on the ground. Of course, they could have been in his car."

"The first murder was in January. That's the week we had a false spring, with high temperatures. And the second was less than four weeks ago—it was warm then too—before the rains started again."

They turned back, walking slowly, toward the church.

"What about this monster in the château? You think he's the killer?"

"There is no monster, M'sieur Inspecteur. You'll know that when you talk to Pouchet. The villagers take several bottles of Calvados up there with them. That's how they're able to see a monster and hear a bell tolling!" He opened the wooden gate and motioned for Damiot to go ahead. "I'll stop at the gendarmerie and pick up the key to those gates at the château. Pouchet's getting deaf. Never hears the bell."

"You have a key?"

"For emergencies. The lawyers in Paris arranged that years ago. From time to time, if nobody hears from Pouchet, someone goes up to check. Never been anything wrong. He just forgets to contact them."

"Do these lawyers know about the monster?"

Bardou hesitated. "No, M'sieur. Nobody's told them."

"Would anyone object if I went inside the château?"

"A Chief Inspector from Paris? Certainly not!"

"Let me warn you! I've no intention of getting involved. I came to Provence for a rest."

The gates, as before, were closed and padlocked.

Damiot peered through the wrought-iron grille at the shaded entrance drive between the rows of poplars, and saw the castle rising in a blaze of sunlight above the distant courtyard.

The pigeons circling the towers were the only signs of life.

Nothing had changed, although the walls of the château seemed a much lighter color today. Almost golden! More like he remembered them in the past.

He turned to see the dog scampering off in pursuit of some

animal, real or imagined, into thick underbrush edging the wall. "Fric-Frac!" Clapping his hands. "Come here, Madame!" He watched her trot back, tail waving. "Maybe I should lock you up in the car while we're here." The dog whimpered, as though she understood. "All right! Promise to behave and you can come with us." The tail wagged again.

Directly opposite the gates, on the other side of the road, was an open meadow ringed by a copse of young trees with the forest beyond. That meadow was said to have been cleared, hundreds of years ago, for the crowds that came to attend the public trials held by visiting judges in the courtyard of the château. The gallows must have stood in the center of the field. When he was a kid he had dug up old coins there. Probably valuable. He had no idea what had become of them . . .

The first girl had been murdered somewhere in that meadow. Maybe he should take a closer look . . .

No! This morning, with Bardou, he would visit the château, but afterward he was going to forget the Courville monster. He only wanted to see inside the castle because of his memories.

Turning back to the locked gates, he leaned down and saw that the padlock, chained on the inside, was a recent model. He straightened as he heard a car approaching, chugging noisily, from the direction of the village.

As it came closer he saw that it was a black, older-model Peugeot, covered with a layer of mud and dust that made it appear gray. Bardou's face was barely recognizable through the bird droppings on the windshield.

He moved away from the gates, Fric-Frac at his heels, as the car slowed to a stop.

Bardou got out. "I have the key but I'd better ring the bell. Pouchet doesn't like to be surprised, and there's no telephone." He went to the right gatepost and fumbled among the ivy leaves until he found a button, which he pressed several times. "This rings somewhere in the kitchen, but unless the old man's nearby he won't hear it." He produced a key from his pocket. "Why don't we drive up to the château in my car? Leave the other one here."

"What about the dog?"

"Bring her along." He turned his key in the padlock. "Pouchet has a dog."

Fric-Frac capered when she realized she wasn't being left behind.

Damiot opened the door of the other car, motioned for the dog to jump in, and sat beside her as Bardou slid in from the other side.

"I'll drive round to the back." Bardou exhaled spurts of pungent tobacco smoke as he talked. "The old man's usually there, unless he's off in the forest. Hunts for most of his meat and raises the rest. You must have known Pouchet when you lived here . . ."

"There was a gamekeeper who chased me off the place many times. I used to climb the fence to steal walnuts. There wasn't any wall in those days. When was that built?"

"I've no idea." He sneezed.

Damiot wondered, as the car rolled up the drive, whether the wall had been put up to keep people out or to keep someone—something—inside? "Why weren't you here last night, with those villagers? You must've suspected what they'd be doing."

"It was raining. Thought nothing would be happening, so I went to bed early. Had a feeling I was catching a cold . . ."

"Where are you staying?"

"They've put me at the Hôtel Courville. Small room in the back. No heat, and the bath's down the hall. That's how I got this cold."

They followed the left branch of the drive around the edge of the circular courtyard, past the entrance to a long allée whose marble statues and fountains were engulfed by weeds.

"Have you asked, at the Hôtel Courville, who was staying there the night of each murder?" Damiot asked.

"Who was . . . Mon Dieu! I hadn't thought of it. I should find out who was there both nights . . ."

"And who checked out next morning. He may have been driving a black Ferrari."

"Black Ferrari? Thanks for the tip."

Fric-Frac's nose twitched, sniffing the delicious wild scents pouring from both sides.

Damiot looked up at the stone façade of the castle rising from the cobbled courtyard, eyes pausing on the carved entrance doors in the center, under a columned arch. His gaze followed strands of ivy up to the balustraded terrace where the monster had appeared last night, then continued on to the stone balconies and small tourelles and, higher and higher, to the massive circular towers thrusting their pointed roofs toward the sky. "There was a bell in at least one of those towers when I was a boy."

"They say there used to be bells in three of them, but the last one was removed years ago because the beams had rotted. They were afraid it would fall and the whole tower might be pulled down. I've checked every tower and there are no bells in any of them."

"What did those villagers hear last night?"

"Nothing!" His voice was harsh. "They imagined the whole thing."

"Did they?" Damiot noticed that the old tiles on the roofs had weathered to a greenish bronze and that many were missing. With the winter rains, the number of holes might cause serious damage to the interior. Ceilings could collapse and floors would warp . . .

Bardou slowed his car, following the drive along the western side of the château toward the rear. "They say this place is some sort of historical monument. Protected by the government."

"I wouldn't doubt it. Must go back at least three centuries."

"I've been inside, but there's nothing except some old pictures and furniture. Pouchet lives in a room off the kitchen."

"No women around?"

"Never saw any." He turned the car right, into an open area extending from the kitchen yard to a distant row of stables.

Damiot recalled the last time he had been here. He had been caught by a gamekeeper, clutching a canvas bag filled with mushrooms he had picked in the forest. That gamekeeper was a tall man, muscular and rough. Damiot had been dragged, protesting, into the cavernous kitchen, and when they asked his name he told them the truth. Some of the servants had known his parents, and one of the cooks gave him a slice of cold game pie. He remembered to this day the delicious taste. They had let him keep the mushrooms, and his father sliced them into an omelette for the family dinner that night . . .

The car slowed to a stop near the open kitchen door, unchanged since his last visit, scattering several chickens. Their squawks roused a family of ducks at the edge of a pond.

Damiot heard a dog barking—the same deep sound he had heard last night—and saw Fric-Frac's ears lift in response.

She was the first out of the car, eager to investigate everything.

He looked around, recalling earlier visits, as Bardou headed toward the kitchen door. The rear gate, behind the stables, was out of sight from here. One of the stable doors stood open but the garages were closed. In the old days they held a row of expensive cars.

He noticed that a dovecote near the stables had collapsed and fallen to the ground. The metal aviary where peacocks had been caged was rusted and empty, its doors hanging open.

"Pouchet! Where are you?"

Damiot turned to see Bardou coming from the kitchen.

"He's not inside. Can't be far, leaving his door open."

"I heard a dog . . ."

"Big mastiff. He keeps it chained inside."

The silence was abruptly torn apart by a terrifying scream.

The dog in the kitchen went into an uproar of barking.

Fric-Frac shot across the yard toward the stable.

Damiot went after her, limping because of his haste, as the scream was repeated. He realized that Bardou wasn't hurrying.

"Somebody's been hurt!"

"They'll be dead before we get there. Pouchet must be butchering this morning."

"Of course! I haven't heard that sound in years." He paused for Bardou to catch up, then walked beside him toward the stables, where Fric-Frac had disappeared through an open door.

"The old man does his own butchering when he needs fresh meat."

"Who's out there?" It was a harsh male voice, from inside the stable.

"It's me! Bardou." He led the way inside, into cool shadow.

As Damiot's eyes adjusted to the dim light slanting down from one dusty window, he noticed an old car parked inside the door and saw Fric-Frac, crouched on the earthen floor, facing a curious scene.

Two white pigs were hanging from wall hooks, their throats cut, dripping blood into white enamel pans.

A brute of a man, tall and completely bald, turned to face Bardou. "I've been expecting you this morning." There was a knife in his hand.

Damiot saw that there was blood on the knife blade, spattered over the old man's right arm and hand. Blood on his leather apron and spots of blood, gleaming like rubies, on his boots.

There was also blood in the air. That sweet, sickening, unmistakable smell . . .

At the same instant, he had an image of two young girls with slashed throats.

"Bonjour, Pouchet!" Bardou stepped closer. "Brought an associate with me this time. M'sieur Damiot's from Paris . . ."

"A policeman from Paris?" Cold gray eyes inspected Damiot's face. "What's Madame Bouchard's dog doing here?"

"Came with me," Damiot answered. "I'm staying at the Auberge." He glanced down and saw that the dog was drinking from one of the small puddles of blood on the floor. "Fric-Frac! Get away from there."

"All dogs do that," Pouchet muttered. "Fresh blood's good for them."

"You had visitors last night?" Bardou asked.

"Salauds! They came over the wall again."

"Did you talk to them?"

"Never went near 'em." He rested the bloody knife on a wooden trough and untied his apron, letting it fall to the floor. "Didn't get to bed 'til after I saw 'em leave." He thrust his hands into a pan of water and splashed his reddened arms.

Damiot watched the water turn pink.

"They claim they saw the monster again," Bardou continued. "On the terrace this time!"

"They saw nothing. As usual." Pouchet laughed, his voice a deep rumble in his massive chest. "Same as they always see. Nothing!"

"Have you ever seen this monster?" Damiot asked quietly.

"There is no monster, M'sieur." He picked up a coarse towel and dried his hands. "They tell those stories in the village to make a little excitement for themselves."

"I agree," Bardou nodded. "This monster business is nonsense."

Pouchet grunted and dropped his towel onto the bench.

"Is anyone living in the château?" Damiot asked.

"Been nobody here for years." Pouchet moved ahead of them, toward the open door. "Only me."

"What about the de Mohrt family?"

"None of 'em alive any more." He led the way outside, into bright sunshine.

Damiot saw now that the old man's work clothes were worn and faded. "You didn't see the monster yourself last night?"

"I told you, M'sieur!" The old man turned toward him, angrily. "There is no monster. Why are you asking me all these questions? You say your name is Damiot?"

"That's right." The gray eyes were studying his face.

"You're that boy used to come here and steal my walnuts. Your family had a restaurant where Bouchard and his wife opened their Auberge. You're the Damiot boy!"

"Then you knew my parents?"

"Used to walk down to the village through the fields and stop by their kitchen door. Your father and I drank many a pastis, sitting on those back steps." Holding his hand out. "The Damiot boy . . ."

Damiot grasped the huge hand and shook it, aware of hard muscles under the roughened skin.

"Your father used to talk about you. He was proud of you. Said you were a famous policeman."

"Chief Inspector Damiot's here for a holiday," Bardou explained.

"Chief Inspector!" Pouchet laughed. "Come up in the world, since you left Courville."

"What became of that cook who used to be here?" Damiot asked.

"Which cook?" The old man scowled. "There was more than one!"

"Was it Madame Léontine?"

"The fat one! Léontine Guibert . . ."

"And wasn't it you who caught me one morning, stealing mushrooms?"

"That's right! The others got away."

"You hauled me into the kitchen and Madame Guibert gave me a slice of game pie . . ."

"Bet you thought I was going to thrash you!" The old man laughed. "Fat Léontine went back to her family when those lawyers in Paris decided to close the château. All the other servants left years ago."

Standing there in the bright sunlight, Damiot was overwhelmed by the past. Memories, long forgotten, came rushing back . . .

"What are you doing here?" Pouchet asked. "With Bardou!"

"Told him I was driving up to see you this morning," Bardou answered. "M'sieur Damiot asked to come along."

"I wanted to see the château again. Haven't been inside since Madame la Comtesse was alive." Damiot lifted his eyes toward the stone mass of the castle rising above them. "They used to say, in the village, there were a hundred rooms here."

"Don't know 'bout that." Pouchet shook his head. "Most of 'em have been closed for years. I keep a few rooms cleaned and dusted, on the chance the family lawyers show up from Paris, unexpectedly. Wait here! I'll fetch my keys . . ."

He watched the old man stride across the cobbled stable yard toward the kitchen door. Must be in his late seventies, but his back was straight and he walked without a limp.

"You talked him into it," Bardou murmured. "I'd like another look at the place myself."

Damiot noticed Fric-Frac sniffing at the ground.

The caretaker had left a visible trail on the soft earth. Prints, from his heavy boots, that seemed to be damp.

The dog was licking at one of the footprints.

He realized that it was stained with blood.

10

As they went through a mirrored gallery after inspecting the enormous ballroom, Damiot noticed that Pouchet, marching ahead of them, had changed his boots.

Bardou remained silent, walking beside him, staring at everything.

The tall double windows on opposite walls were closed but not curtained, and the mirrors between them reflected a pattern of bare tree branches tossing in the sunshine. The effect was dazzling, as though the walls were not solid.

A row of chandeliers in the ceiling held no candles.

"We're in the west wing!" Pouchet opened another door. "Where the family used to live."

Damiot followed him into a spacious room with paneled walls and a huge marble fireplace facing another row of tall windows.

"Not much left here . . ." The old man hesitated, squinting at the furniture lined against a wall. "Nobody can remove anything unless they have written permission from the lawyers."

Damiot squinted at the high ceiling, with its carved figures surrounding paintings of nymphs and fauns. This west wing of the château must be near the terrace where he had glimpsed the monster . . .

The old man swung the door open. "Next is the salon where Madame la Comtesse liked to sit. I came here every morning to get my orders for the day."

They followed him into a smaller room, bright with sunshine from floor-to-ceiling double windows. The light was accentuated by white-painted woodwork, walls covered with faded yellow satin, white marble fireplace, and a recently polished parquet floor. The Louis Seize furniture was arranged as though the Comtesse might appear at any moment to take her place on the small sofa near the fireplace.

Here all the paintings were portraits. Two of the faces—men in fancy wigs and uniforms—seemed familiar.

It was the face carved on the gateposts! The de Mohrt face . . .

Faint wheel tracks on the parquet floor. The old man must push a small cart from room to room with his cleaning materials.

Damiot remembered being brought here one Christmas, with other children from the village. They had been lined up to sing carols in the old *langue de Provence* for Madame la Comtesse and, afterward, had been given cakes made with nougat and glacéed fruit . . .

". . . same furniture when the old lady was alive," Pouchet was saying. "People came after she died, packed everything from the other rooms into cases, and shipped 'em off to Paris." He crossed the sunny room as he talked. "Next to this is the library." Opening a door, into a darker room. "The old lady and her grandson, the young Comte, were always reading in here . . ."

Fric-Frac darted ahead of Pouchet.

Damiot followed, Bardou bringing up the end of the procession.

More tall windows in the library, but here the sunlight was absorbed by the dark woodwork. Rows of empty bookshelves reached to an elaborately carved ceiling. Black marble fireplace and another parquet floor, this one of an even darker wood than the walls. There was no furniture here.

Damiot sniffed the air. "Someone's living in the château?"

Pouchet looked back, scowling. "I live here, M'sieur."

"I smell cooking."

"That's a cassoulet for my dinner. Been on the stove all morning. The smell comes through the cracks in these floors."

"Cassoulet?" It was not, he was positive, a cassoulet but something made with truffles. The distinctive odor was unmistakable. As he followed Pouchet through the library, he noticed something red on Fric-Frac's left leg, trailing on the floor as he walked. "Here, Fric-Frac!" He reached down and removed a strand of dark red yarn caught in her black curls.

Did Pouchet have a sweater this color? Or was there a woman here?

He rolled the strand into a little ball and thrust it into his pocket.

The old man led them through a long passage, windowless and bare, toward a door at the far end.

Damiot watched Fric-Frac dart to a side door that must lead to an inner corridor. She pressed her nose against the crack at the bottom and growled. "No, Fric-Frac! Here! This way . . ."

She turned from the door, reluctantly, and followed him into what had been the dining room.

Was there something on the other side of that door? A cat? Or had someone been standing there, listening? Was it the monster?

Now Fric-Frac was following an invisible trail across the parquet floors toward the nearest windows. The sunny terrace outside must be the one he had watched last night, from the hill. He followed her to the windows. "Can I get through here?"

"Mais certainement, M'sieur," Pouchet answered. "All these windows open from inside."

He turned the knob, raising a metal rod that released the double windows, grasped a handle, and opened the window without a sound. These hinges had been oiled recently.

Fric-Frac dashed out and scampered across the terrace.

Damiot saw Bardou and Pouchet heading toward a door at the far end of the dining room. Catch up with them later. Meanwhile he could inspect the terrace unobserved.

The dog ran back and forth, sniffing the air.

He realized that the corner where the monster had appeared

was straight ahead. As he walked in that direction, moving casually in case anyone noticed from the window, he saw that the terrace floor was white marble, cracked and stained from centuries of rain.

Approaching the corner, he could see the cobbled courtyard below. From here, the château seemed to be surrounded by impenetrable forest. Dark and menacing, even in bright sunlight. Checking to be sure he wasn't watched, he peered at the hill rising above the trees in the back. That was where he had been last night, looking down on the monster.

Walking toward the rear on the side terrace—Fric-Frac racing ahead—he passed a row of double windows and glimpsed more empty rooms inside. He reached the northwest corner and looked down at Bardou's car, parked in the kitchen yard.

The ducks and chickens had resumed their greedy scramble for food, and a wisp of smoke was rising from one of the chimneys, probably the kitchen chimney, but there was no smell of truffles cooking back here.

Something brushed against his right trouser leg.

Looking down, startled, he saw Fric-Frac. "Good girl! You've been a great help today. My new assistant!"

She wagged her tail and, nose to the marble terrace, resumed her exploration of some invisible trail. As Damiot followed, he wondered what scent she could have found. She had reached the front corner of the terrace again and was sniffing where the monster had stood last night.

He went closer and stooped to examine the weather-stained surface. Solid marble with no fresh scratches. Impossible for anything to sink out of sight here. And yet, he had seen it happen.

Fric-Frac moved on, investigating each crack in the marble. Back across the terrace, more slowly, toward another row of double windows.

These must be the windows where that light had come from last night.

The dog had found another scent and was following it straight to the closed windows. A human scent, or . . .?

The windows opened unexpectedly, and Pouchet stepped out, peering suspiciously from side to side. "There's nothing out here."

"I wanted to see the view," Damiot explained. "And the dog wanted to get out."

"Dogs usually want to get out." Pouchet moved closer to Damiot as Bardou came through the window. "The place doesn't look the way it did when the family was alive. In those days we had gardeners."

"Wasn't there a side entrance to the east? A gate in the fence?"

"You know about that?" The old man looked surprised. "They kept it when they built the new wall. Nobody remembers that gate anymore, so it's never locked. I go that way when I drive down to the village."

"You never told me you've got another entrance!" Bardou complained. "Is there a road on that side?"

"More like a cow path. Wouldn't advise you to use it." Pouchet winked at Damiot, excluding the outsider. "Brings you down near the railroad tracks, but it's easy to lose your way."

"Been ringing that bell in the front every time I drive up here." Bardou's voice was harsh, as though his cold were getting worse. "You never answer, so I have to unlock it myself."

Pouchet laughed. "That bell hasn't worked in years!"

"I'll be damned."

There was a sudden piercing shriek from the forest.

Fric-Frac barked at the shrill sound.

"What's that?" Bardou asked, staring toward the trees.

"One of the peacocks," Pouchet answered. "Used to be kept in a cage but they escaped."

The scream was repeated and Fric-Frac barked again.

From inside the château, another dog responded.

"That's my dog barking." Pouchet motioned for them to follow as he went through the open windows. "This is where the family spent their evenings. Would be cold in winter, so they always had a fire going."

Damiot went ahead of Bardou, the dog darting in front of them, into a larger salon with a row of crystal chandeliers overhead, along the center of the empty room's ceiling. More portraits, several of them full-length, were hanging on the wall facing the windows.

Some of the faces were similar to those in the other salon. The sitters were dressed in elaborate costumes and wigs. They had the same aquiline noses and piercing eyes. In one, the subject had long black hair hanging down to the epaulettes of his Napoleonic uniform.

It was the face he had seen last night! That portrait he had glimpsed at the Tendrell farmhouse . . .

". . . received important guests in this salon," Pouchet was explaining. "I remember many times bringing 'em here to pay their respects to the Comte before showing them up to their rooms. The Comtesse preferred the small salon. So this was never used after her husband died . . ."

Damiot noticed that there were no candles in the chandeliers or candelabra. One electric bulb, suspended from a hook, its cord plugged into a wall socket.

So there was electricity here!

Had someone turned that bulb on last night? Held it up to throw light through those windows and cast a shadow across the terrace? Was the monster nothing more than a shadow!

He would like to come here again. Without Bardou! Through that gate in the east wall. Pouchet was deaf and wouldn't hear his car . . .

Maybe tonight? And bring a pocket torch.

He saw Pouchet near the fireplace, whispering to Bardou about one of the carved female figures. Laughing as he fondled an enormous marble breast. Nasty old man's laugh . . .

That east gate led down, by way of an untraveled back lane, to the village. Near that alley behind the town hall where the second girl's body had been found.

Some old men who lived by themselves became strange . . .

Pouchet had been on these premises for years, promoted from gamekeeper to inside work. Now he was the caretaker. He had always been considered bad-tempered, even when he was younger. Scaring kids away. Shouting and waving his gun at them . . .

Damiot remembered that crack of sound he had heard yesterday, beyond the locked front gates, as Jenny rode past on her black mare. Did Pouchet wait there mornings, watching for the English girl? She had called him "one of those strange old men . . ."

He studied another portrait. What possible connection could there be between these paintings and that face in Tendrell's portrait?

Damiot saw that Pouchet had opened another door and that Bardou was already leaving the salon. "Come along, Fric-Frac!" As he hurried after them with the dog, he realized that his hip was numb from all the walking.

Fric-Frac ran ahead through what seemed to be a central corridor. High ceiling with a line of skylights down the center, crusted with grime. Some of the panes were broken and had been covered on the outside, blotting out the light. The caretaker closed the door behind them.

"When was that new wall built?" Damiot asked, facing him. "In the old days there was only a wrought-iron fence."

"Must be five years ago, after the old Comtesse died," Pouchet answered. "The lawyers had it put up because of poachers."

"There've always been poachers."

"I've told 'em for years we needed a wall, and they finally listened to me."

"Why didn't you leave your dog outside last night to scare those villagers away?"

"She's too old. Was afraid they might harm her." Pouchet moved on, down the long corridor. As Damiot followed with Bardou, he saw that rain had leaked from the damaged skylight and had rotted sections of the parquet floor.

Bardou sneezed again. "My cold's getting worse!" He moved closer to Damiot, lowering his voice. "Eh bien, M'sieur Inspecteur! Nothing suspicous here."

"No . . ." His eyes were on the vigorous old man striding ahead.

"I told you there wasn't any monster. Those drunken villagers! None of them saw anything!"

"Of course not . . ."

11

Damiot glanced across the table at his guest. "Not eating?"

"No appetite." Bardou took another swallow of wine.

"I can understand why not." He set his knife and fork down, the *croquettes de volaille* barely touched. "This food's a disgrace!"

"I can't taste anything."

"Lucky for you. I, unfortunately, can taste everything! At least the wine's not bad. The chef couldn't get his hands on that." There were no other customers. "We'd have done better at one of the cafés. Unfortunately, the Auberge only serves dinner. I should've remembered about this place. The Hôtel Courville was never famous for its kitchen."

Bardou whipped out his handkerchief and sneezed.

"Why don't you spend the rest of today in bed?"

"I may do that, M'sieur Inspecteur." He blew his nose violently, put the handkerchief away, and brought out his cigarettes.

Damiot signaled for the waiter to bring their check. "What else is happening at the local gendarmerie?"

"Very little. We have more activity in Arles. Of course I'm only involved with these murders." Lighting a cigarette. "There's one man on duty over the weekend in case of an emergency, which is unlikely. I'll phone in this afternoon and tell him I've caught a cold. I should be all right by Monday morning."

"Drink the rest of that wine. It'll warm your blood." He watched Bardou empty the carafe into his glass. "Actually, mon ami, you should be drinking Calvados. Better than anything to ward off a virus."

"That's what I'd be having at home. My wife fixes a hot toddy when I feel a cold coming . . ." He tossed off the last of the wine.

Damiot checked the bill that the aged waiter placed in front of him and pushed several notes across the table. "Monsieur Bardou has caught a cold. Send a hot toddy up to his room in half an hour, made with your best Calvados."

"I'll bring it myself!" The old man shuffled back toward the bar.

"That's very kind, M'sieur Damiot."

"Tomorrow you'll wake up with no sign of a cold."

"Tell me, M'sieur Inspecteur! Have you turned up any clues? About these two murders . . ."

"I haven't been looking for any. I know very little about those girls who died." He got up, reaching for his hat and waterproof. "I suppose autopsies were performed?"

"Oh, yes!" Bardou rose, snatching his hat and overcoat from the banquette, and followed him into the shabby lobby.

Damiot glanced at the faded-brown plush sofas and tarnished mirrors as they walked toward an ugly marble staircase. "Were either of those girls pregnant when they were killed?"

"No. I saw the autopsy reports."

"You like police work, mon ami?"

"It's all right. My wife says I've no ambition. She's always after me to try for a promotion. Maybe you could advise me about applying for a transfer to Paris . . ."

Damiot grunted.

"I've never been to Paris!" Bardou paused at the foot of the steps. "Thanks for lunch, even if I didn't have any appetite."

"You'll feel better tomorrow. Get to bed."

"A bientôt, M'sieur Inspecteur . . ."

"A bientôt!" He turned back toward the street entrance, beyond the unattended reception desk, as Bardou started upstairs.

In the light filtering through a row of glass-curtained windows, Damiot saw that the restaurant was empty except for three people at a distant table, two men and a woman.

Aurore Bouchard! In serious conversation with two older men. They appeared to be businessmen, too well dressed to be locals. All three talking with animation, hands gesturing, unaware of his presence.

Damiot hurried on before he could be noticed, out of the hotel and into the afternoon sunlight.

Stopping at the charcuterie, he saw, behind the piles of pâtés and canned hams on display in the window, several customers in the brightly lighted shop.

Hercule Mauron stood behind the counter, weighing a sausage

for an old woman. The fat boy had become a fat man. Laughing as he talked, his great belly bouncing under a white apron. Hercule Mauron! He was Monsieur le Maire now . . .

Damiot turned from the window and started across the square.

As he approached the Peugeot, he saw Fric-Frac perched on the back of the seat, tail wagging. One window was slightly open so that she would have air. He tapped on the glass, "I won't be long!"

Circling the fountain, he noticed for the first time that the marble bowl was cracked. Which explained why there had been no water spraying.

He continued across to Avenue de la République, where one shop window was filled with books and magazines. Inside he bought a Paris newspaper and a Simenon mystery he had never read.

The clerk smirked primly as she gave him his change. "Merci, M'sieur Inspecteur. I certainly hope you will find the monster that killed those two poor girls! All of us young women are afraid to venture out after dark. I hurry straight home every evening after work!"

"That's very wise, Mademoiselle." He clutched the book and newspaper in his hand as he went toward the door.

"Au 'voir, M'sieur Inspecteur!"

As Damiot reached the sunny street, he was gritting his teeth with annoyance. How did she know who he was? Somebody had spread the word. Someone like Madame Sibilat . . .

Entering a nearby hardware shop, he asked the aged clerk for a pocket torch. All the man had in stock was a small metal cylinder that he claimed was popular with children. Damiot bought one of the cylinders. It could be useful tonight if he went back to the château.

Leaving the shop, he decided that while he was here he might as well pay another visit to that florist at the end of the avenue.

Opening the door with its jangling bell, he saw that the shop was empty again. There was a stir of movement in the rear workroom. Was Sibilat observing him from between those curtains covering the door? Or was it . . .

Madame Sibilat came through the curtains. "Ah! It's you again, Monsieur Inspecteur . . ."

"Madame! Is your son here this afternoon? There's something else I wished to ask him."

"He drove down to Nice to pick up some flowers at the airport. I would know anything that my son knows."

"In that case, perhaps you can tell me who left a bouquet of roses on Lisette Jarlaud's grave."

"Why would you ask my son a thing like that?"

"Because, from the green paper around them, I suspect they came from this shop. I'm sure you would know."

She sputtered. "They—they were white roses and they were placed on the Jarlaud girl's grave by a young farmer. He had never been in the shop before, but I recognized him. Achille Savord! The Jarlaud girl had many such friends. Young and old . . . You should question them—all of them—not my son. I can tell you for a fact, he would have nothing to do with her sort!"

"And did the Jarlaud girl ever come here to buy flowers?"

"As a matter of fact she did! But only once. Last year . . . My son was off somewhere, and I was alone in the shop. She wanted a small bouquet for her daughter's birthday. Everybody knows she had two children. And no husband! I let her have a few carnations that were not too fresh."

"Merci, Madame. For the information."

She looked startled. "Information? But I . . ."

"Bonjour, Madame." He left the shop without glancing back.

Heading toward the square, he saw that the sky was churning with clouds. Another storm rolling down the Rhône valley?

Damiot realized that he was hungry. He had barely touched his lunch, and it would be hours before dinner would be served at the Auberge.

His hip throbbed from all the walking at the château. Back at the Auberge he would soak in a hot tub and have a long nap. Rest his aching bones, in preparation for another visit to the château after dinner. Meanwhile, perhaps, a sandwich or . . .

Madame Mussot's! Would she still have her apricot tarts?

Damiot walked to the pâtisserie on the corner and was enveloped by a familiar mouth-watering aroma as he opened the door. Madame Mussot and a young girl were busy behind the counter, serving several customers. Madame smiled when she recognized him.

He hung his hat and waterproof on wall hooks and then sank cautiously onto one of the metal chairs as he glanced at the trays of pastries in the display cases.

"M'sieur Damiot!"

"Madame!" He got to his feet as she came from behind the counter, hand outstretched, beaming in welcome.

"I've been expecting you!" She shook his hand firmly, kissing him on both cheeks. "Ever since they told me you'd come back."

"You're looking well, Madame."

"No complaints! Everything goes as usual. Mine is still the only pâtisserie in Courville. So there's no competition! I know exactly what you'll be wanting. Told the girl to set them aside, this morning, when I heard you were here. It will only take a moment." She turned and, waving the girl ahead, marched her toward the kitchen.

Damiot realized as he sat down again that he was smiling in anticipation.

Madame Mussot must be in her late seventies but, in spite of her gray hair, looked twenty years younger. Petite and slim, as though she never touched her own pastries! She had been his mother's closest friend and confidante.

Madame returned with a platter of tarts, followed by the girl with a tray holding a coffeepot and dishes. Damiot stared at the golden apricots in their nests of pastry. "Six of them?"

"You ate five last time." Madame placed them on the table as the girl set a plate in front of him and poured the coffee.

"In all Paris, Madame, I've never found apricot tarts like yours!"

"Bon appétit, M'sieur. Pardon . . ." She hurried toward the counter, where more customers were waiting.

He had never been able to analyze the golden glaze covering the fruit, but there was a hint of lemon and, he suspected, honey. Finishing his first tart, he finally tasted the coffee, relaxing in a glow of contentment, savoring the moment.

He poured a second cup and reached for another pastry.

"Caught in the act!"

Damiot looked up, startled, to see a girl in a pale green dress. Long blonde hair . . . "Mademoiselle Tendrell!" He lurched to his feet, still holding the pastry in his fingers.

"I never imagined I might find you here, Monsieur Inspecteur! Devouring apricot tarts in public."

"But, I—I'm . . ."

"The incriminating evidence half-eaten!"

Damiot laughed as he placed the remainder of his pastry on

the plate. "Won't you join me, Mademoiselle? I was hoping to see you again."

"Were you?" She sank onto the other chair, hanging her shoulder bag over the back. "I've been doing my usual Saturday chores for our cook. Madame Mussot's is always my last stop."

"Have one of these apricot tarts. They're my favorites." He glanced at the remainder of the tart on his plate.

"They're also my favorites!" She took a tart in her fingers and bit into it. "We enjoyed meeting you, last night, Allan and I . . ."

"I look forward to seeing Monsieur Tendrell another time."

"You must come up to the farm again. Perhaps dinner, one night next week? Allan has so few friends here. He's painting this afternoon because the light's rather good, but one of the farmhands told me it should rain tonight."

"More rain?"

"Allan says he had enough rain in England for the rest of his life. It's very bad for arthritis . . ."

As Jenny chattered, Damiot signaled for Madame Mussot's assistant, motioning for more tarts and fresh coffee, but missing nothing that the English girl was saying.

"Are you enjoying your stay at the Auberge?"

"Indeed, yes. The food is excellent."

"Michel's a first-rate chef. At least Allan thinks so. I'm not really into food . . . I suppose like all the other males, you've fallen in love with Aurore!"

"Is that what usually happens?"

"My father is most certainly in love with her! For a time last year, I thought they might be getting married. Which of course would be fine! But unfortunately," she continued eating the pastry as she talked, "Aurore has this passion for Michel! Perhaps because her husband was also a chef. Of course, Michel will never marry her. He's rather a Don Juan, you know."

"A Don Juan?"

"Women know it but they still fall for him. Allan gets very uptight if Michel so much as looks at me."

"You like this young man?"

"Like him? I find him amusing. Intelligent and unpredictable. Actually, I s'pose, I see Michel now and again because it would annoy Papa if he found out. We meet when I know Allan will be busy painting in his studio. That's the only time I can take the

80

car. I tell him I'm going down to the village, but instead I drive into the hills, where Michel and I have a bottle of wine at some roadside café and talk for hours. Or, if I'm certain that Allan's going to be out for the evening, I phone Michel at the Auberge and tell him he can come up to the farmhouse."

"What if Aurore answers the phone?"

"I call in the morning after she leaves to do the marketing or during the dinner hour, when the phone only rings in the kitchen."

"Isn't that risky?"

"I enjoy taking risks. Like riding my mare across the fields in an electric storm. Dangerous, I s'pose, but utterly thrilling!"

"I saw you yesterday morning, racing past the château."

"I'd just had a smashing argument with Allan at breakfast, about Michel. Papa suspected I had seen him the night before. Actually, that was one time I hadn't! It's all so terribly involved, because Allan's in love with Aurore and she's in love with Michel. And, I suspect, Michel isn't in love with anybody but his handsome self."

"Then you're not in love with him?"

"Certainly not! Our relationship is disgustingly innocent."

Damiot watched Jenny finish her first tart, licking flakes of pastry from her lower lip. "I've been eating Madame's apricot tarts since I was a boy. Madame says I managed five the last time I was here." He served himself another one. "You told me last night that someone watches you ride past the château . . ."

"That strange old man. He's completely weird!"

"The caretaker? Pouchet . . ."

"He's the one!"

"You've seen him through the gates?"

"He keeps out of sight, but I sense someone lurking in the shrubbery. I think he stands there, mornings, waiting for me . . ."

"Why would he do that?"

"I've read stories, in newspapers, about nasty old men who get their kicks watching young girls. That's all he can do, I s'pose. Watch, not touch . . . You don't think he's the one who did away with those girls, do you?"

"I know nothing about that."

"But you must suspect something . . ."

"Suspicions are not facts. Only facts lead to answers in a murder investigation, but to get answers someone must ask the right questions."

"And do you have questions about our Courville murders?"

"They will remain unasked." He smiled. "Except there's something I'd like to ask you."

"Lovely!" Her eyes brightened in anticipation.

"You mentioned a black Ferrari last night, in relation to those two murders."

"Yes . . ."

"Where did you hear about this car?"

"I've seen it! Twice."

"What?"

"The first time was several months ago and the last was just before Lisette Jarlaud's body was found."

"Was the first time before or after the other murder?"

"I've thought about that, but I can't remember. In fact, until last night I had never associated the car with those murders. Then, as we were talking, I found myself wondering . . ."

"Where did you see the car?"

"In front of our farmhouse. Both times. I have a habit of walking through the garden just before bed. The fresh air usually helps me sleep. I was standing there, breathing deeply, when I heard a powerful motor approaching . . ."

"From the village?"

"From the other direction. Both nights. Going rather fast, but it seemed to slow as it came closer. I was interested, of course, to see a shiny new black Ferrari. And surprised when it slowed even more as it passed, as though the driver were looking at me."

"You saw his face?"

"I couldn't even tell if it was a man or a woman. Could barely make out a head covered by one of those tight leather skullcap things racing drivers wear, goggles over the eyes and leather gloves on the hands. Gave me the oddest sensation! We stared at each other, I s'pose, for a matter of seconds—though it seemed much longer—and then he revved the motor and roared away. Like one of those unidentified flying objects they report in the papers . . ."

"Most curious. Probably someone from a nearby city driving down to Cannes."

"I s'pose . . ."

"Won't you have another pastry?"

"Perhaps just one." Snatching it, childlike, from the platter. "This'll be my third."

"I'm still one ahead of you." He sipped his coffee. "Have you never been inside the château?"

"Not once! Allan has, although he won't tell me how he managed it. He says there's no monster, but Michel thinks there is . . ."

"Does he?"

"Michel was never inside, either! He's only repeating what he hears in the village. He plays billiards several nights every week, after he finishes work at the Auberge. The villagers talk of nothing but the monster and those two murders."

"And you think there's nobody in the château but that caretaker?"

"I didn't say that. No . . . I suspect there's a woman there."

"What woman?"

"I've no idea. But for months now, I've had a feeling that Allan visits the château to meet someone. And, knowing my dear father, it has to be an attractive woman. I do know that last summer there was a child there . . ."

"A child?"

"I saw him one morning, as I rode past the gates. The shrubbery was so heavy I couldn't really be certain, but it looked like a boy. I s'pose he thought I wouldn't be able to see him because of the leaves. His face seemed to float between the bushes, like a ghost without a body. He had long dark hair and . . ."

"You're positive it was a boy?"

"I s'pose it could've been a girl . . ."

"Perhaps some local child?"

"If it was, I've never seen him in the village."

"Would you recognize the face, if you did?"

"Only the eyes. His face was a blur. But in that instant, before the mare carried me past, I looked straight into his eyes. Children's eyes are the saddest in the whole world! I think when we're very young we know things that later on we forget. Important and terrible things . . . Eat your tart!"

"Yes, I will." Damiot frowned as he picked it up and took a bite.

Could that figure on the terrace have been a child playing a trick on the villagers?

What child?

12

When he returned to the Auberge he switched on the lamps in his room and closed every curtain to shut out the rain. He tossed his Paris paper on the bed with the Simenon. Unwrapping the small torch, he slipped it into a pocket of his damp waterproof, which he then hung in the armoire.

The room was chilly, and he immediately ran a hot tub.

Undressed, he stood before the long bathroom mirror.

His scars were hideous. Each time he looked at them he was repulsed by the damage those doctors had done to his body. He had seen hundreds of dead bodies without flinching, but the desecration of his own flesh repelled him. The livid scars would be with him for the rest of his life.

After a long soak in the steaming water, he slipped into his robe and stretched out on the bed, placing the Simenon within reach of the bedside table. Save that for the first night he couldn't sleep.

He opened the newspaper but, turning the pages, found no crime news.

The paper said it was raining in Paris. Checking the date, he discovered that it was Wednesday's paper. The day before he left Paris! No matter. He hadn't seen a newspaper since leaving the hospital.

Turning more pages, he became interested in a political crisis. Same old politicians, new scandals . . .

He wakened with a start, pushing the newspaper off his face.

Checking his wristwatch on the bedside table, he saw that he had slept for several hours. He flung the paper aside, jumped up from the bed, and went to the nearest pair of windows. Driving rain and a flooded garden! There would be no visit to the château tonight.

He heard a dog barking in the darkness. The forlorn sound

came from the front. Probably a stray, running loose on the avenue.

Damiot closed the curtains, shutting out the rain, and went into the bath, where he splashed his eyes with cold water to bring himself awake.

Studying the menu, he saw that the specialty for the evening was ratatouille.

Only six other guests in the dining room—three middle-aged couples. The chef himself served Damiot, with both of the waiters and the garçon in attendance. One waiter removed the cover from a large earthen casserole on a serving cart. The other set a plate of ratatouille before Damiot, after Michel spooned it from a silver ladle, with fresh asparagus and *gratin dauphinois* in separate dishes.

Damiot sniffed the rich aroma. "Smells magnificent!" He picked up a fork, realizing that Giroud was waiting for him to taste his creation. As he did so he noticed Madame Bouchard at her desk, smiling in anticipation. He glanced up at the chef—remembering what Jenny Tendrell had said about him—as he took the first mouthful. Aurore Bouchard was in love with this young man and, quite obviously, the English girl was at least attracted to him . . .

Giroud leaned forward slightly. "Monsieur?"

"Haven't tasted a genuine ratatouille in years! Can't find anything like this in Paris."

"Plaisir, Monsieur Damiot." Michel Giroud bowed, his starched *toque blanche* stiff as a bishop's miter. He waved the waiters ahead of him toward the kitchen, followed by Claude pushing the serving cart.

Damiot settled down to enjoy his dinner. The ratatouille was excellent, but no better than his father used to make . . .

Or was memory deceiving him?

He remembered his father, after Chez Damiot closed for the night, stirring a big pot of ratatouille and filling three plates. The family eating in the kitchen, sopping up the last drop of the stew with crusts of bread left from other people's dinners. Afterward, he would always help his mother with the dishes. All the tableware from the restaurant. Pots and pans. Two hours of hard work before they could go upstairs, where his father would already be snoring . . .

Damiot finished his carafe of *vin blanc* with a local cheese and asked Jean-Paul to serve coffee, as usual, in the lounge. He left the dining room unobserved by Madame Bouchard, who had disappeared into the kitchen, and went into the lounge.

Relaxing near the open fire, he pondered several questions.

Was it possible that Pouchet was the monster? Or was it that small boy Jenny Tendrell had glimpsed through the entrance gates?

He wondered if Bardou was sleeping after his hot toddy . . .

"Jean-Paul said you didn't want your Calvados tonight."

He looked around to see Aurore Bouchard. "Not tonight. Merci!" Rising clumsily from the low fauteuil. "Won't you sit down?"

"For a moment." She sank onto a sofa, facing him.

"Another excellent dinner!" Lowering himself into the armchair again, favoring his hip. "Pity there were so few people to enjoy it."

"We always expect that in this weather." She clasped her hands on an arm of the sofa. "Why didn't you tell me who you are?"

"But I did, Madame!"

"Yes, of course you did." She smiled. "You even wrote your name in our guest book when you arrived. I simply didn't associate it with the previous owners of this property. In fact, I'd completely forgotten that their restaurant was called Chez Damiot! After Madame Sibilat phoned this morning, I checked through a file of documents and found the names—Pierre and Clémence Damiot . . ."

"I suppose Madame Sibilat told you I placed roses on their graves?"

"She did."

"I noticed fresh flowers on your husband's grave."

"Oh, yes! I get them every Saturday, when I pick up flowers for the restaurant."

"Off the record, what do you think of the Sibilats? Mère et fils?"

She frowned. "The truth is—I do not like them. Either of them!" Facing him again. "Madame is much too inquisitive. Most of the village women have sharp eyes—and sharper tongues. Except Madame Mussot, at the pâtisserie. She's a love!"

"I've known her since I was a child."

"Madame Sibilat's the worst! She asks the most personal questions and expects an answer. I also resent the way she dominates her son. Marc must be in his thirties, but he's completely controlled by his mother. Madame Sibilat is constantly telling him what to do. Even in their shop. I find it uncomfortable to go there, but they do have the best flowers this side of Grasse!" She rose from the sofa. "Eh bien, Monsieur! Now that I know who you are . . ."

He got to his feet. "Yes, Madame?"

"Would you care to see what Julien and I have done to your old home? To your parents' kitchen . . ."

"I would indeed."

"I shall give you a personal tour." She led the way, across the lobby and through the dark dining room with its ghostly tables. "My staff has departed for the night and Michel will be leaving shortly, in spite of the rain, for whatever diversion he may have planned for this evening. Perhaps some billiards or a visit to one of his lady friends. He has many local admirers . . ."

Damiot was aware of a note of irony in her voice as she pushed the doors back, into the brightly lighted kitchen.

"We enlarged the old kitchen. Put in more windows . . ."

His eyes moved from the compact modern ranges to a row of white refrigerators as she talked, noticing the enormous stainless-steel pots, hanging copper pans, and rows of casseroles. Worktables holding electrical equipment—mixers and blenders. "My father would appreciate every change you've made in his kitchen, and my mother would admire what you've done to her dining room. Especially the chairs!"

"I am so glad, Monsieur." She glanced toward a corkscrew wooden staircase that rose from a shadowy corner. "Now would you care to see my own suite?"

"If I wouldn't be intruding . . ."

"Certainly not!" She started up the curving steps. "I suppose these were your family bedrooms?"

"My parents had the large one. Mine was the smallest. The other room, in front, was available for guests." He clutched the polished baluster as he climbed after her. "You added this staircase . . ."

"Julien found it in an old farmhouse that was being torn down. It was his idea to put it here, so that we might have a private entrance to our apartment." She turned to look down at him. "Oh, Monsieur, I forgot! Your hip . . ."

"No problem. I'm walking much better today."

"How thoughtless of me!"

"Not at all." He followed her to the top, hip barely protesting. All the exercise, these past three days, must have done some good.

"Here we are!"

He saw that they had reached a shallow landing with a carved antique door. She swung it open and snapped a wall switch, sending a spill of light from inside the room across the landing. "Come in, Monsieur."

Damiot followed her into a spacious sitting room furnished with Provençal antiques. Warm pools of light from handsome pottery table lamps. "This must take up the space of both our old bedrooms! Mine used to be over there, I think, in the corner. And my parents' room was about here! Where I was born . . ."

"My bedroom's through there." She indicated a closed door. "In the front."

"That would be where our guest room used to be."

"We added a new wing for guest rooms and a lounge. Two rooms downstairs, four above."

"This is very comfortable." He glanced around at the curtained windows, crowded bookshelves, and framed paintings of Provence.

"You've noticed the paintings! These were my husband's favorites."

Damiot saw her tapestry workbag, resting on a small sofa. "I've something here I'd like to show you." He brought out the strand of wool from his pocket.

"What is it?" She moved closer as Damiot held the crimson yarn into the light.

He handed it to her, unexpectedly touching her fingers. "Knowing that you do needlepoint, I wondered if you might be able to tell me anything about this . . ."

"It's pure wool, of course. I haven't seen such a deep scarlet dye in years." She rubbed it between her fingers. "Or felt such a heavy texture. I've never found this color at the only shop in the village where they sell yarn."

"It was caught in Fric-Frac's hair."

"Fric-Frac?"

"Today while we were out. What do you suppose it came from? Some garment?"

"Hard to say." She peered at the ends of the strand. "A sweater or scarf, perhaps. Something old because it's been washed many times. You can see that the color's slightly faded." Handing it back. "Afraid I'm not much help . . ."

"Where is Madame Fric-Frac?" He thrust the yarn into his pocket again. "Haven't seen her tonight."

"I left her in my bedroom before dinner, fast asleep."

"That's because I wore her out today, walking with me. There's also something I'd like to ask you about the Courville monster . . ."

"There I'll be even less helpful!"

"I've been told there's a local legend that says a monster appears at the château whenever there's trouble there or here in the village. But as a child, I never knew of any such legend. Children are always the first to hear and repeat these things. And, of course, believe them! Have you heard this legend?"

"Matter of fact, I have."

"Do you recall where you first heard it?"

"Months ago, I think . . ." She frowned, puzzled. "I believe it was shortly after that first girl was murdered."

"Who told you?"

"I think it was the garçon . . ."

"Claude?"

"One morning when he arrived for work. He's always bursting with gossip he picks up from his family and friends . . . Yes! I'm certain it was Claude who first mentioned a monster at the château."

Damiot glanced toward the curtained windows as a car roared down the drive.

"That's Michel." She shrugged. "Off early for his Saturday night entertainment in the village. Rain or no rain!"

"And I should say good night. Thank you for showing me the changes you've made here."

"I'm so glad you approve." She moved toward a third door. "You can get downstairs through here." Unlocking and opening the door. "This corridor will take you past our other guest rooms to the front stairs. Sleep well, Monsieur . . ."

"And you!" He hesitated, feeling a sudden urge to embrace

her before he went through the door, but restrained the impulse and continued on into the hall. "A demain, Madame!"

"A demain . . ."

Clutching the railing, Damiot went down the curving steps to the lobby and headed for his room. He unlocked the door and saw that someone had turned on the lamps, lighted a fresh fire on the hearth, and straightened his rumpled bed. Probably the garçon again . . .

He circled the room, switching off every lamp except the one on his bedside table. That, with the glow from the fireplace, would be enough.

As he moved in and out of the bath, preparing for bed, he could hear the rain through the closed curtains and shutters, beating against the windows.

Perhaps the weather would clear again tomorrow. Several things he wanted to do. And tomorrow night, if it stayed clear, he would have another look at the château, on his own, without Bardou. Take Fric-Frac with him! She had certainly been useful this morning . . .

Standing before the tall mirror, behind the bathroom door, he examined his scars again and once more was repelled by what those surgeons in Paris had done to his flesh. If only he could get several days of sun—a good tan should hide some of the ugly marks they had left . . .

He slipped into his robe, securing it around his waist. As he folded the tailored cover back to the foot of his bed, he noticed the Simenon waiting on the bedside table. Wouldn't do any reading tonight. Maigret would only keep him awake, he would have to read it through to the end. He began to untie the cord of his robe . . .

Someone knocked softly.

Damiot frowned as he stared at the offending door. Who the devil could be knocking at this hour? Perhaps Bardou was phoning . . .

He crossed the room reluctantly, as the knocking was repeated. "Who is it?"

"Madame Bouchard. I hope you weren't in bed . . ."

"Not yet." He unlocked the door and swung it open.

She stood there in her dark brown robe, the quilted satin gleaming like metal, bronze hair hanging free below her shoulders.

Her beauty made him speechless and he could only stare.

"I thought perhaps you might enjoy a Calvados now. My husband always liked to have a nightcap . . ."

Only then did he realize that she was holding a silver tray with a bottle and two glasses. "I would indeed! Please come in."

She carried the tray without a word toward the lighted lamp and rested it on the bedside table.

He closed the door and followed her. "This is a pleasant surprise."

"There are several things, Monsieur, that I have decided I must tell you." She uncorked the bottle as she talked. "Even though you're not investigating the Courville monster or those murders . . ."

"I swear, Madame, I have no official reason for involving myself in either matter."

"You don't think they're one and the same?" Now she was filling the glasses. "Those two unfortunate girls were killed by the monster."

"I have no opinion as to that. I've been asking questions because, like all detectives, I have a larger curiosity than most. Eh bien! What is this you've decided to tell me?" Accepting one of the glasses from her. "Merci, Madame."

"First of all, there is something I think you should know about Lisette Jarlaud . . ."

"First of all! Shall we sit down?"

"Of course . . ." She sank onto the yellow wool blanket. "I hope you're finding this bed comfortable?"

"In every way." He sat beside her, aware of her perfume again. Fresh and subtle, unlike the heavy scents worn by his wife and his mistress . . .

She raised her glass, the Calvados glowing amber in the firelight. "To your complete recovery, Monsieur! From that surgery . . ."

"I'll happily drink to that possibility." He touched his glass to hers. As they drank, he noticed that her robe, in this light, seemed to have a tawny golden sheen like the pelt of an animal. "You were saying—about the Jarlaud girl?"

"May not be important, but . . . I haven't told this to anyone! Of course, the local police never questioned me. Lisette Jarlaud came here one morning, not long before her death."

"Oh?"

"Two weeks before she died. Only Claude knew about it. He

was alone in the kitchen when she knocked on the door, and came upstairs to tell me that Lisette wished to see me. I went down and found her sitting on the kitchen steps. I suppose Claude overheard what was said. I've never discussed it with him.'' She sipped the Calvados slowly as she talked. ''Lisette wanted to know if I might have work for her. Told me that she was unhappy at the Hôtel Courville—had to make a change—but I wanted no part of her. I'd been aware of her reputation since shortly after my husband and I arrived here. So I explained, as kindly as possible, that I already had two women who worked for me whenever maids were required. I never saw her again but I've wondered, since her death, why she wanted to leave the Hôtel Courville . . .''

''She offered you no explanation?''

''None. I've thought about it many times. Could she have been threatened by someone? Perhaps one of the guests at the hotel . . .''

''They would surely have followed her here!''

''Perhaps she knew they couldn't afford our prices. Also, with only six rooms, our guests are somewhat more conspicuous.''

''But if anyone had threatened her—even someone on the hotel staff—she could have left Courville and found a job in Marseille!''

''With two small children? Surely she wouldn't leave them with her parents.''

''I suppose not . . .''

''Ever since Lisette's death, I've felt that I should tell someone about her coming here. It didn't occur to me at first, because I thought I knew who had murdered her. I thought he would be caught right away, but it's been several weeks.''

''And who did you think had killed her?''

''Perhaps I shouldn't say!'' She swallowed more of the brandy. ''Now that I'm talking to you, I'm not so certain.''

''Why did you suspect this particular person?''

''Because I saw them together one morning, months ago, as I was parking in the square to do some errands. I first noticed him coming from the pharmacie, walking toward his truck parked near the fountain. I was about to speak when I realized that he hadn't seen me because his eyes were on someone else. Lisette Jarlaud had apparently been waiting for him, hidden between his truck and another car, but when he reached her they began to quarrel . . ."

"Who was this man?"

"Must I tell you?"

"Only if you wish."

"He has lived in Courville only a few years. A strange and lonely man. Not at all a friendly person . . ."

"Marc Sibilat?"

"I've said too much!"

"You think Sibilat killed the Jarlaud girl?"

"I wondered about that right after her death, but I'm not so certain any more. And I know nothing about that other girl who died. I've no reason to suspect Marc, except I did see him arguing with Lisette that morning in the square. And he is, well, rather strange . . ."

"In what way?"

She shrugged. "I have an uncomfortable feeling whenever I'm with him—in his shop or when he delivers flowers here—a suspicion that because of his mother he hates all women." She frowned as she faced him. "If that were true—could he be the murderer?"

Now it was Damiot's turn to shrug. "Perhaps he dislikes everyone. Men and women! There are people like that. Any man can be a murderer or, for that matter, any woman. And every human being, in his own way, is strange—has his or her peculiarities—psychopathic or otherwise. Some of my strangest suspects have proved to be completely innocent."

"Forget everything I've said about Marc Sibilat!"

"Let me assure you, I'll not repeat it to anyone." He reached across to set his empty glass on the bedside table.

"Another Calvados?"

"Not just now . . ." He placed his hand on her thigh, feeling the solid flesh under the satin robe. She leaned closer, touching his cheek lightly with her lips.

"Aurore . . ." He took her in his arms and kissed her on the mouth.

"How did you learn my name?" she whispered.

"I have learned many things."

"I'm sure you have . . ."

As he loosened her robe, searching for the invisible buttons, he realized that she was wearing nothing underneath.

"Let me." She pushed his hand away, gently.

"You are very beautiful . . ." He stretched out beside her, accommodating his hip cautiously to her warm flesh.

Her body was reacting. Rhythmically, spasmodically.

Damiot sighed, releasing his worries and tensions of the last weeks. Her body felt firm and warm against his. This woman was more real—more satisfying—than any woman he had known in Paris.

Afterward, relaxing, they drank another Calvados, sipping it slowly.

Aurore was the first to bring up the subject of the murders again. "There must be something that connects those two young women! Lisette and the other one . . ."

"I've known cases where several people were killed and their only link was the killer. None of the victims knew the others but all of them, unfortunately, did know their murderer. If these two met theirs by chance, your Courville monster may never be found!"

"I saw you this afternoon, in the Hôtel Courville."

"I went there for lunch with a friend, but neither of us could eat. He had no appetite because of a cold, and I had none because of the food."

"Their food is unmentionable! I lunched with two businessmen from Paris, and we had so many things to discuss, fortunately, that we barely tasted the miserable food. I saw you and your friend going into the brasserie, but you didn't notice me in the dining room."

"I saw you when I was leaving."

She laughed, throwing her head back, bronze hair flowing over her shoulders. "Perhaps you recognized my companions? I'm told they're well known in Paris."

"Afraid I didn't notice their faces. Only yours." He reached across to set his empty glass on the bedside table.

"Those gentlemen represent an international hotel chain that has bought the Hôtel Courville."

"I see!"

"There's been no announcement because they hope to purchase several adjoining properties, and if word got out prematurely, prices would soar!"

"Naturally."

"It's to be an enormous hôtel de luxe, as in Cannes or Monte

Carlo. With a first-class restaurant and a swimming pool. Of course, this should bring new business to all the shops in the village."

"Why did they select Courville for their new hotel?"

"Because of the traffic on this highway. They had surveys done which show that in the summer there's a constant flow of tourists through the village, between Paris and the Riviera. I've told you, I'm always booked for the entire season. They naturally want no other restaurants in Courville—except those two cafés for the locals—so they've offered me a small fortune for this property."

"Are you going to sell?"

"I have a month to decide. Next week I must drive to Lyon and discuss everything with my attorney."

"Tell me . . ." He found it difficult to ask his next question. "What would happen to this building?"

"They plan to tear it down."

"Mon Dieu!"

"I know. The house where you were born . . ." She sighed. "And the restaurant Julien and I created. Where we were so happy!"

"Do you wish to sell?"

"The money will make me independent. Julien would want that."

"You should sell."

"Is that your advice?"

"Whatever pleases you."

"You are a very kind man."

"Nobody's ever accused me of that before!"

"Nonsense! You're kind and . . ."

"I am a policeman. Obstinate and frequently unpleasant. Always searching for the truth."

"And have you ever found the truth?"

"Once or twice, perhaps . . ."

She leaned closer and kissed him, lightly, on the shoulder. "One thing more, about the new hotel . . ."

"Yes?"

"They want me to take complete charge of their restaurant and advise the architect who is designing the kitchens and dining rooms. Seems for some time they've been hoping to find a woman manager for one of their restaurants."

"That should certainly make you decide." He slipped his arm carefully under her head.

"They had planned to bring a famous chef from Paris to supervise the menus and food, but . . ."

"What about your chef? Giroud's first-class."

"I've discussed Michel with them each time we've talked, and they are very interested. They'll be having dinner here tomorrow night. I'm telling Michel that they're friends of my husband's and I want him to give them a perfect dinner. I will select the menu, some of the dishes he does best. Michel won't know he's being considered for such an important project. If he suspected the truth there could be scenes in the kitchen, and dinner might be a disaster! I've made only one demand of these people. They planned to call their restaurant the Relais de Provence, but I told them that if I do sign their contract they must call it Relais Julien. They've agreed to do that. So it would be Julien's restaurant, as well as mine. Our restaurant!"

"You loved your husband very much."

"We were very close."

"But you are reasonably happy? Running a restaurant . . ."

"Reasonably? Yes . . . What about you? Are you reasonably happy in your métier?"

"Nobody's ever asked me that before." He stared at the ceiling, barely visible in the light from the fireplace and bath. "I've never thought about it. Whether being a policeman satisfies me . . ."

"Did you always want to be a detective?"

"Such a thing never entered my mind! When I first went to Paris, years ago, I had to find a job while I studied law at night. I worked as a waiter, took tickets on a bus, was a telephone repairman . . . Then I went to classes during the day and got a job at Au Printemps as a night watchman. Which gave me more time to study. After three years, quite by chance, I discovered that I could apply for a job at the Préfecture. The fact that I had been studying law was in my favor . . ."

"And now you're a famous detective!"

"The newspapers exaggerate!"

"Do you enjoy your work at the Préfecture?"

"I'm happiest when I'm away from my office. Working on a case. Meeting people. Asking questions . . . That's when I'm really happy." He felt her body, beside him, relaxing again as he talked. "When I'm doing that, every day is exciting . . ." Moving closer, pressing his mouth against her lips, he felt her fingers moving slowly down his spine. He buried his face in the soft cloud of her hair, breathing deeply of her fragrance as his lips found her ear.

Her caressing fingers had discovered the scars on his hip.

She gasped.

He realized that his scars had reminded her of another man. If Julien Bouchard had lived, survived that skiing accident, his body would probably have been scarred.

She was sobbing. Quietly . . .

He kissed her cheek. It was wet with tears.

Her fingers were stroking his scars . . .

"I understand," he whispered.

"Do you? Yes! I believe you do . . ."

" 'But if my queen weeps, I too will weep . . .' "

"You will weep?"

"A famous poet wrote that. Many years ago. He was born in Provence . . ." His lips found her mouth again.

13

Damiot opened his eyes and squinted at the luminous dial of his wristwatch on the bedside table.

Almost nine?

Aurore must have slipped away in the night . . .

He slipped out of bed and hurried toward the nearest windows, the tiled floor cold under his bare feet, flung the curtains apart, and opened the inside shutters.

The gardens beyond the open windows were a glare of sunshine. Good weather again, grâce à Dieu!

Sunday morning? The villagers would be going to Mass.

Leaving the curtains open, moving with purpose, he hurried into the bath and splashed cold water on his face. Brushed his hair and slipped into his robe.

When the garçon brought breakfast, he must ask him where he had first heard the legend about a monster appearing at the château...

Settling into bed again, he noticed the glasses and empty Calvados bottle on the bedside table. They had finished that last night, before they slept...

If only this good weather would last through the night. No matter. Clear or not, he was going to get inside that château. On his own...

His thoughts were interrupted by the garçon's discreet knock.

"Come in!" Pushing himself to a sitting position as a key turned and the door opened.

"Sorry I'm late!"

"Aurore!" Wearing another robe, more tailored, and with her hair brushed away from her face, she had brought his breakfast tray.

She laughed. "I'm the Sunday garçon when we have only one guest."

A small black body skidded across the tiled floor and jumped onto the bed.

"Bonjour, Fric-Frac!"

The dog kissed his hand with the tip of her tongue and barked her pleasure.

Damiot looked up as Aurore set her tray on the bedside table. "Won't you have coffee with me?"

"I've work to do." She smiled as she collected the glasses and brandy bottle. "Will you be dining with us tonight?"

"Most certainly! I'm going out this morning but I should be back late in the afternoon."

"Good."

"Your friends from Paris will be dining here..."

"I'm breaking the news to Michel over breakfast. He always cooks a special breakfast every Sunday, which we have in the kitchen."

"I want to drive up to the château after dinner, and I was wondering if I might take Fric-Frac with me?"

"By all means!"

"What time will your guests arrive?"

"Around eight. They're spending the day in Cannes."

"Then I shall have an early dinner."

"Enjoy the sunshine today!" She carried their glasses, with the empty bottle, toward the door. "It's all for you."

Damiot smiled as he watched her leave. She hadn't even mentioned last night. The next move, obviously, would be up to him.

He bit off the end of a croissant as he filled the small porcelain bowl with coffee. Fed a piece of croissant to Fric-Frac before he tasted the steaming black brew.

"Eh bien, Madame la Duchesse! I won't be taking you with me this morning, but tonight, weather permitting, we'll have another look inside that château. Unless you have some other engagement?"

She sat up and pawed the air, hoping for more of the croissant.

"There's much to be done today. I've told everyone I wouldn't involve myself, but it seems no one's doing anything to solve these murders or put an end to this monster business. You agree?"

She barked and wagged her tail, eyes on the croissant.

Damiot broke off another piece and gave it to her. "I must learn the facts to satisfy my own curiosity about both—murderer and monster."

She barked again.

Standing in the narrow street, facing the small house where Blanche had lived, eleven years ago, he realized that the sun was much warmer than yesterday. He slipped out of his waterproof and tossed it into the car.

Blanche had been born in Courville, although he hadn't known her when he lived here. Of course, there was nine years' difference in their ages. She was only twenty-three when they had met . . .

Damiot pulled the metal handle beside the door, and heard a bell tinkle inside.

Perhaps Blanche had gone to Mass. More than likely she was married by now. With three or four children . . .

"Oui, M'sieur?"

Damiot saw a tiny old woman, thin and dark, with narrowed suspicious eyes. "Pardon, Madame. I'm looking for Blanche Carmet."

"Blanche Carm . . ." She slammed the door.

He returned, puzzled, to his car and, swinging it around, drove back toward the square. Pausing at the corner of Avenue Mireille for the traffic light, he heard organ music coming from Saint-Sauveur.

Perhaps if he waited outside the church, he might see Blanche Carmet coming out from Mass. He slowed to a stop and walked toward Saint-Sauveur. In this bright sunlight the church looked almost as it had when he was a boy.

The music of the Mass flowed out to meet him as he went up the gravel path around the side, into the cemetery. Making his way between the headstones, he noticed that the red carnations on Julien Bouchard's grave still looked fresh.

And so did the roses he had left yesterday . . .

Damiot touched the headstone on his father's grave as he listened to the shrill, untrained voices rising above the wheezy rumble of the organ. To his surprise, he recognized the end of the Mass . . . Repulsed by the cold headstone, he left the graves and headed back toward the church.

The interior of Saint-Sauveur would be unchanged from his childhood. Warm candlelight on the old paintings, the statues, and the curiously decorated walls.

It had seemed a different place, cold and dark, when he attended the requiem masses, three weeks apart, for his parents . . .

He waited at the corner of the church until the first rush of villagers came through the portal blinking at the sun, pausing for a word with the priest. This was a new man. Younger than the last, but already showing a priestly paunch under his chasuble.

The two Sibilats emerged slightly apart from the others. Madame, in black, holding a missal in one black-gloved hand. Sibilat, wearing a gray suit that, with his slicked-down hair, made him seem younger. Madame had noticed Damiot and was whispering to her son.

Damiot glanced away, checking other faces, before Sibilat had a chance to look in his direction. Some of the villagers had noticed him, and more heads were turning. None of the young women resembled Blanche Carmet . . .

He looked back toward the Sibilats, who had already reached the street. Madame seemed to be arguing with her son, the shiny black feathers on her hat swaying up and down.

Turning toward the church again, Damiot saw that Hercule Mauron and a thin woman, obviously his wife—both dressed in their Sunday best—had paused beside the priest, who was bowing obsequiously to Monsieur le Maire. They continued on toward the street without noticing Damiot.

His attention was drawn back to see Aurore Bouchard, very smart in a tailored suit and jaunty hat, coming from the church with Michel Giroud, wearing a dark blue jacket with gray slacks. Damiot hadn't anticipated seeing them here this morning. Aurore had observed his presence but showed no reaction, and Michel, after speaking to the priest, escorted her toward the gate.

They were followed by Jean-Paul, the waiter from the Auberge, with a pretty girl. Probably his wife. He saw Damiot and bowed, turning to speak to his attractive companion, who stared quite openly at the detective.

Damiot wondered if the murderer might be among these people coming out from the dark church into the glare of sunlight . . .

"Monsieur Inspecteur . . ."

He turned to face Marc Sibilat, who had returned across the grass.

"You were waiting to see me?"

"Matter of fact, I've been visiting my parents' graves again." He saw that Sibilat was nervous, fumbling with his tie. "Why did you think I wished to see you?"

"My mother told me you came to the shop yesterday. Asking about those flowers on Lisette Jarlaud's grave . . ."

"I suspected, from their wrapping, they'd been bought in your shop. Madame remembered that she had sold them to a young farmer."

"Achille Savord."

"She said he came in one day while you were out."

"I'd gone somewhere in the truck to make a delivery."

"Can you tell me anything about Savord's relationship with the Jarlaud girl?" Damiot asked.

"I know nothing about that. Although I have heard, of course, that Lisette had—relationships—with many men in Courville."

"And you, Monsieur? Did you have a relationship with her?" He glanced away and saw that the last of the villagers had departed. The priest, hesitating at the portal, was observing him with undisguised curiosity. Hearing a deep sigh from Sibilat, Damiot faced him again. "Well, Monsieur?"

"Several times. My mother doesn't suspect. She thinks I never knew Lisette. Has no idea that I used to take her in my truck to other towns so that we could go to a cinéma without being recognized . . ."

"Where did you sleep with her?"

"In the back of the truck, usually. We would park on a side road or in some field. But I always had to be home before midnight or my mother would ask questions. Lisette's parents never cared what time she got in."

"You're a grown man, yet your mother treats you like a child."

"If only my mother had died, instead of my father. Poor man! She always told him what to do. Watched him, every minute!"

"You were seen recently talking to Lisette Jarlaud, here in the square. Apparently quarreling with her."

"Lisette waited for me in the square. Many times! When she saw my truck parked. Usually to ask for money . . ."

"Would you give it to her?"

"If I had it. I felt sorry for her. Two small children to support."

"What about the other girl? The one found in that field."

"Annie Deffous . . ."

"You know her name!"

"I was afraid to tell the local gendarmes when they questioned me. Didn't want to get involved. But when I learned that you had come from Paris, I knew I would have to tell you."

"Where did you know this Deffous girl?"

"When I lived in Toulon."

"Toulon?" He watched the priest go, finally, into the church.

"Before I came to Courville. Annie worked there in some shop, as a bookkeeper."

"What sort of shop?"

"She never told me."

"Where did you first meet her?"

"When I was walking one evening on the Quai Stalingrad."

"And after that?"

"Many different places. She never said where she lived or anything like that. Whether or not she had a family . . ."

"How did you arrange to meet?"

"She would tell me when she would be free and where I could pick her up in my car. Usually some street corner. I would take her to a restaurant for dinner, and afterward to one of the waterfront hotels."

"Didn't your mother suspect?"

"My father was alive then and she was more concerned about him. Anyway, I always told her I was spending the night with a friend from medical school."

"How long ago was this?"

"The summer before my father died. Three years ago."

"Why did you stop seeing the Deffous girl?"

"She told me she was pregnant."

"Your child?"

"Annie swore that it wasn't. Said she knew who the father was and he had agreed to pay for everything. Told me she was in love with him and she wouldn't be able to meet me any more."

"Did you try to see her after that?"

"Why should I? Matter of fact, I was glad we were finished."

"Why?"

Sibilat shrugged. "I was never in love with Annie. Never intended to marry her. She was as demanding as my mother. Telling me where she wanted to go for dinner, which movie to see."

"You never saw Annie Deffous again?"

"Not until she turned up in Courville. Came into my shop..."

"When was this?"

"The day before her body was found."

"Your mother saw her?"

"Fortunately, she was busy in the kitchen. I built a new kitchen in the back purposely, so I could have a few hours' peace every day without having to hear my mother's voice. Annie showed up when my mother was cooking dinner. Mon Dieu! If I hadn't been there that afternoon, they would have met."

"What did the Deffous girl want with you?"

"Nothing, really. She had noticed our sign—Sibilat Fleurs—as she drove into the village. I'd told her many times that I wanted to open a florist shop. So she stopped, and there I was!"

"What did she tell you?"

"We only talked for a moment because I was afraid my mother would hear our voices. Annie said that she'd come here to see a friend."

"Someone in the village?"

"She never told me that, but she implied the person had money."

103

"Man or woman?"

"From the way she talked it had to be a man."

"What, exactly, did she say?"

"Only that she was seeing somebody about money he owed her."

"A man who owed her money . . ."

"She had taken time off from her job to drive up here. She wouldn't know how long she'd be in Courville until after she contacted her friend. Asked me about a cheap place to stay, and I suggested that motel behind the town hall. But when I phoned in the evening, she wasn't there. Her body was found next morning. I had no idea at first that the dead girl was Annie. I can tell you, Monsieur Inspecteur, it was a shock when they asked everyone to try and identify the body. Fortunately there were several of us lined up, and nobody noticed that I recognized her. I told them I'd never seen her before. I swear, Monsieur, I didn't kill Annie."

"In that case, nothing can happen to you. On the other hand, if you did kill her, someone will eventually find out."

"Then I've nothing to worry about! Except I'd better get home before my mother becomes suspicious. I'll say that you questioned me but there was nothing I could tell you."

"Did you see what sort of car this Deffous girl was driving when she came to your shop?"

"Yes. It was a gray Dauphine. An old model . . ."

"Au 'voir, Monsieur." Damiot held out his hand.

Sibilat appeared to be surprised by the gesture. "Merci, Monsieur Inspecteur." He shook Damiot's hand and hurried down the path.

So Sibilat had known both those girls. Annie Deffous and Lisette Jarlaud.

Florists worked with sharp knives, and Sibilat had studied for several years to be a doctor. A surgeon . . .

These seemingly weak types, dominated by women—mother or wife—frequently exploded with sudden violence. Even murder . . .

14

"Graudin speaking . . ."

"Wasn't sure you'd be home, Sunday morning."

"M'sieur Inspecteur! You're back in Paris?"

"I'm still in Courville." He heard small children screaming in the background as Graudin talked. "I was calling to ask . . ."

"How's the hip, M'sieur? Feeling better?"

"Seems to be healing. I've been giving it plenty of exercise. I'm staying at the Auberge Courville."

"Auberge Courville . . . I'm writing that down."

"It's a new place. Some people have taken over the building where my parents had their restaurant. The house where I was born! There's a phone, if anyone wants me. Don't know the number. I'm calling to find out if anything's developed with those two cases I was working on before I went to that damn hospital . . ."

"Everybody at the Préfecture is talking about you!"

"What?"

"The Chief announced at some meeting yesterday that you're investigating two murders there."

"Merde! How the devil could he . . ."

"He told them that when they take vacations they do nothing but eat and sleep. Always come back to work overweight. But not Chief Inspector Damiot. He gets involved with two murder cases and . . ."

"I am not investigating any murders! You can tell that to anybody who asks. Including the Chief! Tell them I'm going to stay here—eating and sleeping—for another two weeks!" He slammed the phone down and, still furious, turned away from the public phone in the lobby of the Hôtel Courville.

As he stalked toward the desk, he realized that he had learned nothing from Graudin about the two Paris investigations!

A man was typing behind the registration desk.

"Inspector Bardou's room?"

"Room seventeen. Second floor, rear . . ."

The upstairs corridor smelled of bad plumbing and ancient dust.

Climbing the stairs hadn't bothered his hip. So he must be improving! In fact, this morning he was feeling much better in every way. Perhaps it was because of what had happened, last night, with Aurore . . .

He found number seventeen and knocked on the door.

"Who's there?" Bardou's voice was muffled.

"Damiot!"

There was a shuffling sound from inside before the door opened.

"M'sieur Inspecteur! I was in bed."

"Good." He saw that Bardou was wearing wrinkled cotton pajamas, his feet bare. "How's your cold?"

"Much worse . . ." He headed back toward his rumpled bed. Damiot closed the door. "Didn't that toddy help any?"

"Nothing has helped." He collapsed onto the side of the bed. "Don't get close to me, you'll catch my cold. Sit over there." Motioning to the only chair that wasn't piled with clothing.

"I'll stand, if you don't mind." Damiot realized that he was still seething with rage over his call to Paris. Mustn't get angry with Bardou. The man looked miserable. "I must warn you again, I've no intention of getting involved with the local police. In any way!"

"I understand that, M'sieur Inspecteur." He lighted a Gauloise as he talked. "I've told everybody you're here on vacation . . ."

So he had reported his presence to whoever was in charge at the gendarmerie! Damiot restrained his fury.

"They already knew you were in Courville."

"Did they?"

"Seems they checked with Paris when they realized you were the famous Chief Inspector Damiot."

"Merde!"

"They thought you'd been sent to solve the two murders, but Paris informed them you're here for a rest."

"Exactly what I told you yesterday!" Damiot moved about in the cramped space, avoiding furniture. "But I do have one or two ideas about those girls who were murdered, and I've come across several bits of information. I'm going to look into them because of my professional curiosity about all crimes, but whatever I learn I shall turn over to you."

"To me?"

"You must get all the credit. Understand?"

"That's very generous, M'sieur Inspecteur!"

"Generosity has nothing to do with it! I have no desire to get involved. Now then . . . Did you ever hear of a young farmer named Achille Savord?"

"No. Who's he?"

"One of several locals who apparently enjoyed the favors of that Jarlaud girl."

"Nobody's mentioned him to me."

"Savord must have cared for the girl, because he's the only one who placed flowers on her grave."

"I thought her family put them there."

"Madame Sibilat, at the florist shop, tells me she sold them to Savord. You should have a talk with him."

"I'll certainly do that, M'sieur Inspecteur . . ."

"What's the name of that man you said would be on duty this weekend at the gendarmerie?"

"Porel."

"Phone him after I leave here. Explain who I am and . . ."

"He already knows! Everybody on the staff would like to meet the Chief Inspector from Paris."

Damiot gritted his teeth. "Tell Porel I want to have a look at that girl in the morgue. I'll stop by this afternoon. Now! For your private information . . . The unidentified girl in the morgue was from Toulon."

"Was she!" Bardou found a pad and pencil on the bedside table and scribbled notes as Damiot explained.

"Her name is Annie Deffous."

"Annie . . . I know several of the Toulon gendarmes. They came to Arles last year, to break up a ring of kidnappers."

"Call them this afternoon. The Deffous girl worked there, as a bookkeeper in some shop. She arrived here the day she was murdered, driving a gray Dauphine. Your friends in Toulon can get the license number for you. You should send it, with a description of her car, to every gendarmerie in Provence. It has very likely been abandoned in the hills. You'll be able to find out where Annie Deffous was staying, now that you have her name. Maybe it was this hotel! Ask why they didn't report her missing when they found her luggage in the room where she must have spent part of the evening, waiting for someone. Check what phone calls she made. She apparently came to Courville looking for somebody who owed her money . . ."

"Man or woman?"

"Had to be a man. Could be someone in the village or living nearby. That's all I can tell you at this moment."

"More than anybody else has learned in two months!"

"Don't let anyone suspect you got this from me."

"No, M'sieur Inspecteur."

Damiot went toward the door. "Handle this right and you'll get a promotion."

"I spoke to the manager on the phone this morning. Had him check who was staying here when those two girls were murdered, but there was nobody here both nights."

"Of course he could've used different names each time!"

"And the manager doesn't remember any guest driving a black Ferrari. Too fancy for this hotel . . ."

"Make those calls."

"Right away!" Bardou stubbed out his cigarette and reached for the telephone.

Damiot was smiling as he closed the door, escaping the cigarette-fouled room, and started down the corridor toward the stairs.

He was no longer angry about his call to Paris.

The ham sandwich was excellent and the beer, as before, not too cold. The proprietor, his squat body wrapped in a long apron, was busy sluicing down the sidewalk with soapy water.

Damiot watched three ancients, their heads protected from the sun by faded berets, playing a game of *boules* in the far corner of the square, beyond the pissoir. They had probably been here every Sunday, weather permitting, for years!

As he finished the sandwich, washing it down with the last of his beer, Damiot wondered again why that old woman had slammed the door in his face when he asked for Blanche Carmet. In the old days, when he was growing up, everybody in Courville knew where everyone else lived! And everybody was friendly. At least to other villagers. But, of course, he was an outsider now . . .

Perhaps the Carmet family had moved to some nearby village . . .

The proprietor returned from the street with his empty water bucket. "Another beer, M'sieur Damiot?"

"You know who I am, do you?"

"The whole village must know by now! That you were born here and they've sent you from Paris, to find out who killed those two girls . . ."

He felt his anger rising again. "That's a local matter. No concern of mine."

"Of course! Whatever you say, M'sieur Inspecteur."

"One beer's enough today." Dropping a ten-franc note on the table.

"The radio says we may get more rain tonight." He set his bucket on the floor and counted out change.

"Have yourself a beer." Damiot pushed most of the change across the table. "Do you know a local girl named Carmet? Blanche Carmet?"

"M'sieur knows Blanche Carmet?"

"Met her last time I was here. She seems to have moved since then."

"Not far! One of those old houses at the far end of rue Woodrow Wilson. Around the corner, third from the end. You can't miss it!"

Damiot glanced at the solitary billiard player and rose from the table. "I suppose Monsieur Giroud plays billiards here?"

"Michel? Several nights every week. When he doesn't play here he goes to the other café across the square. Gives his business to both of us." Walking with Damiot toward the street. "Always buys a bottle of my best wine. He knows every good year. As well as the bad!"

"I'm not surprised. He's a fine chef."

"Wouldn't know 'bout that." He hesitated, arms akimbo, in the open doorway. "Can't afford the prices they charge at the Auberge. A demain, M'sieur Inspecteur!"

"A demain . . ." He started toward the corner. The air was even warmer with the sun directly overhead, and the old men playing *boules* were moving slowly in a haze of heat.

There were small shops on both sides of the street. All were closed for Sunday. No sidewalks here, and the line of shops ended in a row of houses, close together, edging the cracked pavement. He approached the door of the third house from the end.

Reaching out to grasp the rusty handle, he heard a bell respond inside when he gave it a pull. The door was opened, barely a crack, by a thin-faced woman with glossy black hair, wearing a black silk kimono.

"Pardon, Madame. I'm looking for Blanche Carmet . . ."

"Blanche?"

"I was told she lives here."

The door opened a little more. "You're a friend of Blanche?"

"I knew her several years ago." He saw that the black kimono was embroidered with scarlet flowers and trimmed with fringes of the same color. "The last time I was in Courville."

"Then you're an old friend!" She laughed. "Come in, M'sieur." Moving ahead, through a narrow hall. "You can wait in our salon."

He closed the door and followed, aware of her overpowering perfume, into a dimly lighted room furnished with divans and ottomans upholstered in crimson velvet. The place looked like . . . a whorehouse!

Madame motioned toward a divan. "Would you care for something to drink, M'sieur?"

"Not at the moment."

"Make yourself comfortable. I'll find out if Blanche is awake . . ."

"Merci, Madame." He sank onto a divan as she left the room and was immediately engulfed by waves of scent. They seemed to rise from the velvet upholstery, which must have been saturated for years with perfumes from many female bodies.

Blanche Carmet in a whorehouse?

That's why the old woman had slammed her door. She had thought he was looking for a prostitute and, apparently, he was . . .

Eleven years ago Blanche had said that she was twenty-three. Now she must be thirty-four. He tried to remember what she had looked like. Brown hair and blue eyes. Big-boned girl, solidly fleshed but attractive. He had enjoyed being with her several times while he was here. She had been extremely satisfying in bed. Could she even then have been working in the local bordello? He had driven her home, late at night, but never met any members of the family. She said it was her home, and he had asked no questions . . .

"Thought it must be you."

Damiot looked up to see a plump woman with short blonde

curls, standing in the doorway. Breasts barely covered by a pale pink kimono, pink satin slippers on her bare feet.

"Blanche?" He got to his feet, clumsily.

"I heard you were back." She moved toward him, smiling tentatively. "Wondered if you'd come see me . . ."

"You've put on a little weight."

The kimono billowed as she walked. "Some men like a big girl. Others like thin or crippled girls or . . ."

He shrugged. "Chacun à son goût!" They sat down on the divan. "How long have you been working here?"

"Six years now. There was nothing else for me in the village." She rested her small hands in her lap. "I got your letter."

"Why didn't you answer?"

"You wrote that you were getting married."

"So I did . . ."

Someone overhead was running a bath, and there was a smell of fresh coffee. The place was coming alive. Girl's voice, clear and sweet, singing a popular song he remembered hearing in Pigalle. "I went to that house where you used to live . . ."

"Oh?" She giggled nervously. "What happened?"

"When I asked for you the woman banged the door in my face."

"She would." Throwing her head back and laughing. "Been some time since anyone looked for me there."

"I'm staying at the Auberge."

"I know." Her laughter subsided. "Madame saw you yesterday, when she was shopping. You were in the pâtisserie with that English girl. M'sieur Giroud had already told us you were staying at the Auberge. He's the chef there."

"You know Giroud?"

"Michel? He was here last night. Always asks for me." She smiled. "Says he only likes girls who look as though they enjoy eating. And I do! Not like that woman at the Auberge who's always after him."

"Woman at the . . ."

"She owns the place. Madame Bouchard! Michel says she needs more flesh on her bones."

"Does he?"

"Michel's a pleasant fellow! All the other girls like him but he asks only for me. He phones at least twice a week when he knows what time he'll be finished at the Auberge. Phones from the kitchen, during the dinner hour, so Madame Bouchard never suspects anything." She giggled again. "That English girl's after him also, but Michel says she's skinny as a boy! That's what he says, but I think he makes love to all of 'em! Not that I care . . ." She shrugged. "He still comes back to me!"

"Do you know a young farmer named Savord?"

"Achille? He comes here Saturday nights. Always asks for Clara. Achille's a nice boy. Très gentil!"

"Not a rough type?"

"Certainly not! He sometimes brings little gifts for Clara's new baby . . ."

"What about the Jarlaud girl? The one who was murdered. Did you know her?"

"I've seen her in the shops, but we never spoke. Most of the men in the village knew her. Even though they deny it! Madame didn't like her, of course, because she took business away . . ."

"Eh bien! I must be going." Damiot got to his feet. "Wanted to see you again. Find out how things were with you."

"Not bad. As you can see." She pushed herself up from the divan. "Madame looks out for us. Only at the moment, things are slow. Everyone's afraid to go out, nights, because of those murders. Even the men!" She walked ahead of him toward the entrance, her hips swaying under the kimono. "Maybe you'll catch the killer while you're here . . ."

"I'm on vacation. Not looking for any murderer." As he followed her through the hall, he took two hundred-franc notes from his wallet and folded them in the palm of his hand. "I came here to rest after I left the hospital."

"You've been ill?"

"Last month, in Paris, I had to have surgery on my hip."

"Mon Dieu!"

"But I'm much better now."

"How's your wife?"

"She's left me."

"For good?" She turned to face him as she opened the door.

"I don't know."

"You're a fine man. If you want her, she'll come back."

"Au 'voir . . ." He held out his hand.

The unexpected gesture surprised her. "Will I see you again?" She shook his hand.

"Perhaps . . ."

"You are also a kind man." She pulled her hand away.

Damiot realized that the hundred-franc notes were gone.

"Take care of yourself, M'sieur Inspecteur!"

Local gendarmeries were always housed in the town hall. There would be a small courtroom, an interrogation room, and a jail. He wondered what poor bastards were behind bars here today. Some farmer who had stolen a neighbor's sheep. The village drunk . . .

This empty corridor stank, like all municipal corridors. It was a combination of many things, dominated by disinfectant and the unmistakable scent of poverty and fear, left behind by the unfortunates who had passed through here.

Damiot walked into a room where Gendarmerie was painted on the gray wall in crude black letters, and looked inside.

The room was small, with a row of files against one wall, and several wooden benches. Facing the door, between two windows, a low platform supported a long table that served as a desk. Low arched doorway in the wall opposite the files.

A man slumped in a chair at the desk was snoring.

The gendarme appeared to be in his twenties. Black hair, one clump hanging down over his forehead. Thin face and long nose.

Damiot cleared his throat.

The eyes opened. "M'sieur?"

"I'm . . ."

"Chief Inspector Damiot!" He struggled to his feet. "Forgive me, M'sieur! I must've dozed off . . ."

"You are Porel?"

"That's right, M'sieur Inspecteur. I knew you'd be coming in this afternoon. Inspector Bardou phoned half an hour ago. Did you know he's identified the first victim?"

"Has he?"

"Told me on the phone. Her name's Annie Deffous and she came from Toulon. Inspector Bardou talked with the gendarmes there. They have no record of her name, but he's asked them to check on her and get back to him."

"Looks as though he's making progress."

"Inspector Bardou's a terrific guy!"

"Did you know this Deffous girl?" Damiot asked, glancing toward the nearest windows as though his question wasn't important.

"No, M'sieur Inspecteur. I've never been to Toulon."

Damiot faced him. "But you did know the other girl! Lisette

Jarlaud." He saw Porel's face crimson. "Someone mentioned that you knew her."

"I guess everybody knew Lisette."

"You slept with her, didn't you?"

"Once or twice . . ."

"Only once or twice?"

"Four or five times, maybe. Half the men in the village slept with Lisette."

"I'd like to have a look at that unidentified girl who, it seems, has now been identified. What did you say her name was?"

"Annie Deffous."

Damiot followed as Porel swung a heavy door open into a cool corridor where one small bulb glowed in the ceiling. Their footsteps echoed on the stone floor.

"We usually don't keep a dead body here more than a few days. In fact, this is the first since I came on staff." He opened another door and snapped a switch that lighted several ceiling bulbs.

Damiot blinked as he entered a narrow, white-tiled room. The windows at the far end had been plastered over but never painted. There was an old-fashioned autopsy table in the center, and the smell of disinfectant was overpowering.

"Didn't like to look at her at first, but I've gotten used to it now." Porel walked to a tier of three large drawers and yanked the center one out with a harsh clatter of metal.

As Damiot moved closer he felt cold air strike his face.

Annie Deffous, even in death, was a pretty girl. Delicate nose, thick eyelashes, and a pleasant mouth that seemed about to speak.

Damiot frowned. It was still a shock, after all these years, to see the dead body of a young person or a child. He recalled, as he circled the open drawer, that Tendrell had said the murderer's skill with a knife showed knowledge of anatomy. The cut across the throat, neat and precise, had almost severed her neck.

A slit from the *médecin-légiste*'s scalpel extended from the breastbone down to the mound of Venus. The long red hair, tucked like a pillow under her head, looked dull and lifeless. It had continued to grow for a time after death, and the dark roots matched the pubic hair. The Englishman had been right—her hair was dyed.

"Who performed the autopsy?" he asked.

"Doctor Mondor, from Salon. He does all our police work. There's no doctor here in the village."

Damiot peered at the hands. "See this callus? Middle finger, right hand. Took years of pressure to cause that. Pen or pencil. She must've done some sort of clerical work."

"I never noticed that!" Porel leaned down for a closer look. "You're right about her work. Bardou's found out she was a bookkeeper. But you knew that from looking at her hand!"

Damiot straightened. "I've finished."

Porel closed the drawer and turned toward the door again.

"One thing more, while I'm here."

"Certainly, M'sieur Inspecteur!" He opened the door.

"I'd like to see where the other girl's body was found." He went ahead, into the corridor. "Behind here, wasn't it? In the alley?"

"I can show you the exact spot." Porel switched off the light in the morgue and closed the door. They continued on through the corridor. "This takes us to the alley."

Damiot followed, between stone columns, toward a distant door. "What hour of the day was the Jarlaud girl's body discovered?"

"Early morning. Two children stumbled over it as they took a shortcut to school . . ." He turned a key in the lock and opened the door.

The sunlight was dazzling, the air warm, after the cold interior.

He walked with Porel toward a mass of bushes that formed a green oasis sheltered by tall poplars. "This was the spot?"

"The body was found in here." Porel thrust the bushes apart with both hands and moved between them into an open space where daylight barely reached. "We made marks on the ground to show the exact spot, but of course the rains have washed all that away." He turned to Damiot. "There are photographs, if you'd like to see them."

"Another time . . . This alley must've been convenient for all concerned. Too narrow for cars to pass through, and no people around after dark. Lisette Jarlaud was able to come here unnoticed, after her day's work at the Hôtel Courville. Anyone could meet her without being seen! The alley runs behind all the shops on this side of the square. Any one of a dozen men could've slipped out and met her here . . ."

"That's right, M'sieur Inspecteur. We've questioned all the shopkeepers."

"And anybody could come out for a rendezvous—as we did, just now, from that rear door of the town hall!"

"That's possible . . ."

"I suppose you met Lisette here?"

"Well, I . . ." His voice choked in his throat. "You won't report me?"

"I've already told you. This is Bardou's investigation—not mine. I won't report you to anybody."

"In that case, M'sieur Inspecteur, I will tell you—in strict confidence—I did meet Lisette here. But only twice! The other times we always drove into the hills in my car."

For a moment, as they walked toward rue Voltaire, visible at the end of the alley, neither spoke. Damiot remembered days when he had run through this alley, avoiding the square, on an errand for his parents or up to some mischief of his own. But never at night . . .

As they reached the street, he glanced at Porel again. "I think I'll drive up and have a look at the spot where that other girl died."

"Want me to come with you?"

"That's not necessary."

"I will tell M'sieur le Commissaire that you were here."

"If you must." He turned down rue Voltaire toward the square.

As Damiot drove into the hills, he missed having Fric-Frac at his side, looking out the window. Perhaps when he returned to Paris he would buy himself a dog. Exactly like Fric-Frac!

Sophie had never wanted any kind of animal in their apartment. Afraid it would soil the rugs or damage the furniture.

Olympe always had a cat. Curled up on fancy lace cushions in her boudoir. Fat and jealous, with long white hair that stuck to his trousers. He wondered if she'd taken that damn cat to Mexico.

As before, the gates of the château were closed and padlocked. Through the grille he could see the distant castle beyond the dark tunnel of trees, like a mirage in the dazzling sunlight. A commercial truck roared past, in the opposite direction.

Damiot swerved the Peugeot across the highway, between the trees and toward the field where the girl's body had been found, parking at the edge of the wood. He got out and walked through the cropped grass into the field.

The presence of several cows, grazing at the far end, explained why the grass wasn't higher. Their heads turned in unison to inspect the intruder, but their jaws continued to chew.

This open field, surrounded by a dense forest, was the size of several Paris blocks. Impossible to guess where Annie Deffous had been murdered. There would be nothing left, after two months, to indicate the spot.

He walked along the edge of the wood, parallel to the road, and saw that the moist earth was deeply pitted by hoofs.

This was a perfect place for the murderer to rendezvous with his victim. They could park their cars and nobody would see them from the road or hear the victim's screams.

After Annie Deffous died, the murderer would somehow have had to get rid of her car. He wouldn't be able to drive it anywhere, because he might be noticed walking back to pick up his own car.

The dead girl's car must be somewhere nearby. There were several openings between the trees through which a small car could pass . . .

There would be deep ravines in there. The murderer must have looked the place over, checked the terrain, before he arranged to meet the Deffous girl here. Probably that same afternoon, before the murder. Which meant she had been able to contact him and he had instructed her where they could meet that night, probably at a café in some nearby village. After a few drinks she would have followed his car up here in her gray Dauphine.

The murderer had to be one of the villagers. Only a local would know it was safe to come here for what he planned to do. Would know that everyone avoided this field after dark, because of its unpleasant history.

He realized that the grass was whirring with sound in the hot sunlight. Cigales! Must be hundreds of them . . .

In the old days there had been a gibbet here. Criminals were tried in the great courtyard of the château by a judge who traveled from village to village. People came from all over the surrounding countryside to attend the trials. It was because of those trials that people had called the château by another name. Castle Death . . .

He peered around, visualizing how it must have been.

Crude wooden gallows in the center, with several bodies dangling. Hundreds of people enjoying the free spectacle, eating and drinking. Their horses tied to trees around the edge of the field, among rows of coaches, carriages, and carts. Booths selling food, wine, and cider. Fortune-tellers, mountebanks, pickpockets, thieves . . . Certainly there would have been children underfoot. And dogs . . .

Everyone dropping coins. Losing them through holes in their pockets . . . The same coins he had found here hundreds of years later. And lost again.

There would have been musicians and singers. The noise must have been tremendous . . .

He gazed across the field at the peaceful herd of cows. They had accepted or forgotten his presence.

Suddenly a cloud of color rose from the grass. Orange, yellow, and black.

Butterflies! His eyes followed them as they rose higher and higher. He had never seen so many! They floated in a mass, their colors brilliant against the dark forest.

Damiot realized that the sky was filling with black clouds. Pushing down from the Alpilles.

No matter. He was coming back to the château tonight.

Even if it rained.

15

His father pounding a medallion of veal with a wooden mallet. Complaining, as usual, that the quality of meat wasn't what it used to be. His mother smiling, seated near the kitchen windows, shelling fresh peas from the garden. It was the old kitchen, with only two small windows. As usual, she was singing as she worked . . .

Damiot opened his eyes and saw a glare of light in the tiled bath.

The pounding continued.

Someone knocking at his door!

"Who is it?" he called.

"Claude, M'sieur. You have a telephone call."

"Be right there!" He pushed himself up from the bed and checked his wristwatch on the bedside table. "Almost six-thirty!"

He had slept longer than he intended, after his hot bath.

Securing the cord of his robe, he hurried toward the lobby, into a symphony of aromas flowing from the distant kitchen. The dominant scent was fresh rosemary . . .

He picked up the phone at the reception desk, glancing toward the dim restaurant where the two waiters were arranging their tables for dinner. "Damiot speaking."

"M'sieur Inspecteur! It's Bardou . . ."

"Thought it might be. How're you feeling, mon ami?"

"Much better. I'll be on the job tomorrow. If it's not raining."

"Is it raining now?"

"For the past hour."

"Merde! I've been asleep. What's happened?"

"I've talked with the gendarmerie in Toulon. That Deffous girl was missing for two months. But it seems nobody suspected foul play, because she told people she was taking a long vacation and had no idea when she'd return."

"Does she have a family?"

"Nobody, far as they've learned from her neighbors. She lived alone, in the house where she was born. Both her parents are dead."

"What about friends? Men in her life . . ."

"Nobody seems to know anything. The neighbors say they've never seen anyone go into the house. Except one young woman with a child who came to visit her sometimes on weekends. But they've no idea who they were. My friends at the gendarmerie did find out where she was employed. The place is closed today, of course, but they'll question the owners and her fellow workers tomorrow. And you were right! She was an accountant for a shop that sells hotel equipment and supplies. Been with them several years . . ."

"What about her car?"

"My friends are checking the license number. They'll call back tomorrow, when they get it."

"Good work, Bardou."

"Merci, M'sieur Inspecteur."

"When are you going to report this to the Commissaire here?"

"In the morning. Can't reach him tonight."

"Let me know what else you learn."

"I'll certainly do that, M'sieur Inspecteur."

"And get rid of that cold!" He put the phone down and headed toward his room, where he pushed back the curtains and saw that the garden was drenched with rain, the paths flooded again.

Curious how a young woman could drive off for a vacation and not return in two months, yet nobody reported her absence to the police . . .

Annie Deffous must have been one of those odd young women who lived only for her job—a human computer, who never made an error—until, one day, something happened and the perfect mechanism ground to a stop.

He had known young women in Paris, with good jobs during the day, who prowled after dark in search of excitement. They frequented certain cafés on the Champs-Elysées and in Montparnasse, but they never considered themselves whores because they seldom accepted money and avoided the streets favored by prostitutes. Could that be how it was with Annie Deffous? Had she met some man and followed him from Toulon to Courville, hoping for marriage, only to find death waiting? Perhaps she had been genuinely in love with this man . . .

But how did she connect with Lisette Jarlaud? Could the two girls have known each other? Anything was possible . . .

Rain slashing against the windowpanes.

No matter! He was driving up to the château tonight.

As Aurore led him to his usual table, shielded by the low partition with its row of plants, Damiot was aware of several things.

Aurore was wearing her most attractive dress tonight. Some kind of woolen material, soft yellow, with a skirt that seemed to flow as she walked ahead of him. A simple gold chain around her neck.

Many of the tables were already occupied.

Marc Sibilat and his mother, the old lady in black silk and that same feathered hat, sat at one of the window tables. Sibilat nodded, but Madame only frowned as she spooned soup into her mouth.

Aurore pulled the chair out from his table.

"Merci, Madame." He sat down. "I saw you at Saint-Sauveur this morning."

"Michel and I attend Mass every Sunday." She placed a menu within reach. "He's more religious than I. His family wanted him to become a priest. Did you learn anything at the church?"

"Matter of fact, I did." He glanced toward Marc Sibilat and saw that he too was eating soup. "One or two things . . ."

"The salmis de faisan is very special tonight. That's what I had Michel prepare for my guests from Paris."

"So this is the big night!"

"They'll be arriving shortly, from Cannes. I've given them the double suite next to you. Bon appétit!" She turned back toward her desk, inspecting each table she passed.

Damiot unfolded his napkin and settled down with anticipation for another pleasant dinner as Jean-Paul came to take his order.

"An apéritif, M'sieur Damiot?"

"Dry vermouth, please."

Madame Sibilat was now talking to her son, gesturing with a jeweled left hand as she continued to spoon her soup.

The other table shielded behind potted plants, where the Tendrells had sat, was empty.

Damiot picked up the menu—noticing that ratatouille was listed again—as he heard a car passing the restaurant windows and going toward the parking area. The visitors from Paris?

Madame Sibilat, soup finished, was darting glances at Damiot as she continued to lecture her son. Both hands were free to gesture now. Marc Sibilat hadn't finished his soup and was eating slowly, saying nothing. Pale eyes never lifting to look at his mother.

Jean-Paul returned with the vermouth as a crash echoed through the dining room from the kitchen. "M'sieur Michel is nervous tonight. Madame expects friends from Paris for dinner. So there will be many crises. Pardon, M'sieur . . ." He headed toward the swinging doors as angry voices were heard.

Damiot tasted the vermouth, his attention drawn toward the lobby, where the new arrivals had appeared. As they came into the light he saw that it was the English artist and his daughter. Aurore went to welcome them and the garçon darted to take Jenny Tendrell's umbrella, that same green silk one, and their coats.

He wondered if Jenny had told her father about their meeting, yesterday, at the pâtisserie . . .

She was wearing an attractive dress. Her father was in another tweed jacket, a woolen shirt, and a clumsily knotted tie, his gray slacks without any streaks of paint.

As they followed Aurore through the restaurant, Jenny glimpsed Damiot and waved, flashing a smile. Tendrell turned at once to see whom she was greeting, and nodded as Aurore led them to a window table.

He was amused to see Jenny Tendrell slip into a chair facing the kitchen. Her father hadn't realized that she would be able to observe the chef at work, from time to time, through those swinging doors.

"No great tragedy in the kitchen." Jean-Paul was smiling again. "M'sieur Michel threw a mixing bowl at the sous-chef because he was slow making a sauce. Fortunately the bowl was empty! M'sieur has decided?"

"Let me see . . ." He reached for the menu and, after a brief discussion of each course, ordered rabbit pâté, sorrel soup, and the salmis de faisan with a bottle of Château Vignelaure.

When Jean-Paul returned to the kitchen, Damiot saw that the other waiter had brought the Tendrells what appeared to be some sort of cocktail, probably one of those strange British concoctions made with gin. There was even one called "gin and French!" Whatever that might be . . .

As he ate, savoring each course, he continued to observe the Sibilats and the Tendrells.

Madame Sibilat gave no indication that she enjoyed the food—although she devoured everything—but continued without pause the tirade she was directing toward her silent son. He seemed to answer in monosyllables, eating slowly and, apparently, without appetite.

Jenny Tendrell kept glancing toward the kitchen as she sipped her cocktail. The waiter took their dinner order, which Tendrell gave after consulting his daughter. As he questioned the waiter about one dish, Damiot saw Jenny flash a dazzling smile toward the kitchen, where the chef must have appeared briefly at one of the round portholes in the swinging doors. She glanced at Damiot, realized that he had been watching, and winked.

Her father noticed none of this.

Dinner, once again, was a series of perfections, crowned by the ragout of pheasant garnished with a puree of chestnuts. Damiot was giving his complete attention to his meal when he sensed someone approaching his table and looked up to see the Englishman. "Ah, Monsieur Tendrell!"

"Do you mind?"

"Please . . ." He motioned toward the other chair and, as Tendrell sat down, realized that the Englishman's back would be turned to his daughter.

"Are you enjoying the salmis? This chef, Michel, does it rather well." Lowering his voice. "What's been happening, Monsieur Inspecteur?"

"In regard to what?"

"The murders, of course!"

"I wouldn't know about that . . ." He continued to eat as they talked.

"And the monster? Have you told the local police that you saw it?"

"I have said nothing. Not a word."

"Jenny tells me that she spoke with you yesterday afternoon."

"I happened to be at Madame Mussot's when your daughter arrived. We had a very pleasant conversation." As he talked, he saw that Michel had come from the kitchen, unnoticed by the Englishman, and was circling the restaurant, bowing to the men, kissing the ladies' hands. "By the way, I paid another visit to the château yesterday afternoon. Inspector Bardou permitted me to accompany him on a brief tour of the interior with the caretaker, who turns out to be an acquaintance from my youth."

"And what did you learn?"

"Little of any importance. Inspector Bardou was hoping to find some trace of the monster. I went along because I hadn't been inside the château in thirty years." He rested his knife on the plate. "You have been there yourself more recently."

"I? What the devil do you mean?"

"That portrait I noticed, Friday night, in your home . . ."

"What about it?"

"The face is very like several of those family portraits hanging in the château. The de Mohrt face."

"You are a clever man, Monsieur Inspecteur. Very observant. Yes, I did copy certain features from those portraits. The eyes and . . . Nothing wrong with that, surely? The caretaker, Pouchet, allowed me to enter."

Damiot shrugged. "Like the monster, Monsieur, it is no concern of mine."

Tendrell glanced toward his own table and saw that Michel was talking to Jenny. He immediately got to his feet. "I do wish, Monsieur Damiot, that you would forget about the monster. It simply doesn't exist! Don't waste time at the château. Enjoy your holiday!" He hurried back to his table.

Damiot noticed that the Englishman did not offer his hand to the chef, who after a few words bowed and moved on to the Sibilats' table. He leaned down to kiss Madame Sibilat's jeweled claw.

Why had Tendrell warned him away from the château? Telling him to forget about the monster . . .

He was distracted by the sound of a powerful motor in the drive as a car rolled toward the parking area.

Aurore also heard the arrival and dispatched Claude to help the newcomers with their luggage.

The guests from Paris had arrived.

16

Damiot followed the road parallel to rue Voltaire and the old railroad tracks until he found the lane that would take him up to that side gate of the de Mohrt estate.

He had come up here alone many times, carrying messages from his father. Avoiding this lane and darting across the fields . . .

The caretaker had said he always walked down to the village through these same fields. He should make it easily in half an hour. At the end he would only have to cross those old railroad tracks to reach the alley where Lisette Jarlaud's body had been found.

Did the old man have some local woman living with him and not want the villagers to find out? Certainly, Damiot had smelled cooking yesterday, and it wasn't what Pouchet had said. Not a cassoulet!

This rain should keep Pouchet out of his way tonight. The old man probably retired early. Fortunately, he wouldn't hear any noise overhead inside the château. Or had be been feigning deafness? He certainly seemed to have all his other faculties . . .

The villagers would stay indoors tonight because the monster never appeared unless the weather was clear.

Damiot slowed his car as he glimpsed the open side gate through which he had entered the de Mohrt estate so many times in the past. Swerved off the lane, onto what was little more than a winding cow path, and drove on more carefully, peering from side to side.

The Peugeot nosed out finally into an open area parallel to the east wing of the mansion. Pouchet's quarters were at the rear, to Damiot's right, the front courtyard to the left.

He turned the car toward the front. Slowed to a stop at the edge of the forest, facing the cobbled courtyard, and snapped off his headlights. Bringing out the new torch from a pocket of his waterproof, he got out. His hip was aching again.

When he reached the protection of the columned archway above the tall entrance doors, he turned off his torch, Fric-Frac close behind him.

Impossible to see anything of the entrance drive through the rain, and no sounds came from the distant highway. He removed his hat and shook off some of the raindrops.

Suddenly, from the forest, came a piercing scream. Fric-Frac barked and the scream was repeated.

Damiot realized that it was one of the peacocks. The bird must have sensed the intruders. He put his hat on again.

Another sound now. Dogs barking. From inside the mansion? Pouchet kept a mastiff downstairs, at the rear, but this sounded like two dogs.

Fric-Frac barked again.

"You have friends here, Madame?" Damiot asked. "Was that a dog you were sniffing yesterday, under all those doors?..."

She was wiggling with excitement, as though she knew they were about to have some sort of adventure.

Damiot brought out his key ring and found the device he always carried for such an emergency. He moved closer to the tall double doors and bent to inspect the lock.

Not so old as he had anticipated. Antique locks could be difficult to open, but this had been installed recently. He worked with his small device, and after a moment felt the lock snap. Grasping the ornate knob, he turned it and swung the door open.

"All right, Madame la Duchesse! We go inside, but not a

sound from you." He aimed the beam of light across the marble floor as Fric-Frac ran ahead into the great entrance hall.

This was where he had entered, yesterday, with Pouchet and Bardou. Tonight he would follow the same route, room after room . . .

His footsteps echoed faintly as he crossed the high-ceilinged entrance hall, glimpsing his own dark figure repeated endlessly in distant mirrors, and went up the broad marble staircase.

Fric-Frac whimpered impatiently at the top of the stairs. He joined her on the balcony and opened the door into a small salon.

The dog darted inside and Damiot went after her, closing the door before flashing the beam of his torch around. Holding it down toward the parquet floor, avoiding the uncurtained windows.

It was the yellow salon that had belonged to the old Comtesse! Why was this one room furnished and none of the others?

Moving on—salon after salon, through corridors and passages— he was aware of the silence, interrupted only by the rain striking against windows and dripping from leaks.

He aimed the spot of light at several paintings. All portraits. Variations of the de Mohrt face. Their eyes watching him . . .

No sound came from behind any of the closed doors.

Continuing through the seemingly endless rooms, he wondered again if there had been a dog running loose yesterday. Or was there a woman living here with Pouchet? Had she been following their progress from room to room? Listening behind all those doors . . .

Fric-Frac had stopped to sniff at another door. She began to paw at this one. Damiot switched off his torch as he moved closer.

The only sound was Fric-Frac's nails scratching against the wood.

He grasped the cold metal handle and flung the door open. Fric-Frac shot ahead, growling, into the darkness.

Something moving? Little more than a whisper of sound. Was it a door closing?

He snapped his torch on and sent its thin beam across the floor.

No sign of the dog.

Another faint whisper of movement. From his right . . .

Damiot aimed the torch in that direction and saw Fric-Frac trotting toward him, tail wagging. They were in another corridor.

He switched off the torch again. Then waited in the dark for a repetition of the sounds, but he heard only rain striking the overhead skylights.

He snapped on his torch. Better have a look behind that door he had sensed closing.

Fric-Frac bounded ahead and nosed the crack under the door. Damiot swung it open and stepped inside. Into an empty room he had never seen before. Medium-sized, a row of high windows opposite the door, with a second closed door at one end, white marble fireplace at the other.

As he started toward the closed door there was a distant and surprising sound. A telephone ringing? Faint but unmistakable . . .

He froze as the sound was repeated.

A telephone in the château? Bardou had said Pouchet didn't have one.

The sound was not repeated a third time. Somebody had answered it.

If there was a woman living here she would probably insist upon a telephone. Women couldn't live without one . . .

Moving again toward the door, he heard a dog barking in the depths of the mansion.

Fric-Frac answered.

Pouchet kept his mastiff chained downstairs in the kitchen, but this sounded closer.

Another barrage of barking.

Fric-Frac responded immediately.

No way to stop her. Would Pouchet hear?

Was the old man's dog running loose? It would be dangerous to come upon a mastiff in one of these dark corridors. A beast that size could kill a small dog. Snap her neck with one crunch of its jaws . . .

This was becoming risky. Should he go back the way he had come? He had taken so many turns he wasn't even certain which wing of the château he was in.

"Merde! We're lost."

Reaching the end of the room, Fric-Frac at his side, he opened the door into still another windowless passage. The dog ran ahead again.

The next door opened into a small salon, bare of furniture, with a row of tall, rain-spattered windows.

As Damiot started across the salon, toward more closed doors, there was the faint sound, far away, of a bell tolling.

The same bell that had tolled before the monster appeared!

He opened one of the doors and found himself in a long corridor, with closed doors on both sides. Rain drumming overhead on a row of skylights.

The tolling bell was much more distinct now. As though he were approaching its source.

Which way should he go? Start back the way he had come? He had no idea which direction that might be. What door should be open next?

The bell was much louder. Its deep, metallic clanging seemed to shake the walls. He could feel the vibrations beneath his feet, through the floor.

Fric-Frac howled, her head raised, ears laid back.

This time the other dogs didn't answer. Or was their barking drowned by the tolling bell?

Then, as suddenly as it had begun, the bell was silent.

For a moment his ears continued to hum. Then, gradually, he began to hear the rain again. Splashing against those overhead skylights.

Did the tolling bell mean the monster would appear on the terrace tonight? Surely not in this rain!

There had to be a bell in one of those towers above the castle. But Bardou said he had checked every tower . . .

Could Bardou be covering for someone? Was he too involved with this business of the monster? It had to be a hoax!

He kept going, Fric-Frac scampering ahead. All he could do was continue until he came to something familiar. A room remembered from yesterday . . .

The next door opened into yet another windowless passage, with water dripping from a paneled ceiling and the floor damaged in several places. It would have taken many storms to do so much damage. Must be careful where he stepped . . .

Far in the distance, probably on the highway, he heard the motor of a speeding car. From the sound it was a commercial truck with a powerful engine.

He continued through another long corridor, with more dripping skylights and a rotted floor, the car sounding much closer.

Coming up that front drive to the château?

The roar of the motor increased, louder and louder, until it seemed to be inside the mansion.

This was impossible!

He glanced down and saw Fric-Frac cowering at his feet. "It's all right, Madame." He stooped and picked her up. "Nothing's going to hurt you." He tucked her trembling body under his left arm as he went toward the next closed door. Awkwardly changing the torch to his left hand, he gripped the handle and pushed the door open.

As he stepped into the adjoining room, the roar of the engine filled his ears. He reached to take the torch in his right hand again.

The thunder of sound enveloped him as the dog began to squirm and struggle in his arm. Crossing the room, he tried to restrain her.

The torch slipped from his fingers, its beam of light flashing crazily as it rolled across the floor and disappeared through a hole.

Now there was only darkness and the roar of the motor.

Rubber tires screeching. Brakes shrieking . . .

The black Ferrari?

Damiot took another step forward, cautiously. Then another. Heard rotten wood splinter. Felt the floor collapsing under his foot.

The dog slid out of his arm.

"Fric-Frac!"

There was a sharp flash of pain as his hip twisted.

"Mon Dieu!"

He tried desperately to save himself, but toppled backward. His head struck the floor with a crash that exploded into the roar of the motor . . .

17

"Welcome to the Château de Mohrt, Monsieur Inspecteur!"

"What?" Damiot struggled up awkwardly from a sofa.

"I am Nicolas Frédéric César Philippe Etienne, Comte de Mohrt . . ."

Damiot peered from side to side into the shadows, but there was no one visible.

"I have followed the illustrious career of Chief Inspector Damiot for several years, with constant and growing fascination . . ."

Where was the voice coming from? He pushed himself up to a sitting position on what he discovered was a pillowed sofa. As the voice continued, he looked around at one of the most incredible rooms he had ever seen.

Heavy stone columns supported a vaulted ceiling, and rare Oriental rugs covered the floor. Expensive furniture—fine antiques and sleek modern pieces. Fire of logs in an immense stone fireplace. The place resembled a museum but was obviously lived in because there was a glass and chromium table desk with piles of documents, papers, filing folders, an antique astrolabe, and a pair of tall shaded lamps.

Turning his head slowly, Damiot saw that the walls were a solid mass of books and paintings. Behind the desk, floor to ceiling, was a magnificent tapestry. There were no windows or doors . . .

". . . ever since I lived in Paris and read about your latest murder investigations in the newspapers . . ."

Damiot turned, sensing a whisper of motion at the far side of the room. Fric-Frac began to bark and darted in the same direction.

There appeared to be an open space between two of the stone columns, evidently the entrance to a corridor or passage.

And slowly, out of the darkness, a curious figure in a small wheelchair rolled into view. Body hunched under some sort of brown robe. Long black hair hanging to the shoulders. Damiot remembered those wheel tracks he had noticed yesterday on the marble floors. "Monsieur le Comte?"

"Welcome to Castle Death, Monsieur Inspecteur! That's what the villagers have called my ancestral home for centuries. Château de Mohrt sounds exactly like Château de Mort. But I would not care to be called Count Death!" He laughed.

Damiot realized, as the compact wheelchair came closer, that it was controlled from a small plastic device resting on the Comte's lap. He saw now that the face was an infantile version of the de Mohrt face. The deep-set eyes and prominent nose were like those in the portraits, but the mouth belonged to a petulant child.

"I've looked forward to meeting you, Monsieur Inspecteur, since I learned last week of your arrival in Courville."

"You honor me, Monsieur le Comte."

"Please, call me Nick, if you will. The family title is much too pompous." The wheelchair reached the end of the desk. "My friend, Allan Tendrell, was the first to call me Nick. Actually, I find it more to my liking . . ."

"As you wish. Nick . . ."

The Comte didn't seem to have legs under the rough-textured material of his robe, and no feet were visible on the metal footrest. With his left hand he controlled levers under one chromium arm of the wheelchair.

"Sit down, Monsieur." His voice no longer came from the invisible speakers. He motioned toward a fauteuil facing the desk, then glanced down at Fric-Frac. "What a fine dog! I observed her yesterday when you came here with that detective from Arles. I'm told that her name is Fric-Frac and she belongs to Madame Bouchard at the Auberge. I've suspected for some time, from Allan Tendrell's descriptions of her, that he's in love with her. The lady, not the dog!" He maneuvered his wheelchair behind the desk to face Damiot. "Please!" Gesturing toward the armchair again. "Make yourself comfortable . . ."

Damiot lowered his hip carefully into the fauteuil, and Fric-Frac immediately jumped into his lap.

"I trust you suffered no injury when you fell?"

"No damage done. Apparently I struck my head and for a moment lost consciousness. When I wakened I found myself here."

"Pouchet picked you up and carried you."

"Did he!"

"Must be in his late seventies—no one seems to know—but he still has the strength of three younger men! I suppose I owe you an explanation. In fact, several explanations!"

As the Comte settled back in his leather-padded wheelchair, Damiot was reminded of the Balzac statue by Rodin. Same kind of monklike robe.

"First! About this little joke I've been playing?"

"Joke, Monsieur?"

"My attempt to frighten the villagers would, I was certain, never deceive Chief Inspector Damiot for an instant. So! I will confess to you at once. I am the only monster here." He reached under his desk to click something, and a metal panel slid out from the side, parallel to his wheelchair.

Damiot leaned forward to see a console with rows of dials and levers—the sort of elaborate control board he had observed when he visited television or recording studios in Paris.

"For example, Monsieur l'Inspecteur!" He flipped a lever.

The great bell tolled immediately. It seemed to come from every corner of the room. The deep, metallic clang was deafening.

Fric-Frac put her ears back and howled.

The Comte snapped the lever and the bell was silenced. "There are no bells in any of the towers. I played this tape to attract the villagers' attention. So they would be certain to see the monster . . ."

"And the monster? That can't be another tape!"

"In good time, Monsieur Inspecteur. Tonight, just for you—in those dark rooms—I added a second element . . ." He pressed a lever.

The roar of a speeding car filled the room. Shrieking brakes and screaming tires.

Fric-Frac cringed in Damiot's lap.

The Comte touched the lever and the roar of sound was cut off.

"You gave me one hell of a scare for a moment, when I thought there was a car inside the château!"

Fric-Frac shook her head, as though freeing her delicate ears of the unpleasant noises, and jumped to the floor.

"Speakers and microphones are hidden in every room. In fireplaces and behind wall panels. I can send my voice, or any kind of taped sound, into all of them. And I am able to hear everything!"

"It was you, Saturday, behind those doors?"

"That must have been my dog. I was in the laboratory, observing your progress from room to room. There are also hidden cameras. I was watching you and listening to what you said. Pouchet, as you must have noticed, is somewhat deaf, and I wanted to be certain that you didn't as yet suspect my presence."

"I knew someone was here because Fric-Frac was sniffing under the doors. Your electronic equipment is most impressive."

"I designed much of it myself. Technicians from Paris installed everything. This also is one of my designs." He patted the metal arm of his wheelchair. "Completely electronic! With this I can do everything but walk. It's being manufactured and sold—mostly to hospitals and clinics. All profits are used to provide similar wheelchairs for individuals who can't afford them . . ."

"But, Monsieur le Comte! I was informed that you had died, some years ago, in a motor accident."

"My beloved grandmother was the one who started that rumor."

"The old Comtesse?"

"She did it out of kindness. Let me explain . . . First about the motor accident! My father had three passions—racing cars, beautiful women, and champagne. I suspect in that order! He took me along, one sunny morning, to test a new racing car he had bought. On his way to show it to his current mistress, after enjoying a bottle of champagne with breakfast. We were on one of those endless Roman roads where you can see the horizon. There was no traffic and my father was not at fault. One of the tires burst and we crashed into a tree. My father managed to get off with nothing more than a sprained ankle, but I wasn't so fortunate. I regained consciousness in a hospital, where I remained for many weeks. I was informed much later, after I recovered from spinal surgery, that I had not been expected to live. It wasn't until the following year that I learned, from my grandmother, that I would never walk again. Which, for some time, I had suspected . . ."

"How old were you?"

"Twelve."

"Must be difficult, at that age, to comprehend . . ."

"I was terrified. But grand-mère refused to accept the verdict of those doctors in Rome. Which renewed my courage . . ."

As he listened, Damiot realized that the Comte was even younger than he had first thought. Probably in his late twenties.

". . . chartered a plane and flew me back to Paris, where she had the most eminent specialists examine me. After more surgery, I was told that those other doctors were wrong. I would be able to walk."

"Doctors! They recently stuck a metal pin in my hip."

"I read about you in the Paris papers. Your meeting with that gangster! Valzo . . ."

"And I suppose, like me, they put you through endless therapy?"

"Every day, hour after hour, for months. And I did walk, eventually, after a fashion. Only, by the age of fourteen, my walking did not improve any further because my legs had stopped

133

growing. I have the legs of a twelve-year-old! Unable to support the torso of a man."

"You mentioned only your grandmother. What about your parents?"

"Grand-mère was the last relative I had left. The de Mohrt line comes to an abrupt conclusion with me. My mother died when I was two—here in the château. Pneumonia, I was told, probably caused by these drafty corridors. The old Comte, my grandfather, had died before I was injured in that accident, and my father was killed two years later, in another racing car. We were good friends and his death was very difficult for me. My only family after that was my beloved grand-mère. She lived with me in Paris until the doctors placed her in a Zurich sanatorium. I stayed with her there until she died."

"I remember the Comtesse with great affection. I knew both your grandparents . . ."

"Pouchet has told me. Your father and my grandfather were friends."

"My father worked with the local Maquis during the occupation, when your grandfather was head of the underground in this area."

"And you brought messages to him from your father."

"Many times."

"I wasn't born then, of course, but grand-père taught me the motto of the Provençal Maquis. 'Race of eagles' . . ."

" 'Never vassals!' "

"He told me that I—his only grandson and last of the de Mohrts—must always be an eagle, never a vassal." The Comte shrugged and smiled. "It is difficult, with these legs, to be an eagle, but I have not as yet become a vassal to any man. And never shall!"

Damiot noticed, for the first time, a telephone on the desk. "This must be the phone I heard ringing earlier . . ."

"That was when Allan Tendrell called. I told him you were here and he said he would drive over. Of course, at that point you hadn't crashed through the floor, and I didn't suspect I'd be meeting you. Allan's a good friend. And such a beautiful daughter!" He seemed to relax as he spoke of Jenny Tendrell. "I've seen her, but as yet have never met the young lady. Allan thinks that would be indiscreet, and I agree—at least for the moment." He smiled. "But I wait inside the gates, many mornings, to watch her ride past. That was where I saw you for the first time. You were parked there, last Friday, when I was waiting for Jenny."

"I heard a crack of sound in the shrubbery and thought it was some animal moving about . . ." The special lens at the center of every detective's mind was bringing images into focus. "And, of course, your friendship with Monsieur Tendrell explains how he knew I was here yesterday. He mentioned it this evening, when I saw him at the Auberge."

"I was the one who told him. Allan frequently drives over after dinner. But Jenny has no idea that I exist."

"Tendrell has been painting here, hasn't he?"

"Working on my portrait. His version of the de Mohrt faces you've seen in all those ancestral paintings. Allan should be arriving at any moment. Perhaps, meanwhile, you'd like a glimpse of my laboratory?"

"I would!" He started to rise.

"Don't get up, Monsieur! You can see from where you're sitting." He reached down to the console again. "Probably the finest private laboratory in Europe!"

There was a metallic sliding sound, and the heavy tapestry moved back to reveal a solid wall of plate glass.

The Comte pressed several buttons on the console.

Lights flashed in an elaborate modern laboratory where everything seemed to be made of glass or chromium. Colored vapors flowed through twisting tubes, and sparks darted across curiously shaped machines. Small animals, roused by the lights, stirred under transparent domes. No sound came from beyond the wall of glass.

"I had a scientific mind, even as a small boy, and read every book in grand-père's library. Then, in Paris, during my long convalescence, some of the top professors from the Sorbonne became my tutors. I studied everything! Greek and Latin, as well as the modern philosophers and scientists. English literature, in addition to the French and Russian. At first I was terribly discouraged and depressed. Life seemed completely hopeless. Until I finally realized that I had no desire to die. Once that decision was reached, I devoted every hour to science. Especially the technology of outer space—probably because of my earth-bound legs—electronics, and of course atomic and solar energy. Energy fascinates me! When I returned here from Paris, I brought a staff of the finest young technicians and engineers along with me. They installed the audio system you heard earlier and built this laboratory for me . . ."

"Most impressive!"

"I could probably make a solar bomb device in there, but of course I never shall! I am interested in life—not death. I'm busy in my laboratory for long hours every day, with two assistants who live on the premises." He touched the console again.

Damiot heard the tapestry sliding across the glass wall. "Then you're not alone here?"

"Certainly not! I have people to work with me during the day, dine with me in the evening, and argue with me most of the night. We have some delightfully complex and esoteric conversations! And, of course, there are others who look out for my physical comforts. After the death of grand-mère I dreaded coming back to the château, but during her fatal illness she made me promise that I would live here. My doctor, a specialist in matters of the spine, flies down from Paris whenever I need him. Which happens less and less frequently . . ." He glanced past Damiot, beyond the circle of light. "Ah! Here's Pouchet!"

Damiot looked around, the back of his head paining slightly as he turned, to see the tall figure of the old man, wearing a dark suit and holding a sleek gray mastiff on a leash.

Fric-Frac jumped down and ran, barking, toward the huge animal.

"Fric-Frac!" Damiot called. "Come back here."

"It's all right, M'sieur Inspecteur." Pouchet laughed, leaning down to pat her head. "They will be friends."

"Lautrec likes other dogs," the Comte explained. "It's people he doesn't care for. At least most people."

"You call him Lautrec?"

"He has such magnificent legs! I couldn't resist naming him Lautrec. I'm sure that Monsieur Toulouse would approve."

Fric-Frac had seated herself next to the mastiff, who lowered his great body to collapse majestically beside her. Now he was licking the top of her head with his enormous tongue.

Damiot smiled. "I thought I heard more than one dog barking."

"Pouchet keeps another mastiff in the kitchen. Her barking is useful to cover Lautrec's, and if anyone sees him roaming through the grounds, they think he is Pouchet's dog. But it is Lautrec who keeps intruders out and accompanies me when I hunt. The other dog is very old. Never goes outside. But she can still bark!''

Damiot glanced back at the caretaker, standing erect beside the mastiff.

"Pouchet tells me . . ." the Comte continued.

He saw the old man turn at the sound of his name, his left ear toward the Comte.

". . . your father used to drink pastis with him."

"That's right!" Pouchet nodded. "We sat on the kitchen steps behind Chez Damiot whenever I walked down to the village. Madame Damiot, your mother, would bring two glasses on a tray and . . ."

A buzzer sounded, softly but urgently.

"That should be Allan!" The Comte set his glass down. "There are signals on a master control panel when anyone enters the château. Lights flash as he passes through each room."

"I'll go and meet M'sieur Tendrell." Pouchet looked toward the Comte again. "Should I leave the dog here?"

"Yes. Take off his leash."

Pouchet bent to unfasten the leash from Lautrec's collar.

"Would you care for a drink, Monsieur Inspecteur?" the Comte asked. "Calvados, perhaps?"

Damiot laughed. "How did you know I prefer Calvados?"

"I too have been learning things, Monsieur." He pressed another section under the arm of his wheelchair.

"Yes, M'sieur le Comte?" A woman's voice, coming out of the air.

"A bottle of our best Calvados, Madame Léontine. And a bottle of whisky for Monsieur Tendrell."

"Right away, chéri!"

"Madame Léontine Guibert?"

"Grand-mère brought Madame Léontine to Paris after my accident, and she's been with me ever since. Feeding me. Always complaining because I never put more flesh on my bones, in spite of her cooking. She even makes these robes I wear . . ." He looked across the room. "Here she is!"

Damiot struggled up from the fauteuil as he saw the aproned figure, short and plump, bearing a tray with bottles and glasses. "Madame Léontine . . ."

"If it isn't young Damiot!" Her eyes danced as she came toward them. "As handsome as ever! The last time I saw you,

you came to sing carols for the old Comtesse. I gave you an almond cake and hot cider."

"I remember your almond cake. That was in the yellow salon . . ."

"I've had the yellow salon restored," the Comte interrupted. "All grand-mère's furniture and her favorite paintings. I sit there many evenings, in the twilight . . ."

As Madame Léontine rested her tray on the desk, Damiot saw that she was wearing an old-fashioned shawl. It was the color of that strand of crimson yarn Fric-Frac had picked up yesterday. "You look the same, Madame."

She laughed. "The hair is white and the legs aren't so good . . ."

"My doctor keeps an eye on her." The Comte was uncorking the Calvados bottle. "Madame Léontine took care of me day and night after I was released from that last hospital in Paris."

"I'm still looking after him, grâce à Dieu!" She stood, hands folded over her apron, watching the Comte with obvious adoration as he poured two drinks. "I'm seventy-eight but strong as I was at forty!" She picked up a glass of Calvados and presented it to Damiot.

"Merci, Madame. Your cooking smells delicious!"

"How could you know that, M'sieur?"

"Yesterday afternoon you were preparing something with herbs and truffles. Was it chicken?"

"Two chickens! For dinner."

"Smelled incredible . . ."

"And it was!" The Comte laughed, filling the third glass with whisky. "Although Madame refuses to go near the electronic ovens I've had installed for her . . ."

"Food tastes better when it's cooked over a wood fire." She picked up the glass from the desk and turned to face the dark entrance passage. "Whisky for the English M'sieur!"

"Just in time, am I?"

Damiot looked around to see Tendrell materialize from the darkness.

"Monsieur Inspecteur—we meet again!" The Englishman accepted his drink from Madame Léontine. "Thank you, Madame."

Damiot rose from the armchair to shake his hand. "You knew all the time that the Comte was here!"

"I also knew you were coming closer and closer to the truth.

That's why I told you to stay away from the château." He sat on a sofa near the desk, facing them. "It could only be a matter of time before you discovered my young friend."

Damiot sank into the armchair as Madame Léontine left the room.

Tendrell raised his glass. "Cheers!"

"Santé!" the Comte responded.

"Santé . . ." Damiot took a large swallow of Calvados as he turned to the Comte. "How long has Monsieur Tendrell known you were here?"

"More than a year," Tendrell answered. "I trespassed one day to have a closer look at the castle, and Nick tried to kill me."

"Nothing of the sort!" The Comte laughed. "I sometimes hunt in my wheelchair along the edge of the forest, with Pouchet and Lautrec in attendance. But I only hunt for food—rabbit, wild boar, or pheasant. I stun them with another device I've invented. Lautrec guards them until Pouchet ties them up. One day I very nearly got an inquisitive Englishman!"

"Frightened the devil out of me!" Tendrell gulped his whisky. "We became friends after Nick almost bagged me that day."

"I desperately needed someone new I could talk to evenings. I'd seen Allan drive past the gates many times and watched Jenny on her black mare. Pouchet had told me that she was his daughter. I was a complete surprise to Allan, but he was already like an old friend."

Damiot glanced at the artist. "So you've known all along about the monster?"

"And begged Nick repeatedly not to continue with his little joke."

"Then you did see it Friday night from that hill?"

"Of course! But I've denied seeing anything when it appears. Even to Jenny! I hope, Inspector, that you will persuade Nick to put an end to this ridiculous charade."

"Now, Allan!" the Comte protested. "I've been enjoying my public performances."

"The whole thing could so easily get out of hand. When you first had the idea, I thought it was amusing. Playing a joke on the villagers. But now I'm not so certain."

"Help yourself to that whisky, mon ami. And more Calvados for Monsieur Damiot."

Tendrell rose from the sofa and picked up the Calvados bottle from the desk. He filled Damiot's glass as he talked. "My daughter, by the way, has no idea that the Comte exists. Although she's getting terribly suspicious because of the evenings I spend away from the farm. Fortunately, we have only the one car, so Jenny can't follow me." Replenishing the Comte's glass. "I suppose, one day soon, I shall have to tell her the truth and bring her to meet Nick."

"I look forward to that day! Meeting your delightful daughter . . ." The Comte picked up his drink. "Merci, mon ami."

"Inspector Damiot, I wish that somehow you could convince Nick that he mustn't play this little game." Tendrell filled his own glass to the brim. "He should destroy his monstrous toy!"

The Comte stared at his glass, frowning. "Why must I destroy my beautiful monster?"

"Because the thing is evil. Even though it's only a clumsy contraption of cloth and metal!"

"Clumsy? It's nothing of the sort!" Lifting his glass to Damiot as he talked. "We designed it here in our laboratory. One of my assistants created the head, the wig came from Paris, and Madame Léontine made the costume." He sipped the Calvados, then abruptly set his glass down. "Would you like to meet my monster, Monsieur Damiot?"

"I would indeed."

"Splendid!" His eyes gleamed mischievously as he got to his feet. Standing erect, his waist was barely level with the top of the table desk. "You shall judge for yourself whether he is clumsy." He produced two oblong metal objects from somewhere in his wheelchair. Snapped and shook one, causing it to shoot out into a curiously shaped crutch. "I designed these too. Collapsible and much lighter than any others."

Damiot saw that the crutch was made of flexible metal, jointed and shaped to support the arm. Like no crutch he had ever seen.

The Comte snapped a second crutch into shape and slipped both of them up his voluminous sleeves before circling the desk. "I'll be with you in a moment, Monsieur Inspecteur!" He crossed the room, moving awkwardly, followed by the mastiff.

Under his long brown robe, the Comte appeared to have the muscular shoulders and torso of a grown man, but his invisible legs must be those of a child. This was the boy Jenny Tendrell had glimpsed through the entrance gates! Damiot watched the stunted figure swaying from side to side until it vanished into the dark passage with the mastiff.

Fric-Frac, left behind, came to sit at his feet.

"So now you know the truth!" Tendrell murmured. "I've no idea what Nick was telling you before I arrived, but I must add that, in my opinion, he's an authentic genius. Many of his inventions are already being produced by a corporation he owns in Paris. I think the idea of creating a monster amused him, after the long hours he spends with his colleagues on more serious projects . . ." The Englishman moved around the room, glass in hand. "But the whole thing's become much too dangerous. I hope, Monsieur Inspecteur, that you're able to make Nick put his toy away and forget it!"

"He won't listen to you?"

"No, indeed!"

"What about the murders of those two girls?"

"Nick had nothing to do with their deaths."

"How can you be so positive?"

"You saw him! It would be physically impossible."

"With Pouchet's help, he might have reached that field across from here in his wheelchair."

"Nick has killed no one! He could never get down to the village in his wheelchair, to that alley where the Jarlaud girl was found."

"Pouchet has a car."

"Nick did not kill Lisette Jarlaud. I know that for a fact."

"Do you?"

"I was with him that night. We spent the evening together. I didn't arrive home until long after midnight. Pouchet had to help Nick to bed and it was necessary for me to drive rather carefully."

Damiot was distracted, as the Englishman talked, by a whisper of sound from the passage. A monstrous figure loomed out of the dark. Damiot recognized the great head with lank black hair hanging down to the huge shoulders. A long, multicolored cloak, not unlike the Comte's robe, swaying with the body in an awkward rhythm that made the strange figure seem even more ominous.

Fric-Frac growled.

Tendrell turned and saw the approaching figure. "Ah! The famous Courville monster! In person . . ."

As the towering figure came closer, Damiot realized that the face was a skillfully painted mask with black holes for eyes, hollow waxen cheeks, and a crimson slash of mouth.

Tendrell set his empty glass on the desk. "Startling, eh?"

"Amazing!" Damiot jumped to his feet and crossed the room with Fric-Frac growling at his heels. "No wonder the villagers thought this was real!" He circled the slowly moving figure as Pouchet and the mastiff followed the monster out of the darkness.

Now the tall figure began to sink slowly toward the floor.

Fric-Frac barked.

Damiot stepped back, away from the collapsing monster. "This is what happened Friday night on the terrace!"

The figure shot up again to its full height.

"There you are!" The Comte's voice, muffled, from under the cloak. "Tall as a giant or flat as a pile of rags. Pouchet?"

The old man stepped forward. "Here I am, M'sieur le Comte."

"Take this thing off me!"

The old man lifted the cloak away as it began to collapse again.

Laughing, pleased with what he had done, the Comte lunged free of the contraption. "That wasn't clumsy, was it? The figure's designed on the principle of a toy I used to have when I was a child. A simple mechanism lifts the head and shoulders." He circled the desk on his crutches and climbed into the wheelchair as he explained. "That's why the monster never appears in bad weather. It could be torn apart by the wind and damaged by rain." He reduced his crutches to their original size and returned them to their compartments in the wheelchair.

Damiot watched Pouchet carry the collapsed figure away through the passage. "Your trick has been a great success, Monsieur! This monster you created did not, however, kill those two girls."

"That's quite obvious," Tendrell observed, refilling his glass.

"But the question remains—who did? And why, Monsieur le Comte, did you play this trick on everyone?"

"Because of the stories Pouchet heard in the village about a monster lurking in the château. That gave me the idea."

"And when did you hear about this monster?" Damiot sat in the armchair again as Fric-Frac returned to stretch out at his feet. "Who was the first to tell Pouchet about it?"

"I've asked him that myself, but he doesn't remember. It was after the death of the first girl that he told me what the villagers were saying."

"You never heard it prior to her murder?"

"Never."

"So there is no ancient legend about a monster in the château?"

"Not to my knowledge. Certainly I'd have known about it when I was a child. One of the servants would have told me, even if the family hadn't. I did of course hear tales of criminals tried here, in our courtyard, before they were hanged in that field where the first girl was murdered . . ."

"I heard similar stories when I was in school," Damiot interrupted, "but nothing about any monster."

"I created my monster to keep the villagers away from here, but unfortunately, the first time I showed him down in the courtyard nobody saw him. I had Pouchet light the monster from behind with a lantern, but there was nobody to see. The following night I played the tape of a tolling bell, certain that the sound would attract someone's attention. Pouchet saw a car pass on the road and, after a moment, drive back. The driver got out and stood close to the gates. So I made the monster move up and down. The fellow ran to his car and sped away. He must have been from the village, because the following night, Pouchet reported that several people were gathered outside the gates. We did our performance for them and they departed in a hurry! The next night it rained, so we didn't give them another show until the first clear night."

"With an equally gratifying reception!" Tendrell exclaimed.

"This time there must've been a dozen villagers watching," the Comte continued. "Allan, of course, knew what I was doing from the start. He was on the hill last Friday night when you turned up. What did you think, Monsieur, when you saw the monster?"

"I was certain that the murderer had arranged it, whatever it was, to confuse and frighten the villagers."

The Comte laughed. "You are quite right as to my purpose, but I am not the murderer." Motioning toward the bottles on the tray. "Help yourselves, gentlemen!"

"No more, at the moment." Damiot glanced at his unfinished drink as Tendrell picked up the whiskey bottle to refill his own glass.

"I would never kill anyone, Monsieur Inspecteur," the Comte continued. "My passion is for life. I am interested only in living!"

"Why did you let people think you had died?" Damiot asked quietly. "After your accident."

"Grand-mère started that rumor to save me from having to meet people. She told some reporter in Paris that I had died, and he printed the story. This was after I had had several unfortunate experiences. One day, on the street, I heard a woman call me a monster! Grand-mère and I constantly discussed my future. She knew how difficult it would be for me to face strangers: Unlike the great Lautrec, I had no wish to ease my despair in absinthe or bury myself in the soft, impersonal world of prostitutes. It was grand-mère who, before her final illness, suggested I build a high wall around this family estate, install whatever laboratories I might require for my work, and establish a private world of my own. Madame Léontine prepares my favorite dishes, and Pouchet is my guardian, confidant, and friend. I am a reasonably happy human!"

Tendrell perched on the arm of the sofa, nursing his whiskey. "The villagers, of course, would think you quite mad if they learned you were living here. That you had tricked them with your monster . . ."

"They are the mad ones! Believing in a monster."

"They are superstitious!" Damiot protested. "Foolish! And, of course, ignorant. Many of them . . ."

"Ignorance makes fools of men."

Tendrell nodded. "Ignorance—stupidity—that's what is wrong with the world! There should be one Commandment: 'Thou shalt not be stupid!'"

Damiot got to his feet. "I wish, Monsieur le Comte, that you would not show your monster to the villagers again."

"Ah! But I plan to have him make another appearance tomorrow night. If the weather clears."

"I too wish you wouldn't, Nick." Tendrell rose from the sofa's arm. "When ignorant people are frightened they become violent animals, and the villagers at this moment seem ready to explode. They talk of nothing but those murders and the monster in the château. My daughter hears them every time she goes shopping . . ."

"I agree with Monsieur Tendrell." Damiot moved closer to the desk. "It would be wise to put an end to this joke. I suggest that you destroy the Courville monster!"

"Not just yet, Monsieur Inspecteur. And you won't tell anyone, I trust, what I've revealed to you tonight?" He frowned, suddenly childlike, as though he were about to have his wonderful toy taken away. "You won't report to the local gendarmerie that I've played a trick on their friends in the village? Won't tell them that I'm here in residence at the château?"

"No, Monsieur le Comte. Nick . . . I will not tell anyone. Inspector Bardou's the one who must find the murderer—or murderers. Not I . . ."

"Monsieur Inspecteur!" The Comte frowned. "You must have some theory about the murderer . . ."

Damiot shrugged.

"It has to be one of the villagers!" Tendrell exclaimed.

"I suspect," Damiot finally answered, "that whoever started the rumor of a monster in the Château de Mohrt may be the murderer . . ."

The rain had stopped before Damiot came to the edge of the village. He slowed his car as he reached the Auberge.

None of the windows were lighted. Perhaps Aurore had gone to bed.

He had a sudden urge for a glass of Calvados before retiring. His mind was preoccupied with what he had learned tonight in his conversation with the Comte. Another Calvados might help him to relax . . .

He saw that Fric-Frac, beside him, was sound asleep.

Driving on, down Avenue de la République, he noticed that the filling station was closed. He squinted up at the clock on the town hall tower, its hands halted at twelve o'clock. End of time for his village . . .

The new traffic lights were dark for the night.

Swerving off from the Avenue into the Square, he parked near the fountain. Fric-Frac roused immediately but settled down again when he didn't reach to open the door.

Nobody visible on the streets at this hour and no traffic. Metal shutters dropped over every shop, and the apartments above showed no sign of life. Not a light visible in any rooms of the Hôtel Courville, and the two cafés, at opposite ends of the Square, were closed.

Of course! This was Sunday night. He wouldn't get his Calvados.

He looked up at the squat mass of the Hôtel Courville. Impossible to visualize a tall hotel rising above the village . . .

Would Aurore be happy with her new restaurant? The elaborate Relais Julien could never be like the pleasant Auberge she had created with her husband . . .

A light flashed on in a room on the top floor of the hotel. Some salesman unable to sleep? Turning on his bedside lamp to check over the list of calls he had to make tomorrow . . .

Had he known Lisette Jarlaud on some previous visit?

Fric-Frac roused, lifted her head and looked from side to side.

"What is it, Madame?"

She growled softly and stood up, resting her paws on the open window, peering around the silent Square.

"You're hearing ghosts! Everyone's asleep."

She wagged her tail but continued to growl.

Damiot turned and looked back toward the Avenue.

A car was rolling, slowly and silently, its headlights dark, across rue Voltaire and down Avenue de la République.

A black Ferrari.

Damiot felt a chill pass across the nape of his neck. The sleek black shape of the powerful car was strangely threatening.

He was unable to see the driver, who must be hunched down behind the steering wheel. Fric-Frac barked. Damiot had a feeling that the man in the other car was watching him.

He switched on his headlights.

The Ferrari immediately took off with a roar of sound, headlights still dark, and shot down the length of the Avenue into the night.

"No chasing cars, Madame. We must accept the impossible."

He turned the Peugeot around and started back toward the Auberge.

18

Damiot was roused by the crowing of a cock, which was answered immediately by another and another.

The sound flowed back and forth from farm to farm, then faded to silence.

Another cock crowed, and the answering chorus rose and fell again.

Half awake, he smiled at these familiar voices from the past.

He forced himself to avoid checking his wristwatch, because he didn't want to get out of bed just yet . . .

Crowing cocks meant dawn, and from the number of their voices, these must be announcing the first shafts of the rising sun.

Pray God they also meant good weather . . .

He drowsed until the roar of a motorcycle brought him wide awake.

That would be Claude! Breakfast should arrive in another fifteen minutes.

He got out of bed and, after opening the curtains and inside shutters to see bright sunshine in the garden, hurried into the bath.

When the expected knock sounded he was in bed again, wearing his robe and propped in anticipation against the pillows. "Come in!"

The garçon entered with a breakfast tray. "Bonjour, M'sieur!"

"Bonjour, Claude. Where's Fric-Frac?"

"She's not awake yet."

He smiled, remembering their late night, as Claude set the tray across his lap.

"La patronne told me to bring you her special confiture of apricots this morning."

"Madame's spoiling me!" Noticing a handwritten label as

Claude opened the small jar. "I'd like to ask you one or two questions . . ."

"Certainly, M'sieur!" He stood at attention, smiling and wiping his reddened hands on the long apron wrapped around his thin body.

"Think now!" Filling a cup with black coffee as he talked. "Can you remember the first time you heard about this monster that lurks in the château?"

"Mais certainement! It was soon after they found that first girl's body."

"Do you recall who told you?"

"I'm not sure, M'sieur." He shrugged. "Everybody in the village was talking about it. Saying there have been stories for years about a monster in the castle."

"But you hadn't heard such stories before?" Damiot sipped the scalding coffee.

"No, M'sieur. Never . . ."

"Do you happen to know where the Jarlaud girl lived?"

"In an alley off rue Woodrow Wilson, behind the Hôtel Courville. There's a row of old houses there."

"I know the ones. Is Madame Bouchard up yet?"

"Mais certainement! La patronne's the first in the kitchen every morning, and I'm supposed to be the second. Michel is always the last. Of course, I've already taken a pot of coffee up to his apartment! He cooks breakfast for Madame and they eat together in the kitchen while they discuss the dinner menu and Madame makes out her shopping lists."

"Perhaps I'll see Madame when I get my car. Merci, Claude . . ."

"Plaisir, M'sieur Inspecteur! We're busy this morning. Those gentlemen are leaving for Paris . . ."

Damiot spread preserves on a croissant as the garçon departed.

He should visit that alley off rue Woodrow Wilson, on the chance there might be something he could learn from the Jarlaud girl's family.

His forehead ached faintly, but that must be from the Calvados he had drunk last night. There was no pain at the back, where he had struck his head.

He considered for a moment what he had learned at the château.

Everything the Comte had said appeared to be true. Not a

single discrepancy had turned up as they talked through the long evening . . .

He ate the last of the confiture with his spoon and finished a second cup of black coffee, then went into the bath and ran a hot tub.

Bathed and shaved, his forehead no longer throbbing, he had nearly finished dressing when someone knocked on his door. He slipped a tie under his collar and tied it before another knock sounded. "Coming!" As he went to the door he heard coughing outside. Opening it, he saw Bardou, cigarette dangling from his lip, hat in hand, bundled in his gray overcoat with a wool scarf knotted around his throat. "How's that cold?"

"Still have it, but not so bad as yesterday."

"Come in! Another five minutes and you wouldn't have caught me. Eh bien! Any developments?" He closed the door.

"Had another call from Toulon, ten minutes ago. Thought I'd drive over instead of telling you on the phone."

"Did they learn anything?" Damiot finished dressing as he listened to Bardou's report.

"First of all!" He coughed again, standing in the center of the room, head turning as his eyes followed Damiot. "They located that woman and child who visited Annie Deffous weekends. It's the Deffous girl's child. A boy, two years old. The woman's a friend who takes care of him in her home. The child's never lived with his mother, according to the neighbors. In fact, they didn't know she had one!"

"And the boy's father?"

"The woman claims she knows nothing about him. His name or, for that matter, whether Deffous was married."

"If Deffous was twenty when she died and the child is two, she must've been eighteen when he was born . . ."

"My pal's looking for the registration of birth. He talked with the people where Deffous worked."

"Yes?"

"They sell hotel equipment. She started there three years ago, as assistant bookkeeper."

"Hotel equipment? I wonder if through her job she may have met someone from the Hôtel Courville? You might check on whoever does purchasing for the hotel. Find out if they do business with this firm in Toulon . . ."

"I'll do that today. Recently, when the old woman who was

head bookkeeper died, Deffous was promoted and given a raise in salary."

"So she didn't need money!"

"People always need more money." The ash fell from his cigarette, unnoticed, to the tiled floor. "When I reported this on the phone to the Commissaire, he congratulated me for identifying the Deffous girl. Only I wasn't able to explain exactly how I did it."

"Don't try! Tell him you used your powers of deduction. He won't care how you did it, if you find the murderer for him."

"But, M'sieur!" He ejected a spurt of gray smoke from between his lips. "I've no idea who the murderer is."

"Neither do I." Damiot put his hat on and snatched the waterproof from a chair. "I'll walk out with you. Why didn't this woman who takes care of the child report Deffous was missing?"

"She was afraid to. Although she hadn't been paid for two months. What will you be doing today, M'sieur Damiot?"

"Thought I'd drive through the hills again." He opened the door and motioned Bardou ahead. "Driving a car relaxes me. The hip isn't as painful as it was when I arrived last week. In fact, this morning I barely feel it." He closed the door, checking that it had locked, and followed Bardou through the corridor. "Where's your car?"

"Parked in front. I have to stop by the gendarmerie. The Commissaire wants another little chat . . ."

"You didn't tell him you were seeing me?" Dropping his key on the desk as they crossed the foyer.

"Certainly not! I wouldn't do that . . . When I get a license number from Toulon for the Deffous girl's car, I'm having it sent to every gendarmerie in Provence."

"That should get results." Damiot swung open the entrance door and went down the steps after Bardou into bright sunshine. "My car's in the back, so I'll leave you here."

"They told me, when I phoned in, that the villagers are talking about going up to the château tonight if the weather's clear. More of them than usual." He tossed his stub of cigarette away. "They plan to catch the monster this time."

"Will the police be there?"

"The Commissaire wants no part of such nonsense. There's no monster, M'sieur Inspecteur! You and I both know that . . ."

"Give me a call if you learn anything more from Toulon." Damiot continued around the side of the Auberge, toward the parking area. As he passed the windows of the restaurant he heard Bardou's motor sputter before it chugged off.

So the villagers were returning to the château tonight to catch the monster. And the Comte planned to give them another performance . . .

"No, Madame! Stay where you are." Aurore's voice. "No! No . . ."

He saw that she was bathing Fric-Frac in a small wooden tub on a bench near the kitchen door. The dog was covered with suds. Her owner, wearing dungarees and a man's shirt, sleeves rolled to her elbows, was scrubbing Fric-Frac with a brush. Aurore's hair, piled on top of her head, looked more auburn than bronze in the sunlight.

The silver Mercedes that had been parked here last night was gone. So the visitors had departed.

"Poor Madame la Duchesse!"

"With all this sunshine, I decided to give her a bath. She's very unhappy at the moment, but after I've finished she'll race around, barking and capering like a mad creature." She glanced up from her scrubbing again and smiled.

"Any day that begins with apricot preserves like yours promises to be a memorable one."

"They are served only to special guests. Those who, I hope, will return . . ." Looking into his eyes. "Especially you, Monsieur."

"You're very kind." He saw that Fric-Frac was rolling her eyes, trying to attract his attention, as she wiggled in the scented suds. "She even smells like a duchess!"

"That's my most expensive bath oil." Picking up a pitcher and pouring more water over Fric-Frac's back as she squirmed to escape. "Be good! We're almost finished."

"Did your visitors enjoy their dinner?"

"They were delighted! With what they ate and with everything else."

"And your chef?"

"Michel joined us in the lounge after the restaurant closed. Everything was discussed and decided. They will have contracts for him when they return next month. He's to be in complete charge of the kitchen for the Relais Julien. I, naturally, am delighted.''

"Then you will be selling the Auberge?"

"I might never have such an opportunity again. It would be disastrous for me to try and compete with their elegant new hotel."

He glanced up at the rear of the building. "So it's to be torn down . . ."

"Not for at least a year. Eventually this may be a parking lot for the new hotel. Meanwhile, with Michel's help, I'll keep the Auberge open through the summer." She picked up a towel, spread it on the bench, and began to rub the dog dry. "Unfortunately, I will not be able to keep Fric-Frac while I'm getting the new restaurant organized."

"Won't they allow you to own a dog?"

"They don't know I have one. It wouldn't be fair to Fric-Frac. I will have no time for her—to give her the affection she needs and expects. She was always Julien's dog. Never really mine . . ." She continued to towel Fric-Frac. "I've always suspected she's a man's dog."

"That's possible." He smiled as one eye peeped from under the towel. "What will you do with her?"

"I was hoping . . ." She didn't look up as she spoke. "That you might take her."

"You would give her to me!"

Now she raised her eyes. "You're the first person since Julien's death for whom she's shown any affection."

"I am honored. By her affection, and by your generosity."

She let the towel fall away from the dog. "Fric-Frac would be content with you. I'm certain of that."

The dog shook herself, sending drops of water flying. Then she sat up on her haunches facing Damiot, stroking the air with both paws.

"You see! She wants you to hold her."

As Damiot leaned forward, Fric-Frac jumped into his arms. He could feel the small, damp body snuggled against his waterproof as he stroked her head. "I've always wanted a dog exactly like this one."

"You have?"

"I will take her back to Paris with me." He kissed the top of the dog's head, fragrant with the scent of bath oil. "I'm grateful to you, Madame . . ."

"Madame?"

"Aurore . . ." He handed Fric-Frac to her.

She looked into his eyes again as she cradled the squirming dog in her arms. "It has been my pleasure. Everything . . ."

"Bonjour, mes amis!"

They turned, startled, to see Michel, in robe and pajamas, coming down the steps from his apartment.

"Monsieur Damiot!" His eyes gleamed with excitement. "Have you heard about the new hotel?"

"I certainly have. Just now."

"Aurore's to manage their restaurant and I'll be in charge of the kitchen. A three-star restaurant!"

"That will depend upon you, chéri." Aurore smiled as she set Fric-Frac on the towel. "Only your cooking can make it three-star."

"My cooking is already three-star!" He turned to Damiot. "You must come back again, Monsieur! After the Relais Julien has opened and is a huge success! I will prepare for you the finest dinner you have ever eaten!"

"You've already done that." Damiot studied the tanned face, the dazzling smile, the curly black hair. "You should be a great success with the new restaurant, Monsieur!"

"Aurore tells me your family used to have a little café here . . ."

"Years ago, and very small."

"Your father was the chef?"

"A good one, but not so good as you."

Fric-Frac shook herself again, spraying water.

"Mon Dieu!" Michel exclaimed, brushing his robe. "That little monster!"

Aurore laughed. "It's only a few drops . . ."

"Of course, chérie! No harm done." He bent to kiss her, lightly, on the cheek. "Maintenant, I shall cook a three-star breakfast! Create, just for you, an omelette that no one has ever tasted before. I'll call it—Omelette Aurore! So it must be golden, like the dawn! And we will feature it every morning at the Relais Julien!"

"I must be on my way." Damiot started toward his car again.

"You'll have dinner here tonight?" Aurore called after him.

"Three-star? Wouldn't miss it!"

As he opened the door of the Peugeot, he saw that Fric-Frac had jumped down from the bench and was racing around the parking area in a circle.

She was his dog now.

19

The alley had never been given a name. Everybody always called it "the alley." The only alley in the village—except for that one behind the town hall where Lisette Jarlaud had been murdered. She had lived in an alley and died in an alley . . .

The cobbles underfoot were slippery with gray mud that was like snail slime. Two scrawny cats, playing with a dead rat.

He hesitated as he approached the row of tiny stone houses that had been here ever since he could remember. Five of them, with scabrous walls and no shutters at the windows. The curtains hanging inside were clean but faded from many washings.

No idea which house belonged to the Jarlaud family.

Damiot went toward the first door, but it opened before he knocked.

A bearded old man eyed him suspiciously. "Yes?"

"Jarlaud?"

An arthritic forefinger jabbed toward the end of the row. "Last house."

"Merci, Monsieur." He walked on.

There was a stench of sewage and rotted food as he went toward the final house. He knocked on the door twice before it creaked open.

"What do you want?"

He was surprised to see a younger-looking woman than he had anticipated. "Madame Jarlaud?"

"That's right . . ."

"Chief Inspector Damiot." He showed her his badge. "I'd like to ask a few questions about your daughter . . ."

"You're that flic from Paris! Used to live here?"

"That's right."

"Come in, if you want."

As Damiot entered he saw that the lower floor was a single all-purpose room. Two small children, a boy and a girl in clean blue smocks, were playing on the stone floor near an old-fashioned wood stove. There was no electricity, and the only light came from a lantern on a wooden table. He faced Madame Jarlaud as she closed the door.

"Don't know what I can tell you, M'sieur. I've already answered all their questions. The local gendarmes have been here many times. And there was another one they brought from Arles . . ."

"Inspector Bardou?"

"He's the one! Asked all the same questions."

"I may ask the same ones again."

She shrugged.

Damiot realized that she couldn't be more than forty. Faded blonde hair. Traces of beauty that must have been passed on to the daughter. Her body, under a water-spattered apron and old housedress, was thin.

She was aware of his inspection, smoothing her hair as she circled the table on the other side of the lantern to face him again.

"I believe your daughter was employed at the Hôtel Courville as femme de chambre . . ."

"Got the job for her myself, hoping to keep her off the streets. I work in the kitchen."

"And your husband?"

"Does odd jobs, when he can find any."

"These are your grandchildren?"

"The poor loves!" She glanced down at them with affection. "Lisette was their mother, but they'll never know their fathers. Looking at them, so different from each other, I'd say that one day they'll ask questions. Which I'll never be able to answer . . ."

He saw that the girl had straight blonde hair, but the boy's head was covered with auburn curls.

"Their mother was a natural blonde, like me!"

"Since you are employed at the Hôtel Courville, you must've been aware of your daughter's relationships with the other employees . . ."

She stiffened slightly. "What do you mean by that?"

"Was there anyone on the staff who was annoying your daughter? Perhaps even threatening her?"

"Well . . ." Relaxing slightly. "There were several of the younger men, now and again, who got too friendly, but Lisette could handle them."

"Was there any special man she didn't like?"

"Lisette liked everybody! I told her many times there were some she shouldn't trust."

"Could there have been one man who was so annoying that she would try to find a job elsewhere?"

"She never looked for another job!"

"A few weeks before her death she went to see Madame Bouchard at the Auberge and asked if there might be an opening for a femme de chambre. Said she wanted to leave the Hôtel Courville."

"She never told me!"

"Unfortunately, Madame Bouchard had nothing for her."

She frowned. "Why would Lisette do a thing like that?"

"Do you know if there is anyone on the hotel staff who has any connection with the city of Toulon?"

"Toulon?"

"Either worked there or perhaps does business with some company there? Such as hotel supplies . . ."

"I wouldn't know about that. I've never heard anyone mention Toulon."

"Did your daughter ever say anything about a young farmer named Savord?"

"Achille! Such a fine young man. Lisette brought him home many times. He was her favorite. She even talked of marrying him! And I, for one, was hoping she would. They discussed the fact that she already had two kids, but he promised to treat them like his own. Told me he wanted three more."

"What's he like? Achille Savord . . ."

"A nice man. Never quarreling or nasty. And he loves both these babies. Whenever he came here he brought them toys and, if Lisette wasn't ready to leave, he would sit on the floor and play with them. Achille would have made my daughter a good husband! And, of course, one day he's going to inherit his father's farm. I kept telling her to marry him but she wanted to wait a while." Her eyes brimmed with tears. "Perhaps if she'd listened to me she would be alive . . ."

"Thank you for answering my questions, Madame." He turned to leave.

She followed him. "That's all you're going to ask?"

"For the moment." Opening the door. "Good day, Madame."

"M'sieur . . ." She closed the door behind him.

Making his way carefully over the slippery cobbles, Damiot was disgusted by the suffocating smell of poverty. He knew many such bleak alleys in Paris. Only one thing could bloom in such a foul place. The dark flower of death . . .

As he walked toward rue Woodrow Wilson, he wished that he had asked Madame Jarlaud where he could find Achille Savord.

Blanche Carmet should know! She had called the young farmer "très gentil."

Some other questions he would like to ask Blanche.

Prostitutes knew everything about their neighbors, as well as their customers . . .

He waited in the middle of the perfume-scented room until he heard footsteps coming downstairs, and turned to see the same pink kimono looming in the dim hall. It seemed to float out of the darkness into the rosy light of the salon.

Blanche was smiling. "You did come back."

"Sorry to disturb you. Madame said you were with someone."

"He'll wait. Can't you sit down?"

"This shouldn't take long. You told me yesterday you knew that young farmer, Savord."

"Yes . . ."

"Where can I find him?"

She frowned. "You're not going to question Achille!"

"Nothing official. That's why I've come to you first. I don't want anyone in the village to know I'm seeing him."

"You'll be kind to Achille?"

"Kind?"

"He's such an innocent! Clara says he was a virgin when he first came here and she had to teach him everything. Achille was only seventeen! Until he met the Jarlaud girl he saw Clara every Saturday night. Then he stopped. Clara knew he was going with Lisette. Word gets around! But after she was murdered—the very next Saturday—Achille was back here, asking for Clara."

"You think he might have killed Lisette Jarlaud?"

"Achille wouldn't harm anyone. Believe me, he had nothing to do with Lisette's murder"

"Where will I find him?"

"His father has a farm. On the left side of the road, driving south, before you get to the main highway. Achille took us there last year—Clara and me—for a picnic. Such food!"

"What's happening in the village? I hear they're planning another visit to the château tonight."

"The women are stirring the men up to do something about that monster." Her fingers clutched the sleeve of his waterproof. "Is there a monster up there? Killing people . . ."

"Whoever murdered those two girls is certainly a psychopath, but there's no monster at the château. I can assure you of that."

"The villagers held a meeting last night in the schoolhouse. Some of the women made such a fuss that the men have agreed to catch the monster and destroy it."

"And the women? Will they go with them?"

"They'll wait 'til the men come home, and scream at them if they haven't caught whatever it is. None of them will set foot outside after dark, but even a monster wouldn't touch such crows!" She released his sleeve. "Most of their husbands come here. So business hasn't been good since the Jarlaud girl died. The men stay home nights if it rains, and go up to the château when the weather's clear."

"I won't keep you any longer." He moved toward the hall.

She followed him out of the salon. "There's going to be another murder tonight."

"Why do you say that?"

"Today's Monday, and both those girls were killed on Monday night."

"Were they? Nobody's mentioned that before."

"I remember because Michel comes here Monday nights."

"Michel Giroud?"

"He was with me when both those girls were murdered. That's how I know it was Monday." She opened the front door. "I've been thinking about the murders this morning, because Michel phoned to say he'd be here tonight. Soon as he can get away from the restaurant. He pays for the whole evening, so I don't see anyone else. Michel likes to relax after he finishes work. At least two or three hours . . ."

As Damiot stepped out into the late morning sunlight, he

noticed a truck parked across the street. There was a small sign on its side. "Has Giroud ever mentioned going to the château with the villagers?"

"Michel wouldn't get involved with that. He laughs at them. Although he too thinks there's a monster up there!" She hesitated. "You won't be hard on Achille Savord?"

"If you say so . . ."

"I promise you, he had nothing to do with the murders."

"One last thing . . . Do you know anyone who owns a black Ferrari?"

"In Courville? You must be joking!"

"Hope I haven't kept you away too long from Monsieur Sibilat . . ."

"You know everything, don't you?" She giggled as she glanced toward the parked truck. "He can wait."

"You didn't tell him I was here?"

"I don't tell him anything!" Her second giggle followed him as he headed back toward the square where he had left his car.

So both those girls were killed on a Monday night! Was that, like so many other things, only a coincidence?

And Marc Sibilat was waiting for Blanche! Morning was probably the only time he could escape from his mother. Now, there was a real monster!

Damiot got into the Peugeot, backed away from the silent fountain, and eased into the commercial traffic moving south on the avenue.

Marc Sibilat with Blanche. Why not pay an unexpected visit to his mother?

He slowed the Peugeot to a stop close to the cemetery wall, across from the florist shop, noticing fresh red roses in the display window.

Moving cautiously between the rumbling trucks, he crossed the avenue and opened the door. Heard the bell respond in the rear.

The air was chilly inside, after the hot sunshine.

He had a sudden idea as he reached the counter. He would buy some flowers for . . .

"Ah, Monsieur Inspecteur!"

Damiot was smiling, amused by his idea, as he saw the formidable black figure appear from the curtained passage. "Madame . . ."

"My son's not here." She faced him across the counter. "He

always drives to Grasse, Monday mornings, to buy flowers. Takes him hours to select them for our shop."

"I can believe that, Madame. However, I didn't come this morning to see your son."

"No?" Her eyes narrowed. "You wished to see me?"

"It's always pleasant to see you again, Madame. Actually, I came to buy some flowers."

"Forgive me. I thought . . ."

"Perhaps some roses? Like those in your window."

"Of course, M'sieur." She turned to open the display case and lifted out a tub of red roses. "How many?"

"A small bouquet . . ."

"Certainly." She produced a square of green waxed paper from under the counter, spread it flat, and began to select roses from the tub.

"I hear the villagers will be going up to the château tonight . . ."

"They hope to catch the monster before it kills someone else."

"You believe, Madame, there's a monster in the castle?"

"I've told you! My son has seen it."

"Will he be going up there tonight with the others?"

"I couldn't say . . ." She secured the stems of the roses with a strip of tape. "I only pray they catch the beast before more throats are cut!" Returning the tub of roses to the display case and closing the glass door. "Why shouldn't the villagers take matters into their own hands? The police have done nothing! This monster must be destroyed!"

"I suppose the villagers would like the publicity. Hoping it will bring more tourists this summer."

"Is that wrong, Monsieur? If they destroy the monster it will be in all the papers." She folded the waxed paper around the bouquet and handed it across the counter. "That should put Courville on the map. Tourists will come from every part of the world!"

He dropped a hundred-franc note on the counter and watched as she unlocked the cash drawer. "You would have it destroyed for the money you might make from the publicity?"

"Not I, Monsieur Inspecteur. The money isn't important." Closing the cash drawer and counting out his change. "But the monster must be killed before another young woman dies!"

"Good morning, Madame." He turned toward the door with the bouquet of red roses.

Damiot was smiling as he crossed the street. He was certain Madame Sibilat was watching him.

Passing his Peugeot, hurrying now, he went to the side gate, almost hidden under ivy in the cemetery wall. He pushed the wooden gate open.

This morning he wouldn't visit his parents' graves. Do that again before he returned to Paris, but not today.

Crossing the grass in the shade of the ancient trees, he went straight to Lisette Jarlaud's grave. Slipped the waxed paper back and placed the roses on top of the dead ones left by Achille Savord. "Roses from Madame Sibilat. But these are fresh!"

He turned from the unmarked grave and headed back to the avenue. As he got into the Peugeot he glanced toward the florist shop but saw nothing of Madame's inquisitive face.

Driving south, moving slowly in heavy traffic, Damiot glanced down at the empty seat beside him. He realized to his surprise that he felt lost without Fric-Frac.

After he talked with Achille Savord he would continue south and have lunch somewhere. Relax and think . . .

He had collected too many seemingly insignificant odds and ends, that needed sorting out. There must be something important among them. One small fact that might lead to the murderer . . .

He found the Savord farm and turned off the road to follow a lane, dappled with sunshine, between neat apple orchards and vineyards. This was a prosperous farm with hands working in the fields and among the grapevines. He was aware of heads lifting as he passed, eyes following his car.

Approaching the old farmhouse, he glimpsed a barnyard bustling with activity, as he slowed to a stop at the edge of a flower garden. Two young women, their faces shadowed by wide-brimmed straw hats, were at work.

A tall youth, red-haired and muscular, left a tractor he'd been repairing and came toward the Peugeot carrying a wrench.

"Achille Savord?"

"That's right, M'sieur."

Damiot brought out his badge. "I'm . . ."

"That flic from Paris everybody in the village is talking about!" He lowered his voice. "I've been expecting you."

"Have you?"

"I see all those crime films on television, so I know the way you guys operate." He grinned. "How'd you find out I'd been seeing Lisette?"

"You're the only person who left flowers on her grave. I asked the florist, Madame Sibilat, who bought them."

"Easy as that?"

"There's only one florist shop in Courville."

"These are my sisters." Achille motioned toward the young women.

"No need to bother your family. But I've some questions for you."

He grinned, shyly. "What can I tell you, M'sieur?"

"You know a girl named Deffous? Annie Deffous . . ."

"Never heard of her." He frowned. "A girl in the village?"

"She is now. In a refrigerator . . ."

"That one! I saw her when they asked everybody to try and identify her, but I'd never seen her before."

"When's the last time you were in Toulon?"

"I've never been there. Marseille, but never Toulon."

"Who do you think killed those two girls?"

"The monster, of course."

"What monster?"

"They say it hides in the old château. The villagers are going up there again tonight and try to catch it."

"You've seen this monster?"

"No. I'm going this evening for the first time."

As Damiot studied his face he remembered Lisette Jarlaud's two children. The little one had the same curly auburn hair . . .

"If there is a monster," Savord continued, "it should be put to death before it harms anyone else! And if I could be sure it murdered Lisette, I'd like to be the one who kills it."

"I'm told you wanted to marry Lisette Jarlaud."

"She'd have married me, if she had lived. Promised me she would! Only there was another guy. She wanted to marry him. Said she'd talk to him, and if he refused she'd marry me."

"Who was this man?"

"She never told me his name."

"A man in the village?"

"I suppose so, because she said she was seeing him, and Lisette didn't have a car to drive anywhere."

"Didn't you resent her seeing other men?"

He shrugged. "What could I do?"

"You would marry her? Knowing all this . . ."

"Of course!" He hesitated. "She's the mother of my son."

"Oh?"

"Lisette had two kids."

"I know. I've seen them."

"Mine's the boy. I thought if we were married and she came to live here on the farm, she would give up her job at the hotel and her old life. I promised her she could bring the little girl and I would give her a good home. Just like the boy . . ."

"What about your family?"

"I would've told my father that both kids were mine."

"Why didn't she agree to that?"

"She said this other guy could give her a better life. Take her away from here. I guess she really loved him."

"Some older man?"

"I suppose . . . But he told her he was already the father of a child. He'd never married the girl, and hadn't seen her in more than a year. Lisette thought if she told him she was pregnant he might forget the other girl and marry her."

"Was that what she planned to do?"

"So she said."

"When was this? How long before she died?"

Savord scowled. "It was—the last time I saw her . . ."

"She died on a Monday."

"This was Friday night." He turned to Damiot, his young face twisted with emotion. "We drove over to Arles and had a nice dinner. That night, before I took her home, I asked her again to marry me. And that's when she told me about this other guy. If he didn't fall for her story and agree to marry her right away, she would marry me. I never saw her again."

"Maybe he did fall for her story—and killed her."

"I've thought of that . . ."

"You still would've married her? After she told you this?"

"Of course!"

Damiot was surprised at the vehemence in Savord's voice. "Why?"

"Because I loved her, M'sieur! In spite of everything I knew about Lisette. I still love her . . ."

20

Damiot was preoccupied as he ate lunch on a hillside terrace with a view of Aix, the ancient capital of Provence.

The roadside restaurant had looked inviting but the bored waiter was half asleep, the food disappointing, and the local wine barely drinkable.

He tried to sort out the jumble of information he had turned up about Annie Deffous and Lisette Jarlaud. The most important thing he had learned today seemed to be young Savord's account of his last evening with the Jarlaud girl.

Who was this man she had planned to threaten with a false pregnancy? Hoping he would agree to marriage . . .

The same man Annie Deffous had come to see in Courville? Only Deffous had given birth to his child! Some man she had met in Toulon? Some businessman? . . .

Marc Sibilat?

Was Sibilat's story—that the Deffous girl had noticed his name above the florist shop—an attempt to throw off suspicion? Had she traced Sibilat to Courville? Did he identify her because he hoped that would make him appear to be innocent?

Certainly his mother was a shrewd one. Although she apparently didn't suspect her son was with Blanche Carmet this morning. So he was clever enough to deceive the old woman . . .

And what about Achille Savord? He would be going up there tonight, for the first time, he claimed. Was there a murderer hiding under his seemingly ingenuous appearance? Had he killed Lisette Jarlaud when she refused to marry him? Had he told that story about another man to conceal the truth? How could he have been involved with Annie Deffous?

The good weather held through the afternoon, as Damiot returned to Courville after many hours of driving on country roads.

When he parked behind the Auberge, he noticed a scattering of white clouds high in the western sky.

There was no sound of barking from the kitchen as he passed, so Fric-Frac must be asleep. Probably upstairs in Aurore's private suite.

He saw sunlight pouring through the windows of the lounge for the first time, as he turned down the long corridor to his room.

Dropping his hat and waterproof on a chair, he went into the bath and ran himself a tub. Soaked in the hot water, muscles relaxing, then stretched out on the bed, wrapped in his robe, and slept immediately.

It was after seven-thirty when he left his room and headed toward the front. Crossing the circular lobby, he saw that only one table in the restaurant was occupied. Allan Tendrell was having an early dinner with his daughter.

"M'sieur Damiot!"

He turned to see Claude, behind the registration desk.

"Telephone for you, M'sieur." Holding out the phone, across the desk. "It's M'sieur Bardou again."

"Merci, mon ami." He took the phone from the garçon's hand. "Bardou? What's happened now?"

"Wanted you to know. My friend in Toulon called back. Gave me a license number for the Deffous girl's car that has gone out to every gendarmerie in Provence. They've been told to look for a gray Dauphine."

"That may turn it up."

"I stayed at the town hall most of the day, waiting for news from Toulon, but now I'm back at the hotel. The manager says they never buy their supplies in Toulon."

"It was only an idea . . . Is your cold better?"

"Better than yesterday. A bientôt, M'sieur Inspecteur!"

"A bientôt . . ."

As he went toward the restaurant, Aurore came to meet him, smiling, wearing another attractive dress. This one was a soft rose color.

"How was your day?" she asked.

"Pleasant. Except for a miserable lunch."

"We must give you an excellent dinner to make up for that." Lowering her voice. "Allan Tendrell and his daughter are here."

"So I noticed."

"They seldom dine with us Monday nights." She led him toward his usual table. "I was surprised when Jenny phoned this morning for a reservation. Monday is always slow. You three may be our only customers." She went ahead, past the Tendrells' table.

The Englishman glanced up from his food. "Ah! Monsieur Damiot!"

Jenny looked around and smiled. "Hello, Inspector!"

"Mademoiselle!" He hesitated, facing the painter. "Monsieur . . ."

"I was hoping I might run into you tonight. May I join you for a moment after I finish this bit of fish?"

"Certainly, Monsieur. Whenever you wish." As he followed Aurore, he realized that Jenny had once again managed to sit facing the doors. Through the glass portholes, before he sat down with his back to the kitchen, he glimpsed the blur of Michel's *toque blanche* in rapid motion.

Aurore placed a menu on the table in front of him. "Michel has prepared another of his specialties tonight, hoping that it might please you. Civet de porcelet."

"I will most certainly have that!" Unfolding his napkin as she went back toward her desk, pausing to chat with the Tendrells.

Jean-Paul appeared at his elbow. "An apéritif, M'sieur?"

"My usual, merci." He picked up the menu and considered the pleasant problem of what to order.

The hors d'oeuvres provençaux? No soup. Civet de porcelet. Afterward, because of his wretched lunch, he could permit himself a dessert. The frozen nougat with glacéed fruits! One of his mother's specialties . . .

As he sipped the vermouth, several more people arrived for dinner. None of their faces were familiar.

He was enjoying the hors d'oeuvres when Tendrell joined him. "May I?"

"Please . . ." Motioning toward the other chair. "Will you have a glass of wine? Or, perhaps, some whisky . . ."

"Nothing. Merci . . . I've a bottle of wine to finish with my daughter and I'll be doing some drinking later at the château." He leaned across the table, his voice conspiratorial. "I had Jenny make dinner reservations because I wanted to see you, but I don't want her to overhear what we say. Or, for that matter, Aurore! So, if I should change the subject abruptly, you'll understand?"

"Of course."

"First of all . . . I'm concerned for the safety of my daughter."

"What do you mean?"

"You realize, now, that the so-called monster in the château did not kill those two unfortunate young women. The monster is only a puppet—a harmless joke. So! Who did kill them? I didn't want to acknowledge in front of Jenny, the other night, that I've been worried ever since that Jarlaud girl was murdered, because I knew there wasn't any monster running loose. But whoever did kill those two girls still walks the village streets. Scot-free! I worry constantly about Jenny. Wondering when this beast—whoever he is—will kill again. I was hoping you were on to something . . ."

"Absolutely nothing."

"I saw Nick this afternoon. Was worried about tonight. And with good reason! He's determined to do his monster bit again."

"I suspected from our conversation last night that he would."

"Pouchet tells me he heard in the village this afternoon that more of the locals will be coming up there tonight. Quite a number of them, evidently, if the weather remains clear . . . Isn't there something that could be done, Monsieur Inspecteur—anything you can do—that would stop Nick? Prevent this monster nonsense!"

"I have no authority to prevent anything." He continued to eat with appetite as he explained. "The Comte can play his monster trick on the villagers or do anything else he wishes. As long as no one's injured. The Château de Mohrt is his property. He's not breaking any law."

"I realize that, but I am quite genuinely concerned. This whole monster business is childish! Nick, like most geniuses, has an infantile sense of humor . . ."

As the Englishman talked, Damiot saw that his daughter was nodding toward the kitchen doors. She had attracted Michel's attention and neither her father nor Aurore had noticed.

"Will you be there tonight?" Tendrell asked. "At the château?"

"I may drive up after dinner and see what's happening. I too heard that the villagers would be paying another visit. Their wives, apparently, are demanding that they destroy the monster."

"Nick plans to destroy the thing himself before the villagers discover it's a trick. He told me so today! I tried to persuade him to demolish it this afternoon but he wouldn't hear of it. Where will you be tonight? On that hill again? Behind the castle?"

"Tonight I'll drive up the lane to that side gate where I entered last night. That way I can be on ground level, near the front courtyard. Some dark spot where the villagers won't notice me."

"I've never seen that side entrance. Pouchet leaves the back gate open for me and I have a key to the kitchen door. Nick wants me with him tonight for the performance. I'll tell him you'll be coming."

"My presence, I must remind you, will not be official." He reluctantly finished the last morsel of artichoke vinaigrette.

"After the show why don't you join us for a drink? Nick likes you, and he needs to see more people! I'll have him send Pouchet to find you."

"Might be wise not to make definite plans. Let's see what develops."

"You may be right." Tendrell glanced beyond Damiot toward the swinging doors. "That grinning idiot! Keeps looking in here. Staring at my daughter! I'm not about to have her fall for any Don Juan of a chef. I've a suspicion they've been meeting somewhere when she drives down to the village, afternoons, while I'm painting. I suppose I should buy a second car and follow her! Although I must say I don't care for that sort of thing. Suspicious parent playing detective!"

While the Englishman talked, Damiot noticed that Jenny seemed to be amused, sipping her wine and smiling to herself as though she had just played a trick on her father.

"Did you know, Monsieur Inspecteur?" Tendrell leaned forward again, confidentially. "Aurore's selling the Auberge! Signing contracts to manage the restaurant in a fancy new hotel that will replace the Hôtel Courville . . ."

"Is she?"

"Taking her smiling chef along with her! Which, in my opinion, is a great mistake. Michel informed me, as I ordered dinner, that it will be a three-star restaurant!"

"That's not impossible, I should think. He's an excellent chef."

"But such conceit!"

"All first-class chefs have tremendous egos. They too are artists, Monsieur."

"I suppose he's anticipating all the rich American women he'll charm into bed. Aurore should get rid of him when she closes the Auberge. He amuses her for the moment, but I can't believe she's really serious about him. Except, of course, as a

168

chef! And she wouldn't have been interested in him even as a chef, while her husband was alive. Now there was a charming man!" He got to his feet as Claude cleared the table for Damiot's next course. "See you later, Monsieur Inspecteur?"

"Perhaps, Monsieur. Perhaps . . ."

21

The ruts in the narrow lane didn't seem so deep tonight.

Damiot glanced down at Fric-Frac, curled beside him. "Tonight, Madame la Duchesse, you must stay close to me. And no barking! You understand?" He smiled as her tail thumped the leather seat.

The Peugeot rattled across the wooden bridge and followed the twisting road into the hills.

As he slowed through the familiar open gate into the narrow private lane, he wondered if Aurore would be waiting up when he returned to the Auberge tonight . . .

His headlights swept across the spectral white mausoleum where the de Mohrt ancestors were interred. Would the old Comtesse be there with all the others?

Driving on, Fric-Frac snuggling against his waterproof, he thought about the villagers driving up to the entrance gates. Before leaving the Auberge he had heard more cars passing by. Several had sounded like small trucks. One of those, very likely, belonged to Marc Sibilat . . . When Damiot stopped at the kitchen door to get Fric-Frac, Claude had told him that he was coming to the château tonight on his motorcycle but would be delayed because of the people who had showed up late for dinner. Michel had been furious because he himself always tried to leave early Monday nights.

Turning left on the open strip that circled the château, Damiot drove to the same spot, near the front, where he had parked last night. Switched off his headlights and was immediately aware of the silence.

The dog pawed at his waterproof and whimpered to get out. Damiot reached over, opened the door, and watched her jump down, a black shape against the darkness.

He realized that he had forgotten to buy another pocket torch. The other one had never been recovered from that hole in the floor. After meeting the Comte he hadn't given it another thought . . .

He hesitated in the darkness at the edge of the courtyard.

Must be careful here! If he fell on these cobbles his hip could be damaged beyond repair.

The best vantage point for whatever was about to happen should be at the edge of the forest, on the eastern side of the courtyard. From there he could watch the terrace where the monster had appeared Friday night.

As he started to turn, he glimpsed a flash of reflected light in the dense shadow at the base of the castle.

Damiot froze.

Something metallic was catching that glow from the sky.

He moved cautiously toward it—whatever it was.

A solid black object took shape as he came closer. Glints of starlight flashed from several surfaces. It was a car . . .

The black Ferrari!

Damiot rested his open palm on the metal hood, which felt cold and damp. He tried a door but it was locked.

Did the Ferrari belong to somebody in the castle? Someone who drove through the countryside late at night. Through the sleeping village . . .

Was it the murderer?

The Comte or one of his assistants! Not likely that the Comte could handle such a powerful car.

Better have Bardou check those assistants. But that would give away the fact that the Comte was living here.

No matter! This whole business was getting out of hand. Perhaps he should tell Bardou everything he knew . . .

Damiot moved carefully on the cobbles as he crossed the corner of the courtyard, followed by Fric-Frac. He could see her black body against the pale cobbles.

Which meant that he too would be visible to anyone watching.

He moved closer to the edge of the forest and stood there, facing west, in a blot of shadow from the trees. This was beyond the cobbled area, and the earth felt soggy underfoot.

No lights in the castle or glow of lanterns from the drive.

"We'll have a short wait, Madame. I hope that you too had a nap this afternoon." He glanced back into the darkness where the Ferrari was parked.

What if it belonged to an outsider? Someone from a nearby city who had murdered those two girls and then started the story about the monster. Did he come here to watch the Comte's monster and laugh at the gullible villagers, then speed away in his Ferrari?

Was he lurking somewhere in the shadows, waiting for what was about to happen? Watching . . .

"Watching me!" he muttered.

Glancing down, he saw that Fric-Frac had stretched out on the wet grass. "Don't catch cold, Madame. Why do dogs like to get wet? Can you tell me that?" He smiled, remembering the dog he had owned so long ago. "I used to have one that sat in every puddle!"

Fric-Frac growled, softly.

A faint glow of light that seemed to float between the rows of poplars was moving up the distant entrance drive.

"Good girl!" He saw that she was on her feet, ears back, nose pointing toward the drive.

When he looked again toward the moving light, he was able to make out a small group of men beyond the near row of trees, carrying a lantern toward the courtyard.

Would Sibilat be among them? The first to enter! He was certainly muscular enough to scramble over those gates or climb the wall.

Fric-Frac continued to growl.

The intruders were curiously threatening because as yet they had made no sound. It was like watching a silent film . . .

He glanced up at the château but all the windows remained dark.

Nick would be preparing his monster with Pouchet's help, getting ready to make an appearance. And Tendrell was probably stationed at one of those dark windows, telling them what was happening below.

Damiot looked toward the drive again and saw that the villagers had reached the lower edge of the courtyard. They had paused, facing the castle and looking up at the terrace, no doubt deciding on their next move. The single lantern made a timid circle of light.

The dog growled, menacingly. Damiot saw that she was pointing back, toward the side of the château where he had parked the Peugeot.

Someone there? He hadn't heard a sound . . .

A faceless gray figure appeared out of the night. Damiot recognized the walk and the blur of silver hair. "Monsieur Tendrell!"

"We heard your car arrive."

"And I thought I was being quiet!"

"There are microphones everywhere, to pick up every sound." He lowered his voice as he came closer. "Nick wants you with us, so you'll be able to see everything."

"Splendid!"

"I drove without lights and parked near your car." He turned back, Damiot walking beside him. "Knew you wouldn't have gone far."

"Come, Fric-Frac!"

"You've brought Aurore's dog again?"

"Thought she'd be company while I waited. What time does the performance start?"

"Any moment, I should think." He glanced toward the drive as they left the courtyard, keeping in the deep shadow at the edge of the forest. "A few of the villagers have already come up the drive and more are gathered outside the gates. We've been eavesdropping on them through microphones hidden in the shrubbery. Takes them an hour to get enough courage to climb over that wall."

"I'm not surprised." He was aware of the Ferrari, a dark mass to their left, but said nothing to Tendrell.

"I still wish Nick wouldn't do this tonight. I've begged him again not to show the bloody puppet, but he refuses to listen. Here's your car! I'll go ahead and you can follow. Better keep your lights off."

"Right." Damiot got into the Peugeot with Fric-Frac and tailed the Citroën around the castle to the rear. There, in the faint light seeping from the sky, it was impossible to see the distant stables. He took off his waterproof and left it in the car with his hat, before joining the Englishman at the kitchen door.

Tendrell unlocked the door and went inside. Damiot followed, Fric-Frac darting ahead.

A dog barked in another room, beyond the dim kitchen, the sound muffled.

Fric-Frac growled.

"Pouchet's dog?" Damiot asked.

"Locked up for the night. We go up here." Tendrell led the way toward a stone staircase curving into darkness.

Damiot climbed after him, grasping the heavy wooden railing. "Your daughter knows you're here tonight?"

"Certainly not! Jenny went to bed after dinner. Usually she's curious to find out where I'm going, but tonight she was exhausted."

They had reached the next floor, and Damiot saw that they were in a narrow stone passage, lighted by a single lantern.

"I'm certain Jenny thinks I'm seeing Aurore! One day I shall have to tell her the truth, and she'll want to meet Nick. Tonight, fortunately, she was too tired to ask questions. Jenny's an extremely busy girl! Runs everything for me, you know. From the daily menus to a schedule of chores for our staff."

Damiot smiled. Jenny had obviously been acting for her father, pretending to be sleepy. She would be off somewhere, meeting Michel Giroud before he paid his Monday-night visit to Blanche Carmet.

"I came straight here, after she went to her room. Drove round the back, as usual. Never use those front gates..."

Damiot followed as he listened—Fric-Frac trotting beside him—through another stone passage. This one was wider, with a vaulted ceiling and thick columns spaced at intervals. More lanterns.

"... and I'd only just arrived when we heard your car. Nick hopes you'll stay after the performance, for another evening of conversation."

"I would like that."

The Englishman opened a door into an unfamiliar small salon, across a narrow corridor to another door and through a larger salon. These rooms were unfurnished, and heavy curtains covered every window. The only light came from lanterns resting on the floors or hanging from walls.

There was a musty smell of damp.

Damiot made a mental note of each door and corridor, in case he might have to return this way alone.

"You're the first new visitor since I was invited in last year," Tendrell was saying. "Nick's fascinated by your criminal investigations in Paris. He reads everything! Newspapers as well as scientific journals." He paused, hand on the knob of another door. "You will help me persuade him not to do this monster trickery again? Not after tonight. The whole thing's much too risky!"

"I can only try, Monsieur."

"Tonight must be the monster's last appearance. I've a feeling Nick will listen to you." He swung the door open.

The dog darted ahead, vanishing into the shadows.

"Fric-Frac! Come back here!"

"She can't go far," Tendrell said as Damiot closed the door. "This leads to Nick's private suite."

They were in a windowless corridor lighted by candelabra wired for electricity, walls hidden behind faded tapestries.

The Englishman paused in an open doorway, looking into a dimly lighted room. "Here's Inspector Damiot!"

"Come in, Monsieur Inspecteur!" Nick answered.

Damiot followed Tendrell into a small, uncluttered antechamber. The incredible room he had seen on his previous visit was visible straight ahead. More electricity here.

"We've been waiting for you!" The Comte, in another monklike robe, this one gray, held out a welcoming hand from his wheelchair. "I thought you'd be able to see more of our entertainment from up here."

"I should indeed." He shook the extended hand, aware of its surprising strength. His eyes were held briefly by the ancient eyes in the childlike face.

"We are ready . . ." Pouchet's voice.

Damiot glanced around and saw the old man with Madame Léontine in the shadows beyond the pool of light from a shaded lamp, arranging the monster on a chaise longue. The clumsy head was propped against the higher end of the chaise, the long cloak stretching across the seat and hanging down over the other end. "Madame Léontine! Monsieur Pouchet!"

The two servants smiled and bowed.

Damiot glanced toward the Comte. "Even in repose, your monster looks monstrous."

Nick laughed. "That was my intention!"

The mastiff, Lautrec, was stretched out near the wheelchair, Fric-Frac already snuggled beside him.

"Now that Inspector Damiot's here," Nick looked toward

Pouchet as he freed both hands from the sleeves of his robe, "shall we proceed?"

"At once, M'sieur le Comte." Pouchet lifted the puppet and held it tight as Madame Léontine gathered the folds of the cloak into her arms.

"Lead the way." Nick pressed the small device in his lap, revolving the wheelchair. "The rest of us will follow."

"Yes, M'sieur." Pouchet carried the awkward figure, raised like a banner, toward an open wall panel that was barely visible in a dark corner. Madame Léontine trailed behind, clutching the heavy cloak in both arms.

Nick sent his wheelchair rolling after them. "Messieurs!"

Damiot and the Englishman followed, both dogs racing ahead, through a seemingly endless stone corridor with electric bulbs embedded in the ceiling. The musty dampness Damiot had noticed earlier must have come from here.

"This is a secret passage," Nick called back over his shoulder. "The castle's riddled with them and I know every one! I would hide for hours when grand-mère wanted to lecture me for some prank, and even the servants couldn't find me! Unfortunately, most of these passages are too narrow for my wheelchair."

Damiot thought, as the Comte explained, that he was still a child, with his secret passages and his monster. Playing this infantile trick on the villagers. "Monsieur le Comte? Nick . . ."

"Yes, Monsieur Inspecteur?"

"I would suggest that you should not show your monster tonight."

"And why not?"

"Anything might happen. The villagers have been roused to a pitch of excitement that could result in an explosion."

"But it wasn't I who began it! Someone in the village started the rumor of a monster. Not I! The psychiatrists say there are monsters hidden in every man. Lurking beneath the surface and waiting to appear. So I have given the villagers their own monster. Is it illegal, what I'm doing? Am I breaking any law?"

"Nothing like that. But it could be dangerous."

"I enjoy danger!"

"After tonight I hope you will never show your monster again."

Nick glanced back over his shoulder. "Is this official?"

"Certainly not. I'm asking you to destroy the monster for the sake of the villagers. So that peace can return to Courville. People will be able to sleep nights."

"In that case . . ." He shrugged. "After tonight the villagers will have to find their entertainment elsewhere."

"Good!" Tendrell exclaimed. "I've been trying for weeks to persuade him to stop."

"You get your wish, Allan!" Nick laughed. "Chief Inspector Damiot was more persuasive." Raising his voice. "You hear, Pouchet? After tonight we get rid of our handsome monster!"

"Yes, M'sieur le Comte. I heard."

"And a good thing!" Madame Léontine glanced back toward Damiot.

Pouchet swung a door open. Raising the monster higher, he led the procession into a large, empty salon where a lighted lantern rested on the marble floor.

Once again, Lautrec and Fric-Frac ran ahead.

As Damiot followed the wheelchair, he saw that this was the large salon he had entered Saturday afternoon after inspecting the corner of the terrace where the monster had appeared Friday night.

Tonight the heavy curtains had been drawn over all the windows. The dogs were playing games, running and leaping.

"I hope I didn't startle you last night, Monsieur Inspecteur . . ."

"Startle me?" He faced the Comte.

"When you were parked in the Square and I appeared in my Ferrari."

"So that was you!"

"I decided after you and Allan left that I would enjoy some fresh air. I frequently do that, late at night, after the village is asleep. Drive south for a breath of the sea. Last night I went to Monte Carlo and back."

So the Comte could drive the Ferrari! Drive anywhere!

"You're wondering how I handle such a powerful car? I've redesigned the steering equipment so that my miserable legs can manage everything. A new engineering technique that will one day be on the market for every make of car . . ."

"That Ferrari is his other toy!" Tendrell exclaimed.

"Like my father, I have a passion for fast cars."

Damiot saw that Pouchet was carrying the puppet figure toward a pair of curtained windows near the west corner.

Nick laughed. "Pouchet lifts my monster like a holy monstrance! Did you know, mes amis, in early times the word monster meant a divine omen?''

"Can't say I'm surprised," Tendrell answered.

The Comte halted his wheelchair beside Pouchet, who had leaned the puppet against the wall, near the windows. Madame Léontine began to straighten the folds of its cloak. "Monsieur Damiot! Why don't you and Allan stand outside those far windows?" He motioned toward the other end of the salon. "You'll be invisible from below if you keep close to the wall, but you should be able to observe everything."

"Come along, Inspector!" Tendrell headed across the salon. "I've done this before."

Damiot hesitated. "What about the dogs?"

"They can run outside," Nick replied. "Nobody will notice them in the dark." He reached under an arm of his wheelchair. "I forgot the bell!" He snapped a lever, and the castle vibrated as the great bell began to toll.

Both dogs howled.

Nick grinned impishly. "Our play begins . . ."

Damiot turned and hurried after the Englishman, who was waiting beside the curtained windows.

"We squeeze through here." Tendrell carefully lifted an edge of the curtain and slipped underneath.

Damiot ducked under the heavy material into complete darkness, the curtain falling into place behind him. He wondered where the Englishman's daughter would be meeting Michel Giroud. Pushing the curtain aside a few inches, he glimpsed a strange tableau.

Nick was standing now, laughing as he supported himself on his crutches. Pouchet held the puppet, like some bizarre crown, above the Comte's head and slowly lowered it until the robe covered his body. The monstrous head seemed to rest on Nick's shoulders. Madame Léontine swept up the bottom of the robe as Pouchet lifted his lantern from the floor and slid a cover over the light.

"Here we go!" Tendrell whispered.

Damiot felt cold air strike his face as he heard the window open.

The terrace was ghostly in the blue wash of starlight, with a black mass of forest visible against the sky beyond the marble balustrade.

"We'll be able to see everything," Tendrell explained, pausing outside the windows. "Last time I came out here I actually went some distance away from these windows, and nobody noticed me. There's a sort of buttress where we can be in complete shadow. I'll show you." He bent low and darted across the open terrace.

Damiot crouched down and followed.

The bell tolled again.

Now there was that same curious rolling of voices from the villagers he had heard last week when he was on the hill.

He bumped into the Englishman in the dark.

"They can't possibly see us here!" Tendrell murmured.

Damiot straightened beside a mass of stone that seemed to rise toward one of the invisible towers.

Moving toward the balustrade, he saw that a second cluster of villagers was streaming up the drive. The group seemed to contain at least a dozen men, carrying more lanterns.

Turning toward the castle, he glimpsed a blur of motion at the far end of the terrace. As his eyes adjusted to the darkness he could see the collapsed bulk of the monster lurching forward, with Pouchet walking behind awkwardly, like a second monster. Madame Léontine's plump figure, bending low, held the puppet's cloak like a royal train.

The two dogs came running across the terrace, barely visible against the marble floor. Lautrec, after sniffing at Damiot's shoe, raced back toward the others, but Fric-Frac remained crouching beside him. He leaned down to scratch her head as he watched the mastiff join his master.

Peering below, Damiot saw that the second group of villagers had joined the first. Now they all stood together at the edge of the courtyard, staring up at the terrace where the monster had appeared last week.

"In my opinion," Tendrell whispered, "Nick is slightly mad."

"What do you mean?"

"Exactly that! Every genius is touched by madness, but Nick is, I think, somewhat psychotic. That's why I've never permitted Jenny to meet him. He's urged me to bring her here but I've refused. She would very likely fall in love with him. She's seen him driving the Ferrari—as she told you—but has no idea who it was. I'm quite genuinely fond of Nick, but I do think he's mentally disturbed as a result of his accident. Damaged emotionally as well as physically. Deeply troubled by what happened to his body. He jokes constantly about his legs to mask his true feelings. That, I suspect, is why he created this fake monster to frighten people. A monstrous joke, if you will! The living monster hidden under the fake."

The bell tolled again. Much louder. Its deep metal voice rolling across the courtyard and fading away through the forest.

A strange flapping sound came from overhead.

Damiot looked up to see a cloud of doves, roused from their nests, frantically circling above the château like pale gray bats.

Tendrell nudged him, pointing down the drive.

Damiot turned to see a third group hurrying to join their friends. Several villagers had electric torches that they flashed between the tree trunks, sending grotesque shadows dancing through the forest.

No light as yet on the terrace, but he glimpsed Madame Léontine returning toward the open windows. The performance would be startling . . .

A terrifying scream came from the depths of the wood.

Fric-Frac growled.

"Quiet, Madame!" Damiot ordered.

"Those damn peacocks!" the Englishman muttered.

Damiot saw a wave of movement pass through the crowd as heads turned and arms gestured. One man seemed to be the leader. He appeared to be directing the others. Waving his arms and motioning them forward. It was the Mayor—Hercule Mauron!

A muffled crash sounded from the drive.

"They've smashed the gates!" Tendrell exclaimed.

A few cautious cheers rose from the courtyard.

Damiot leaned forward again. He could feel panic in the air. The same mob hysteria he had experienced many times in Paris . . .

Now the villagers were crossing the courtyard toward the château, moving slowly, almost reluctantly. Pointing up at the terrace.

A faint light had appeared there. Pouchet must have slid the cover back on his lantern.

The figure of the monster suddenly shot to its full height against a faint nimbus of light.

A gasp of horror rose from the villagers, followed by silence.

The swaying puppet figure with its enormous head was even

more impressive in silhouette than it had seemed last week from the hill or last night inside the castle.

Pouchet was crouched behind it, holding his lantern.

The villagers below had come to a halt and stood frozen.

Still another group was rushing up the drive. Some of these carried flaming torches.

As he watched, Damiot wondered about Jenny Tendrell again. How could she go anywhere to meet Giroud without a car? The Tendrells had only one car, and her father had driven that tonight . . .

The tolling bell sounded again and the doves continued to circle above the towers, their wings and breasts blood-red from the torches that flushed the façade of the castle with a fiery glow.

The monster appeared to be glowering down at the intruders, its face seeming even more evil in the flickering light from the torches, long black hair swaying as the clumsy head tilted forward.

The last group of villagers had joined the others. Must be forty of them now, gathered together staring at the figure on the terrace.

The giant figure appeared to be withdrawing, its long cloak swaying as the monster slowly moved back from the balustrade. Now the light would fade on the terrace as Pouchet shuttered his lantern.

The monster had made his final appearance . . .

There was a sharp crack of sound.

Frightened birds shot up from the trees, their shrill cries flooding the night air.

"That was a gun!" Tendrell exclaimed.

"Rifle," Damiot muttered.

Uproar from the courtyard. Shouting. More shots. Rifles and small arms.

Damiot froze, watching the monster slowly collapse.

The light from the lantern had been blotted out.

"What the devil are those bastards doing?" Tendrell shouted, staring down into the crowd.

"Never mind about them. We'd better find out what's happened to the Comte." He turned to Fric-Frac. "Stay here, Madame. Until I call you." He saw her tail wag and hoped that she understood.

As they ran across the terrace, a flaming torch rose from the courtyard, arced through the air, and crashed onto the marble floor in a shower of sparks.

"Idiots!" Damiot growled.

The light from the torch rolling across the terrace revealed the monster slumped down, head tipping forward as though it were asleep. The puppet figure must have collapsed over the Comte's head and shoulders.

Pouchet was sprawled behind the monster, and Madame Léontine hovered near the open windows, afraid to venture farther.

The great bell continued to toll. Damiot realized that it had never stopped.

Another torch flew up from the courtyard, cascading sparks, and struck the crumpled figure of the monster. There was a burst of flame as the long wig caught fire. The monstrous head seemed to explode.

"Nick!" Tendrell shouted.

Damiot moved away from the flying sparks and embers, pulling the Englishman with him as the figure of the monster was enveloped by fire.

A third torch smashed on the terrace, and flames sprayed.

"Don't go any closer!" Damiot grasped Tendrell's sleeve. "Nothing we can do to help him."

"Good God!"

Lautrec sprang forward barking, pawing at the monster's burning cloak. Trying desperately to rescue his master. Part of the burning cloth came away, caught in the dog's nails. Lautrec yelped with pain as he shook his paws free, then lay whimpering, close to the blazing figure.

Damiot watched the two metal crutches slide out, unscathed, from under the burning mass. They seemed pathetically small. Moving closer, followed by the Englishman, he stood looking at the charred shape. Impossible to think that only a moment ago this had been a human being.

"What a beastly way to die!" Tendrell exclaimed.

"Only a moment of pain, before he suffocated."

"I think for some time Nick has wished for death."

"He wanted to be an eagle. And he has escaped . . ." Damiot turned as a hand touched his sleeve and saw Madame Léontine, her cheeks wet with tears. "He's dead, Madame."

"Pauvre chéri! Perhaps it's best this way. He was never happy, after the accident. I have heard him weeping many times, in the night, when he thought no one would hear . . ."

"Pouchet!" Damiot went toward the sprawled figure. "Are you hurt?"

"Bullet. My arm . . ." The old man's face was drawn with pain, his eyes blinking from the acrid smoke. "What about M'sieur le Comte?"

"He's dead."

"Mon Dieu!" He turned his face to the marble floor.

"Bloody bastards!" Tendrell shouted.

Damiot looked around to see the Englishman leaning against the balustrade, shaking his fist at the crowd below.

"Murderers!" he screamed. "You killed him! You've murdered the Comte de Mohrt!"

An uneasy hum of voices rose from the courtyard.

Damiot joined Tendrell to look down at them. The crowd became silent as some recognized him.

"We need a doctor here!" He saw Marc Sibilat among those in the front. Their eyes met but Sibilat looked away.

"We have no doctor in Courville!" someone answered.

Damiot looked in the direction of the voice and saw the gross face of Hercule Mauron. "Monsieur le Maire!"

"Are you in charge?"

"Until I can reach Inspector Bardou."

"Doctor Mondor does all our police work, but unfortunately he lives in Salon . . ."

"Send for him. Pouchet's been shot. And there'll have to be an autopsy on the Comte de Mohrt. His body can't be touched until the médecin-légiste examines it."

"Right away, M'sieur Inspecteur." The Mayor looked around, squinting at faces in the crowd. "Someone go for Doctor Mondor . . ."

"I'll get him!"

Damiot saw a familiar skinny figure, wearing a black leather jacket, step forward. "Claude!"

"I have my motorcycle, M'sieur! And I know where the doctor lives!"

"Explain what's happened!" Damiot ordered. "And bring him here."

"Service, M'sieur!"

The crowd moved apart for Claude to leave.

"And you, Monsieur le Maire!" Damiot raised his voice. "I

would suggest you come up here until Inspector Bardou can be reached."

"Well, I—I'm not here officially . . ." Mauron stepped forward, reluctantly. "How do I get up there?"

Damiot glanced behind him. "Madame Léontine! Would you go down and escort Monsieur le Maire?"

"Certainly, M'sieur." She dabbed at her eyes with a handkerchief and, pleased to have something to do, went toward the open windows.

Facing the courtyard again, Damiot saw Claude in the distance, running down the drive toward the gates. He remembered Jenny Tendrell riding past those entrance gates last week. Was it possible that she had taken the black mare tonight when she went to meet Michel Giroud?

The bell continued to toll.

Tolling for Nicolas Frédéric César Philippe Etienne—last Comte de Mohrt . . .

Damiot leaned against the balustrade, staring at the faces. No sign of Marc Sibilat now, but he glimpsed Achille Savord trying to hide behind the others, which was impossible because of his height. "You are responsible for what's happened here. All of you . . ."

A ripple of fear flowed like a visible current through the mob.

"And one of you is a murderer!"

The faces looking up at him, mouths agape, were reddened by the flames from the torches that some still clutched in their hands.

"Whichever one of you threw the torch that killed the Comte de Mohrt is a murderer! Or, perhaps, an autopsy will discover a bullet in his body. Certainly Doctor Mondor will remove a bullet from Pouchet's arm. Tests will be made and bullets can be traced to the guns that fired them." He realized as he talked that some of the villagers were leaving stealthily, darting across the courtyard toward the drive. "If you don't turn those guns in you will certainly be denounced by your neighbors. Many of you know which persons fired their guns and which of you threw torches up here. Someone is going to tell who those persons are!"

The crowd turned in sudden panic and fled across the courtyard, leaving the Mayor exposed, standing alone.

As Damiot watched them pour down the drive, he thought of Jenny Tendrell and Blanche Carmet again . . .

Blanche had said that Michel Giroud was with her when those two girls were killed. Both nights. For several hours . . .

The last of the villagers seemed to be sucked like corks into the mouth of the drive, the light from their torches fading with them.

And suddenly, two things slipped into place in Damiot's mind.

The garçon, Claude, had told him something important the day he arrived, but he hadn't remembered it until this moment.

And Blanche Carmet had said that . . .

Damiot grasped the icy marble balustrade with both hands.

He knew the identity of the murderer! The puzzle was solved!

"What now?" Tendrell asked. "What do we do?"

"Stay here, mon ami." He started across the terrace, the Englishman at his heels.

"Where the devil are you going?"

"There's something I must do. Something important . . ."

"What's more important than this?"

"There's a real monster still to be caught. A monster who has murdered twice!" He continued on toward the open windows but, remembering, turned back. "Fric-Frac! Come! Quickly . . ."

The small black dog sped out of the darkness across the terrace and jumped into his arms.

"Think I'd forgotten you?" He glanced back and saw the mastiff crouched beside the charred shape that had been its master. "You're a good girl. Staying where I told you." He buried his face in Fric-Frac's curls as he carried her inside, and again breathed the fragrance of Aurore's bath oil.

From behind him on the terrace came a chilling sound.

The mastiff was howling. Mourning for his dead master . . .

22

Glancing down at Fric-Frac, curled beside him in the Peugeot, he smiled. She had led him back without faltering, through those endless passages and down the curving stone steps out of the château.

Nick's body would go to the morgue in Courville. Into one of those metal drawers. Next to Annie Deffous . . .

Doctor Mondor would perform an autopsy.

He had a strong hunch that a bullet would be found. A bullet, not suffocation, had been the cause of death . . .

Several of the villagers should certainly come forward and name the ones who had brought guns to the château.

Many things raced through his mind as he drove past the familiar farms and vineyards.

Aurore! Lonely after her husband's death, she had fallen in love with Giroud . . .

Giroud pursuing Jenny. While sleeping with Blanche Carmet and, probably, several others . . .

What about Jenny Tendrell? Giroud had arranged a rendezvous with her for tonight. But where? She must have told Giroud earlier—probably on the phone, when she made reservations for dinner—that her father would be going off somewhere in his Citroën. Confirmed it at dinner, when Tendrell left her alone and Giroud appeared from the kitchen.

Where would she meet Giroud?

The Tendrells' cook might know . . .

Damiot swerved the Peugeot onto a grassy verge as he glimpsed the rows of beech trees leading to the Tendrell farmhouse.

"Here we are, Madame," he whispered, slowing to a stop.

She followed him out of the car, instantly alert, and trotted beside him up the road.

There were no lights in the farmhouse windows facing the highway. No smoke rising from any chimneys and no car parked in the lane.

"Not a sound, Madame. You understand? Stay close to me!" He walked halfway up the lane, then stepped onto the soft earth and continued on, keeping close to the beech trees on his right.

Hesitating when he reached the last tree, Fric-Frac at his feet, he listened for some sound.

Nothing. Not even a bird.

"We'll check the side windows." They crossed a stretch of grass and followed a pebbled path between flower beds. He wished he had been able to inspect this property more carefully, by daylight. His previous visit had been at night and in heavy rain.

Reaching the corner of the house, he saw that no light showed from any windows along the side. Still no sound from inside or from those cottages at the rear, which Tendrell had said were occupied by his staff . . .

He saw that he was approaching a row of tall double windows, which must have been installed when the place was restored. They faced a flagstone terrace where he glimpsed antique statues surrounded by shrubbery. As he came closer, he noticed that the far pair of windows stood open. Their glass panes, pushed back against the shutters, reflected a silver color from the night sky.

Had Jenny left them open for Giroud? Perhaps the two had come out through here and then walked to his car . . .

Damiot hesitated, listening for any sound from inside.

The windows were covered by heavy curtains, and no light was visible underneath.

The silence was broken suddenly by the neighing of a horse. Fric-Frac growled faintly. He reached down to stroke her head, reassuringly. Must be the English girl's black mare. Locked up for the night in the barn.

Damiot waited, his ears straining. There was no other sound.

Then, barely a whisper, he heard something . . . A voice? From inside.

He moved close to the open window. A man's voice . . .

Fingering one of the curtains carefully, until he found the edge, he pushed it back so that he could look into the room.

A shaded lamp glowed on a bedside table. The small circle of light revealed Jenny Tendrell, asleep in an enormous antique bed. The remainder of the room was in shadow.

A dark figure knelt at the foot of her bed.

Damiot leaned forward to see the man's face . . .

Michel Giroud! Hands clasped and head bowed. His voice was a monotone. Only a few phrases were audible.

Damiot recognized the Latin words.

"Mea culpa! Mea culpa . . ."

He frowned, translating in his mind. "My fault! My fault . . ."

"Miserere mei . . ."

"Have mercy upon me . . ."

The Latin was like an incantation.

Moving cautiously, Damiot stepped inside.

"Miserere mei . . ."

Fric-Frac growled. The small sound was like an explosion in the room.

Giroud.

Giroud, with one swift motion, was on his feet. A knife flashing in his hand.

The dog continued to growl.

Giroud raised the knife.

Damiot saw that it had the special blade a chef uses for boning. Long and thin and deadly . . .

"Monsieur Inspecteur!" Giroud bowed slightly, a faint smile on his lips. "From the day of your arrival, I've known that you would be the one to discover the truth. But I did not expect you here tonight . . ."

Damiot saw that Giroud was wearing an expensive black leather jacket, black trousers, rubber-soled shoes. "Let me have that knife."

"A chef never permits anyone to touch his favorite knife." He continued to smile. "You must know that! Your father was a chef."

"The knife . . ."

"You will have to take it from me, Monsieur. I suppose you have a gun."

"No gun. I dislike violence. All violence! But especially murder."

"Without a gun it will be impossible for you to take my knife. I suspect I'm much stronger than you. In better condition."

"That is possible."

"If you attempt to take my knife, I will be forced to kill you."

"You have already killed twice."

"You've no evidence of that."

"I have proof."

The smile faded. "I don't believe you!"

"And tonight you planned to kill again." He glanced toward Jenny, her long blonde hair spread across the white pillows, and saw that she hadn't moved. "Why this girl?"

"She's much too clever. This girl . . . She too suspects the truth. I was afraid she might tell her father—or you—what it is she has guessed about the other two. I'm afraid I talked too much, the last time we were together."

"The last time?"

"I drove up here after dinner, one night last week. Jenny had told me on the phone that her father would be out. He returned after midnight and, as usual, I departed through these windows. Apparently, during the evening, I said something—I've no idea what it was—that convinced Jenny I had killed Lisette Jarlaud. She'd been suspicious for some time, because I'd mentioned last year that I knew Lisette. She has questioned me repeatedly, but this time—without realizing it—I must have revealed more than I intended."

"Murderers are notorious for their egos. Many have been caught because they couldn't resist talking. Boasting . . ."

Giroud's eyes flashed. "I will not be caught, Monsieur Inspecteur. Even by you! I've known, of course, that you suspected me. When I was playing billiards at the café last night, I was told that you'd been asking questions."

"Detectives always ask questions. Even on holiday."

"You'll never be able to prove I killed anyone. You've no evidence! In fact, one of those girls hasn't even been identified!"

"I learned her name yesterday."

"What?"

"It's Deffous—Annie Deffous." He saw Giroud's eyes widen with surprise. "She came here from Toulon. The local police confirmed this today, but have not yet released that fact to the public . . ."

"How did you find out?"

"Does it matter? I've also learned that you worked as a chef in Toulon before you moved to Marseille. That you have a child by Deffous—a son." He must talk fast now, avoid looking at the knife in Giroud's hand, convince him that he had lost. "You gave Deffous money and continued to pay her for a time, even after you left Toulon."

"She bled me! Always wanting more. That's why I had to leave Marseille. But she traced me, finally, through a waiter in Marseille who had been forwarding her letters. She came here to tell me that she would take me to court if I didn't give her money for all the months I hadn't paid her—that or marry her!"

"Why didn't you marry her?"

"Annie? I never intended to marry her. I detested her! When she phoned the Auberge, I told her to meet me that night after I finished work. A café in another village, where I wasn't known. From there I drove up to that field across from the château, with Annie following in her car . . ."

"I suppose you knew that field from earlier visits with other young women. Only you killed this one! Drove her car into some nearby ravine. The police will be searching for it tomorrow." He saw that Jenny was turning in her sleep, moaning softly. "And what about Lisette Jarlaud?"

188

"That bitch! She, too, was after money. Always begging! Constantly spying on me!"

"Was that why she asked Madame Bouchard for a job?"

"You found out about that, did you? Lisette wanted to work at the Auberge so that she could watch me every day! The final straw was when she told me she was pregnant. I would have to give her money. Exactly like Annie Deffous!"

"But Lisette Jarlaud wasn't pregnant. The autopsy proved that."

"Then she lied! As usual . . ." He glanced down at the sleeping girl in the bed. "Jenny's the only one who never lied to me . . ."

"Were you in love with all these young women?"

"What is love, Monsieur?" He shrugged. "This one's the first I might have married. After all, she's the only child of a rich Englishman. The others had nothing! Family or money. I have always needed money, but now, with my job as head chef of that new hotel, I won't need the Englishman's money. I'll have a large salary. Thanks to Aurore!"

"And what about Aurore?"

"A fine person. But unfortunately, I prefer women much younger."

"Fortunately for her!"

"Although I'll not discourage her quite so much, in the future. Aurore's getting a tremendous price for the Auberge."

"All this talk of money!"

Giroud shrugged again. "The pleasures of life are expensive, Monsieur." He raised his knife suddenly. "Your body must not be found here. We will take your car. There's a bridge up the road where it would be possible for you to crash through the railing into a deep gorge . . ."

"What about Jenny Tendrell?"

"She will sleep until I return. I added something to her food at dinner so that she would be asleep before I arrived here."

"You can't kill another girl with that same knife!"

"Why not?" Giroud looked down at the knife in his hand. "The stupid villagers will say the monster did it."

"Too late for that. The police know there is no monster."

"But some of the villagers have seen it. Several times . . ."

"They saw it again tonight. Unfortunately, they killed it."

"Killed it?"

"You were the one who started those rumors about a monster."

"What makes you think that, Monsieur?"

"Because you murdered Annie Deffous and Lisette Jarlaud. The rumors about a monster were started by their murderer to confuse the police and frighten the villagers."

"Those rumors worked! I had heard stories about lights seen at night in the windows of the castle . . ."

"There were lights because someone lived there. The young Comte de Mohrt. Your rumors gave him the idea to create a monster figure that he displayed for the villagers as a joke."

"So that's what it was! I was surprised, of course, when those idiots said they'd seen something."

"They destroyed the monster tonight. Murdered the Comte de Mohrt! Only it was you who killed him. As surely as you murdered those two young women. But you'll not harm this girl, because there is no monster now to blame for her death."

"Jenny knows too much. And suspects even more! I can't allow her to jeopardize my contract with the new hotel. That's the ambition of my life! Head chef for a three-star restaurant!"

"You will never see the new hotel. And you'll not see Blanche Carmet tonight."

"How do you know about Blanche?"

"You were with her both those nights, after you killed Annie Deffous and Lisette Jarlaud. Had an alibi ready, each time. Provided for you by a prostitute! The way you use women disgusts me!"

Giroud shrugged again, his eyes hardening. "You are only a detective, Monsieur. Not a judge." He motioned toward the open window with the blade of his knife. "We must go now."

Damiot wondered if Michel would lack the courage to use his knife, and only make intimidating gestures. Slash at one of his hands, perhaps, or his face. The possibility caused him to relax, although these next seconds would be the most dangerous. He must talk himself out of this corner, as he'd done many times in the past . . .

Giroud seemed to be tensing for attack. Adjusting the knife in his hand.

"I would suggest, Monsieur, that you place your knife on the foot of the bed. Leave here through the window . . ."

"And walk into a trap?"

"There is no one waiting outside."

"I don't believe you!"

"I've told no one what I have learned about you. I came here alone." He kept his voice low, persuasive. "You can get your car and drive away."

"And you will follow!"

"I will *not* follow you."

"It won't work, Monsieur Inspecteur! I'm taking you with me. In your car." He lunged suddenly, the knife flashing.

Damiot, caught off guard, felt the blade slice through the sleeve of his waterproof.

Fric-Frac barked.

Giroud, eyes wild, raised the knife again.

As Damiot stepped back to avoid the blade, he was aware of the small black body hurtling past him.

"Mon Dieu!" Giroud, off balance, was surprised by the dog's attack. Toppling back, he struck against the foot of the bed and slid to the floor.

Damiot saw the knife fly out of his hand, onto the bed. At the same time he was aware of Fric-Frac savaging Giroud's ankle.

Giroud screamed. "That dog! Get her away!"

Damiot moved swiftly to snatch up the knife.

"She's biting me!"

"Here, Fric-Frac!" Damiot ordered. "Come away."

She turned at once and ran toward him.

Giroud rubbed the ankle, then got up and faced Damiot again. "You're going to arrest me?"

"No. I am not."

"What?"

"Here's your knife." He held it out, handle toward Giroud. "Take it and leave. I must, of course, report what I know to the local police, but that will give you at least an hour. Perhaps more . . ."

"An hour?"

He saw Giroud's eyes narrow as he glimpsed a chance for escape.

"Bien! In an hour I will be far away from here." He snatched the knife from Damiot's hand. "The local gendarmes will never be able to find me." He thrust the knife under his jacket. "There is someone in Marseille who will hide me."

"A woman, I suppose . . ."

"But of course!" He flashed an arrogant smile. "Au 'voir, Monsieur Inspecteur!"

Damiot watched him go to the windows, push the curtains aside, and disappear into the night.

Poor bastard . . . He was feeling sorry for him!

"Your murderers are your children," Sophie had said.

Maybe his wife was right. He had felt sorry for many of them.

Fric-Frac pawed at his trouser leg.

"Good girl." He leaned down and stroked her head. "You are the best assistant I've ever had!"

Damiot turned back to the bed and, moving closer, looked down at the drugged girl. Jenny's delicate young face, so vulnerable against the soft pillow, reminded him of that other girl. Annie Deffous . . .

Jenny would never know what had happened in this room. Never suspect she had been so close to death . . .

He straightened the bedcover before he turned away and, Fric-Frac following, went toward the windows. Closed the curtains carefully behind them and started back to his car.

Walking down the lane, Fric-Frac at his heels, he heard the roar of an approaching car. He waited, hidden by one of the poplars, and watched the green Jaguar flash past. It was heading north instead of toward Marseille.

Damiot smiled.

23

He slowed the Peugeot as he approached the château. Glancing down beside him, he realized that Fric-Frac was asleep. Dogs were born with the gift of instant sleep. Something he had never learned!

Tonight he would toss for hours. Always happened when his mind was involved with the finish of an investigation . . .

Fric-Frac growled softly as the Peugeot came to a stop near a row of parked cars.

Damiot saw one of the entrance doors open and watched Bardou, bundled in scarf and overcoat, hurry across the courtyard.

"Who is it? We're busy inside. No time for . . . M'sieur Damiot!"

"Spare a moment, Inspector?"

"But certainly!"

"What's going on?" Damiot asked.

"We're waiting for them to take M'sieur le Comte's body to the morgue. Doctor Mondor hasn't finished his examination."

"Did he find a bullet wound?"

"In the Comte's chest, near his heart."

"I thought so! Now then . . . I've more information, but let me warn you again, I don't want anyone to know I gave this to you."

"Whatever you say, M'sieur Inspecteur, but I still think . . ."

"I know who killed those two girls."

"You do!"

"The murderer—of both girls—is Michel Giroud."

"Giroud?"

"He's the chef at the Auberge."

"Mon Dieu! I didn't even suspect him . . ."

"Used to work for a restaurant in Toulon, where he knew the Deffous girl. Had a son by her. Gave her money for the child's care until he came to Courville. She traced him and drove here to persuade him to give her more money or to marry her. He killed her to get rid of her. And it was Giroud who started rumors about a monster in the château, hoping to confuse the police and panic the villagers. He murdered Lisette Jarlaud when she, too, demanded money, after telling him she was pregnant . . ."

"Will I find Giroud at the Auberge?"

"He's driving north in a dark green Jaguar. Send out word that he's the murderer. He has a knife—probably the same one he used on both those girls. Warn every gendarmerie that he's dangerous. Although I don't think you'll find him alive."

"Why not?"

"He'll either use the knife on himself or drive his car off some mountain road. Have a look through Giroud's personal belongings. He has an apartment above the garage, behind the Auberge. I suspect you'll find letters there from Annie Deffous."

"What can I say, M'sieur Inspecteur? Express my gratitude . . ."

"Not a word. Move fast and you may catch Giroud before he harms himself."

"There's a phone upstairs." Hesitating as Damiot started the Peugeot. "You'll be staying in Courville a while longer?"

"I've made no plans. Let me know when you find Giroud." Making a sharp turn and starting down the drive. "Bonne chance."

It was raining again.

As he passed between the shattered entrance gates and turned left toward the village, he wondered what he should do about Aurore.

Have to explain all this. Prepare her for the shocking news about Giroud . . . That would be a disagreeable job, but better than having her learn from Bardou when he came to search through Giroud's apartment.

Aurore would never know he had been the one who discovered that Giroud was the murderer. Or would she guess?

Perhaps she would come to his room tonight, when he returned to the Auberge. That might be a good time to explain things . . .

Fric-Frac was snoring. "Lucky dog!"

She was his dog! Coming back to Paris with him . . .

Should he drive down to Cannes first? Introduce Fric-Frac to his wife? Talk with Sophie and make decisions?

Why bother! It would be impossible to discuss anything quietly and intelligently, with her mother listening to every word. And the old lady hated all dogs!

His attention was caught by a flash of living color as the car rounded a curve and its headlights swept across a row of young trees. New leaves, glossy from the rain, quivering like small green flames.

Spring should come to Provence in another few weeks, or even days . . .

And he probably wouldn't be here!

The villagers would not be sleeping tonight, knowing that someone among them had killed the Comte. Would they come forward tomorrow and tell Bardou his name? Not likely! They would stick together against all outsiders, and Bardou was from Arles . . .

Might be weeks before that bullet taken from the Comte's body could be traced to the right gun . . .

Had Marc Sibilat brought a gun with him tonight? His mother would probably have thrust it into his hand as he left for the château . . .

Rumors of a monster—started by a murderer—had become a threatening reality to the villagers.

No monster, but two murderers! Michel Giroud and the villager who had shot the Comte . . .

Peering through the rain-spattered windshield, he wondered about Michel Giroud. Had he already sent his Jaguar crashing into some rocky canyon? Or was he sitting in the car at this moment, knife in his hand? He was religious, so he would be praying for his immortal soul. Poor bastard . . .

Blanche Carmet would be waiting for him.

But there was an empty drawer at the morgue. Also waiting.

Giroud had established alibis both times with Blanche—when Annie Deffous and Lisette Jarlaud were murdered. He had come to Blanche afterward and spent several hours with her.

Had told her that he would be with her tonight. After killing Jenny Tendrell, he would have gone straight to Blanche. Another alibi . . .

"Three alibis are two too many!" he muttered. That was the final piece of information that had convinced him Giroud was the killer.

The first—that Giroud came from Toulon—had been given to him by Claude, the afternoon he arrived at the Auberge, but he hadn't remembered that until tonight.

He reduced speed as he reached the Auberge, and Fric-Frac at once roused and sat up.

Turning off the avenue, he glimpsed the ghost of another restaurant through the rain. The old entrance, with his flower garden in front . . .

"Chez Damiot!" Whispering the name as he drove past the row of new windows. The dining room was dark.

Both garage doors stood open, and the space where the Jaguar had always been parked was empty. He eased the Peugeot into the free space, next to Aurore's station wagon, and switched off his headlights.

Getting out of the car, he saw that Aurore's suite above the kitchen was lighted. "Come, Madame la Duchesse!"

Fric-Frac jumped out.

"Wait here! I'll carry you." As he locked the car, a reflected glow of light flooded into the garage. Turning quickly, he saw that the kitchen door had been opened.

Aurore was standing there, silhouetted against the light. "I was waiting for you!"

At the sound of her voice, Fric-Frac scampered across the wet tarmac and bounded up the kitchen steps.

Damiot hurried after the dog, through the driving rain, into Chez Damiot.

ABOUT THE AUTHOR

VINCENT McCONNOR is a writer living in Los Angeles. He is the author of *The French Doll*, *The Riviera Puzzle*, and *The Provence Puzzle*.

"The most important horror collection of the year."
—LOCUS

DARK FORCES

Edited by Kirby McCauley

(14801-x) $3.50

Including a complete new short novel by Stephen King

This new volume of 23 chillers contains new works by a star-studded roster of authors. You'll find spine-tingling tales from Davis Grubb, Ray Bradbury, Edward Gorey, Robert Aickman, Joe Haldeman, Dennis Etchison, Karl Edward Wagner, Lisa Tuttle, Ramsey Campbell, T.E.D. Klein, and many other masters of horror.

Get ready for terror as you encounter slug-like creatures who inhabit New York City's sewers, zombies who become all-night store clerks in California, a young boy who is kidnapped in his very own bed, and a multitude of horrifying beings and events.

Available in September wherever paperbacks are sold or directly from Bantam Books. Include $1.00 for postage and handling and send check to Bantam Books, Dept. DF, 414 East Golf Road, Des Plaines, Illinois 60016. Allow 4–6 weeks for delivery.

MIDNIGHT WHISPERS
by Patricia and Clayton Matthews

Super-selling authors Patricia and Clayton Matthews team up for the first time to weave a tale of danger and passion. MIDNIGHT WHISPERS is the story of April Morgan, a beautiful young heiress whose witness of a traumatic event has erased her memory. From Cape Cod's untamed coast to the jagged cliffs of Ireland, from the lake country of Switzerland to fast-paced, trendy London, April searches for her hidden past—and finds romance. But wherever she goes, she is haunted by a mysterious voice on the phone—"Mr. Midnight," a total stranger with the power to manipulate April's every move—for good or for evil. (on sale September 15, 1981)

SCATTERED SEED
by Maisie Mosco

"Glorious! I laughed, I cried."
—Cynthia Freeman,
author of PORTRAITS and
A WORLD FULL OF STRANGERS

If you loved EVERGREEN, you'll love SCATTERED SEED. The magnificent family saga that began in FROM THE BITTER LAND now continues. Maisie Mosco's superb new novel is the story of proud men and women in love and war, torn between the powerful ties of tradition and the exuberant freedom of their adopted land. (on sale October 15, 1981)

Read all of these fabulous romantic Bantam novels, available wherever paperbacks are sold.

WHODUNIT?

Bantam did! By bringing you these masterful tales of murder, suspense and mystery!

☐	14939	**SLEEPING MURDERS** by Agatha Christie	$2.50
☐	14981	**THE MYSTERIOUS AFFAIR AT STYLES** by Agatha Christie	$2.50
☐	13777	**THE SECRET ADVERSARY** by Agatha Christie	$2.25
☐	13951	**THE RELIGIOUS BODY** by Catherine Aird	$1.95
☐	20271	**THE STATELY HOME MURDER** by Catherine Aird	$2.25
☐	14450	**MURDER BY THE BOOK** by Rex Stout	$1.95
☐	13407	**A QUESTION OF IDENTITY** by June Thomson	$1.95
☐	13651	**IN THE BEST OF FAMILIES** by Rex Stout	$1.95
☐	13783	**SOME LIE & SOME DIE** by Ruth Rendell	$1.95
☐	13039	**A SLEEPING LIFE** by Ruth Rendell	$1.95
☐	13948	**THE FINGERPRINT** by Patricia Wentworth	$1.95
☐	14546	**CASE CLOSED** by June Thomson	$1.95
☐	14930	**THE ROSARY MURDERS** by William Kienzle	$2.75
☐	13784	**NO MORE DYING THEN** by Ruth Rendell	$1.95

Buy them at your local bookstore or use this handy coupon for ordering:

Bantam Books, Inc., Dept. BD, 414 East Golf Road, Des Plaines, Ill. 60016

Please send me the books I have checked below. I am enclosing $_____ (please add $1.00 to cover postage and handling). Send check or money order —no cash or C.O.D.'s please.

Mr/Mrs/Miss_____

Address_____

City_____ State/Zip_____

BD—8/81

Please allow four to six weeks for delivery. This offer expires 2/82.

Ross Macdonald Lew Archer Novels

"The finest series of detective novels ever written by an American... I have been reading him for years and he has yet to disappoint. Classify him how you will, he is one of the best novelists now operating, and all he does is keep on getting better."
—The New York Times

☐	13963	**FIND A VICTIM**	$2.25
☐	13235	**THE GALTON CASE**	$2.25
☐	12926	**THE MOVING TARGET**	$1.95
☐	12337	**THE NAME IS ARCHER**	$1.95
☐	13789	**THE BLUE HAMMER**	$2.25

Buy them at your local bookstore or use this handy coupon for ordering:

Bantam Books, Inc., Dept. RM, 414 East Golf Road, Des Plaines, Ill. 60016

Please send me the books I have checked above. I am enclosing $_____ (please add $1.00 to cover postage and handling). Send check or money order —no cash or C.O.D.'s please.

Mr/Mrs/Miss_____

Address_____

City_____ State/Zip_____

RM—8/81

Please allow four to six weeks for delivery. This offer expires 2/82.